DEDICATION

To our grandchildren...

Already born or yet to come.

ACKNOWLEDGMENTS

Though all the writing and errors are solely my own doing, a number of people contributed to the creation of the text. I would like to thank the numerous friends and family members who were kind enough to comment on various drafts and led me to make material changes for the better. A special mention is reserved for my wife who labored through so many versions that I am sure she has lost count.

OPERATION KOVESH

A Top Secret Operation to Neutralize Iran's Nuclear Capabilities

A NOVEL BY

ANDREW B. LOUIS

For information regarding permission, please write to:
info@barringerpublishing.com
Barringer Publishing, Naples, Florida
www.barringerpublishing.com

Cover, graphics, and layout by Linda S. Duider
Cape Coral, Florida

ISBN: 978-1-7352525-7-5
Library of Congress Cataloging-in-Publication Data
Operation Kovesh / Andrew B. Louis

Printed in U.S.A.

PREFACE

Though the events described here may have some historical precedent, they are totally fictitious, as are equipment and its use. Similarly, any resemblance between the characters in this story and actual individuals would be totally coincidental. Finally, though the geographical locations are real, the characterization of certain countries is vaguely inspired by reality. One should not conclude that the author's views relative to any of these countries matches the views presented here. The entire Middle East has been a war cauldron for most of its history, and yet it remains both the birthplace of western civilization and the origin of wonderful scientific discoveries. Additionally, its contribution to the world of art, through the ages, has been unquestioned. In short, whoever is painted as a villain today could turn out to be a hero tomorrow.

CHAPTER.01

Jesse Benaroya, Israel's Prime Minister, still felt somewhat incredulous at the last twenty-four hours' developments. At this point, he was resting comfortably in the cabin of a large, corporate jet belonging to the Israeli Air Force that was flying him back from Germany to Tel Aviv.

The day had started with a classified phone call from Roger Caldwell, the President of the U.S. He wanted to have a short, secret, and private visit with Jesse. He hoped that both of them could be alone, so that anything that was said would go no further. He apologized both for the short notice and for the request that Benaroya visit him in the U.S., noting that good form would have had him offer to travel to Israel. But he said that the best way to ensure the rendezvous remained totally secret was to invite Jesse to meet him at his Southwest Florida estate, in the Port Royal enclave of Naples: "Away from Jerusalem; away from Washington . . ."

Caldwell explained that it would be hard, not to say impossible, for him to fly to Israel without attracting unwanted attention. He added, "I never seem to be able to go to the bathroom without dozens of journalists following me . . ."

Jesse laughed: "No worries . . . I get it . . ."

"Knew you would."

Caldwell suggested that Jesse should transit through and change planes at Ramstein Air Force Base in Germany. He recommended that Jesse fly the Germany/U.S. leg on a U.S. Air Force Gulfstream 5, which he would arrange. It would include a full bed so that Jesse could have a good night's rest and get to Naples early in the morning.

"Private jets don't draw much attention in Naples . . . Most of my neighbors have one."

Upon arriving at the Naples municipal airport, Jesse indeed noted that there were quite a number of jets parked on the tarmac, remarking: "Not quite as many as in Nice at the time of the Cannes film festival, but still . . ."

His plane taxied directly to a hangar where a black, Suburban SUV, with heavily tinted glass, was waiting. He correctly assumed the car was armor plated but noted that it was not the president's own limousine; Caldwell had thought that his car would attract unwanted attention. Also, the SUV did not have much of an escort, other than the usual single police car, as was the norm when a visitor to Caldwell's place did not require a full motorcade. Yet, seated next to the driver was a member of the Secret Service, ostensibly in radio contact with his base. The car drove south on Airport-Pulling road, veered west toward Tin City and the old part of town and then south again onto Gordon drive. This is probably the most prestigious avenue in Port Royal, the wealthiest enclave within Naples. It is lined on both sides by mansions, each one bigger than the next, with those on the right-hand side of the road, driving south, the most impressive as they sat right on the beach. Those on the other side often had water access as well, but through the myriad of canals that crisscross the old city of Naples.

After they had passed the Port Royal Club on their right, the car arrived at the estate, which Jesse had never visited. He noticed the impressive gates in the center of what looked like three hundred feet of road frontage. A single police car was at the gate, although he could see, just inside the property, a small contingent of police and secret service agents.

As he was expected, his car did not have to wait, and the gate swung open. Jesse was impressed by the long, S-shaped, curving driveway, lined with majestic, Imperial palm trees, weaving through a large park, with a helicopter pad on the south side. He could see flowers, particularly bougainvillea in a variety of colors, as well as a few trees with light, pinkish-purple flowers which he did not recognize. These were early flowering tabebuia, cousins of the ubiquitous yellow variety which flowers profusely in March, usually six weeks or so before the enchanting Royal Poincianas, with their flamboyant, red canopies, justifying their colloquial name in South-East Asia—"flames of the forest." The majestic driveway led to a massive, classic residence, with light cream stucco and red roof tiles. Jesse thought to himself: *repaint it white and it could be dubbed the "Southern White House"— it's certainly big enough.*

The car parked next to a large fountain in front of the center of the house, which Jesse noticed was almost perfectly symmetrical around a center section, with a large, classical, triangular pediment. The driver walked around the car to open his door. Jesse was met by President Caldwell at the bottom of the residence's external imperial staircase. They walked up the first flight until they reached the half-landing; there, the stairs divided into two symmetrical flights initially going in opposite directions and then switching back to get to the common final landing on the terrace—the formal entrance to the residence. They took the left flight and then turned right to face the impressive front door.

The décor inside the house was grandiose, with marble floors and gilded furniture in the entry hall, contrasting with dark, green wallpaper. Paintings on the walls were classical, probably 18th century, but Jesse did not recognize any. He thought to himself that *the decoration, so far at least, qualified for virtually any description other than understated.* They walked to the right of the twin circular staircase, with marble steps and wrought iron banisters, leading to the second floor; the hall there seemed to be decorated in the same general style, though in a lighter color.

They entered a large library which doubled as Caldwell's office. The dark wood of the bookcases made the room look somber despite a light-colored, rice paper wall covering. The office had light beige wall-to-wall carpeting, with a nice Persian rug, probably from the Kerman area, judging by the borderless design. It was in the sitting area in front of the fireplace with two wing chairs in front and slightly to the side of it; they looked like they were from the Louis XVI period. On the opposite wall, Jesse saw a large sofa, which looked quite plush and comfortable, with two armchairs on either side; all were upholstered in the same orangish-colored fabric. In front, a low, Chinese-style table covered in part an extremely fine red and cream Sarouk rug. The curtains around the two windows facing north and on either side of the fireplace were also quite heavy and dark, with a heavy, golden accented valence as well. Similar curtains hung around the two French doors facing west which framed the large and heavily decorated presidential desk from the same period as the wing chairs. The French doors opened onto a patio with a large pool, a jacuzzi-spa at one end and a waterfall on one side. Beyond it, one could see the white, sandy beach and the blue waters of the Gulf of Mexico. The room was lit by a Dutch-style, copper chandelier, in the center of the ceiling, as well as a number of spotlights over the paintings and down onto the sitting areas opposite and in front of the fireplace. Additionally, there was a substantial gilded, crystal, tabletop lamp on Caldwell's desk.

Caldwell motioned for Jesse to sit in the armchair on the left side of the fireplace, while he took his place on the right side. He started the official part of the conversation with very few words: "My friend, I'm going to need your help . . ."

He let them sink into Jesse's mind and seeing no obvious reaction—Jesse was an excellent, though not highly publicized, poker player—he continued. He went on to explain that he had grown tired of the frequent Iranian attacks on U.S. forces and those of its friends in the Middle East, adding: "They've just gone too far. I could tolerate the odd skirmish, but not their systematic, constant harassment."

He mentioned the dozen rocket attacks on U.S. troops in the last two months, and then spent a bit more time on the latest one a few days prior aimed at an Iraqi military base in Kirkuk; it had killed a civilian U.S. contractor and wounded a few soldiers. Jesse muttered words of support but did not want to interrupt Caldwell's flow, with a comment to the effect that Israel had had its share of rocket attacks as well . . . The U.S. President did not miss a beat and read what was on Jesse's mind. He did add that he was fully aware that allies had been hurt as well, not least the Israelis who had defended against missiles fired from Gaza or southern Lebanon, among other Palestinian strongholds. Jesse smiled.

Caldwell then intimated that he was ready to order a retaliatory strike on Iran which would surely surprise the world. He refused to go into specifics but added that he viewed it as an attempt to stop a war rather than start one. He blamed his predecessors, in general, for not having had the fortitude (he did not use that term, but a much cruder form derived from the male anatomy) to deal with Iran. Again, Jesse smiled. Caldwell added, "Iran has never seen an agreement on which they've not cheated . . ."

He continued and argued that the key issue was now simple. The world needed to show Iran that it had two, and only two, options. It would either be forced out of the community of nations if it kept behaving as a sponsor of terrorism as well as a rogue, nuclear arms developer, or it could adopt more civilized manners and be welcomed back into it. Proxy terrorism, in part financed by money which the U.S. gave back to them when they signed the five-party nuclear treaty and partly by the money that was flown to Iran (probably but not officially in exchange for American hostages) was simply unacceptable.

Pausing in his diatribe, he asked Jesse for his thoughts. Jesse suspected that Caldwell was asking for his thoughts with respect to hitting Iran but was not totally sure whether he referred to the announced, unspecified, impending strike or something else. Experience and basic prudence had taught him: "When in doubt, keep your mouth shut."

So, he replied with very general, but supportive comments. He could hardly have done anything else, considering the fact that Israel's views on the situation were pretty much the same as Caldwell's. Even more to the point, Israel had been wishing for some American help for some time. He kept his next question to himself: *Could Caldwell be doing to the Middle East what Reagan did to Eastern Europe?* He paused for a minute.

This seemed to re-energize Caldwell—if that was in fact needed—as he continued to build on his case. He said he did not want a war with Iran. He added that he was pretty sure that neither Israel nor other regional powers such as Saudi Arabia likely wanted a direct confrontation either. He mentioned he believed that all would welcome an Iranian change in behavior. Jesse nodded his agreement, though he kept for himself the belief that nothing would get Iran to change other than another revolution that took the religious leadership back to the sidelines which, in his view, they should never have been allowed to leave.

Cutting to the chase, as he said, Caldwell outlined a plan. The U.S. had already struck at Iranian targets in Iraq and Syria, and the infamous Kata'ib Hezbollah brigades a couple of days earlier. With the benefit of hindsight, as he put it, it really did not make much of a difference, as it had been a classic response which historically had not worked. Though it did incapacitate those few bases for a while and killed a number of individuals, a few in local leadership positions, it also triggered a nationalist revulsion within Iraq. In his view, this was exploited by natural insurgents and led to the attempted invasion of the U.S. embassy in Bagdad. He added that his reply to the attempted invasion of the embassy had been an opportunity to show Iran and the world that the current U.S. leadership was not going to be pushed around: "We didn't follow the example of prior fiascos where reinforcements were not ordered or approved and did not arrive in time; we're showing them we would respond with force."

In fact, the U.S. had immediately sent in military reinforcements, mainly marines, within a couple of days of the attack on the embassy, with promises of more to come, together with at least one Apache helicopter. But he could not explicitly discuss the details of that plan, as it was a work in progress and not yet a completed military action. Time would tell if the show of force was enough, at least in the short term. The arrival of the marines and the presence of the helicopter had convinced the insurgents that the smartest tactic was to retreat and evacuate the site. As could be expected in a world dominated by public relations, the insurgents left declaring victory: "We rubbed America's nose into the dirt."

Caldwell's reaction to the news of the insurgent's claims was, for once, somewhat subdued. He would think to himself that words don't matter—actions would.

Caldwell paused to drink from the cold-water glass to his right. Jesse took the opportunity to offer a few additional comments. He started by expressing sincere hope that the siege of the Bagdad embassy would end without bloodshed, drawing an immediate response from Caldwell: "You can be damn sure of that, except if the blood is that of the insurgents."

Jesse did not reply to Caldwell and went on congratulating him for his decisiveness and his understanding of how things worked in his part of the world. In fairness, there had been prior instances when Jesse had not totally understood Caldwell's decisions, like the prior June when, at the last minute, Caldwell had called back airplanes that were due to bomb Iran in reprisal for shooting down a U.S. drone. *But, then again,* he thought, *a President did not operate alone and thus could not always do everything he wanted*. So, he gave Caldwell mental credit, thinking he might have been pushed within his own administration. Summarizing his view of the region, Jesse simply affirmed: "People need to understand we're dealing with bullies."

He blamed a biased press and the natural reaction of the public that was afraid of war. He added that he understood that people hated war but argued that bullies needed to be confronted. He further argued that appeasers should be called out: "They've forgotten the old Latin proverb: *If you want peace prepare for war.*"

Caldwell smiled and nodded at Jesse's last comment. Jesse went on to suggest that the main issue is that proxy wars are notoriously hard to fight, because you do not know who the enemy is, at least officially. He added: "Remember, Sun Tzu—he wrote *The Art of War*; he clearly says there that the first imperative is to know your enemy."

He noticed that Caldwell did not seem to know who Sun Tzu was, but still went on, gambling that the U.S. President would not interrupt him. The gamble worked. He conceded that today's world was quite different from 500 B.C. when Sun Tzu wrote the book, a time when Chinese kingdoms fought each other almost continuously. There was no real public opinion then; only the opinion of the king and that of his most powerful courtiers mattered. Now, he argued, public opinion seems almost to be the most important factor: "As you know, Mr. President, many people believe, and I do too, that the Vietnam war was lost in Washington and not on the ground . . ."

"You can say that again . . ."

So, the issue, in Jesse's eyes, was that one had to take care in reporting remains biased in favor of Iran and the terrorists, or at least against Israel or the U.S. Caldwell asked, almost colloquially: "What d'ya make of that?"

"Well, gotta be careful. Pick your shots . . ."

"Tough with the Congress I have."

"You and me both. You should try the Knesset."

Seeing that he and Jesse appeared to be on the same wavelength, Caldwell went on to outline his intended next steps, which in fact were the reason he had invited Jesse to join him. First, he mentioned that he would order another visible and dramatic strike: "This will come very soon. Can't miss it."

Though it would be couched as further reaction to the embassy attack, there would be further justification within the general sphere of self-defense and the prevention of further attacks. Caldwell added, "This game has to stop . . ."

The next phase of the plan included Jesse and Israel. Caldwell said: "I want to cripple Iran's nuclear capacity . . ."

Caldwell paused to watch for Jesse's reaction. This time, the venerate poker player could not hide his total surprise. So, Caldwell smiled and went on, arguing that the plan could not be carried out without help and cooperation from at least Israel and Saudi Arabia, and, potentially, from Kuwait as well. More precisely, he said that his main goal was to destroy the Iranian nuclear enrichment capacity. Jesse objected: "That would be an act of war . . ."

Caldwell smiled for a few seconds. Then, he nodded and said that he did not want it to be. Jesse then asked: "Can we have it both ways?"

The U.S. President smiled at the fact that Jesse had used the pronoun "we" rather than "you" in his question. Then, he replied that the only way the whole plan could work was for everything to be done in a covert action, which would be totally deniable: "No possible attribution to you or to us, or even to the fact that several of us had cooperated."

"What if it leaked?"

"Hell would break out . . . Can you imagine the pandemonium, at the U.N.? Everywhere? The U.S., Israel and two Arab states attack Iran? No. We can't have that. It has to be secret and deniable or else it can't be."

"Mr. President, back to the alliance; do you really believe that the Saudis would cooperate with us?"

"My friend, at this point, I don't know for certain. But I sure as hell believe there's a good chance they will, if I ask them in the right way."

He added that he knew they hated what Iran was doing. He had had conversations with them after their oil installations were attacked a few months earlier. He was referring to events when missiles and drones attacked the state-owned, Saudi Aramco oil processing facilities at Abqaiq and Khurais in Eastern Saudi Arabia. The Houthi movement in Yemen—an Iranian client—claimed responsibility, but most of the world concluded that several, if not all, of the drones could not have come from south of the facilities. Expanding on his contacts with the Saudis, Caldwell went on to argue that the Saudis had then intimated that they would be willing to participate in a further retaliatory strike but did not want to risk being directly associated. Jesse noted: "They also want to have their cake and eat it too."

Caldwell agreed with Jesse's cynicism but admitted that he understood Saudi Arabia's internal political dilemma—divergences within the population and rifts within the extended royal family. Yet, he said he had concluded that the U.S. could not go at it alone, twisting the knife a little, saying: "Neither should we . . ."

He explained that, after all, the U.S. had gone from being a large oil importer to becoming self-sufficient and one of the world's largest producers of both oil and natural gas. So, it was no longer dependent upon Saudi oil or oil that transited through the Strait of Hormuz. He noted further the fact that the Europeans did not seem interested in participating in any retaliation. From his point of view, that hesitancy ruled out any rationale for doing anything official at that point. Caldwell simply added, "Just don't understand the Europeans."

"Mr. President, maybe you understand them too well: business, business, business."

Caldwell smiled broadly. At the same time, he said he did not want to live with the risk of a nuclear Iran and was worried about what that could do to Israel. Adding that he was not sure that other administrations would be prepared to support Israel as much as he had, he simply argued that it could be a "now or never" moment, particularly in view of still secret intelligence pointing to still further gains in Iran's march toward acquiring a nuclear weapon. He noted: "Can you imagine the world with a nuclear Iran?"

Jesse understood that the question was strictly rhetorical and stayed silent. Caldwell went on: "I can and I can't stand what I see . . . I don't think it would start with an outright nuclear attack on Israel, but I am sure we would see dirty bomb attacks by terrorists in Israel and Saudi Arabia at the very least. Imagine the mess . . ."

Jesse smiled and thanked him profusely.

Caldwell concluded that he would contact the Saudis as soon as Israel demonstrated that they were on board with the plan. Jesse asked: "Anything specific you're expecting from us?"

"Nope. Not yet at least . . . We all know their key installations. But I'm not sure what is feasible or not. I can't believe an external hit could be both successful and deniable, but you tell me. But I need to know if you're in or out . . ."

"Hmm. I see . . . How long do I have?"

"A few days for an early indication. We're smack in the middle of planning something big for the next day or so. We'll need to keep up the momentum."

CHAPTER.02

Upon returning from the U.S., Jesse immediately called his "war council." It included General Ariel Landau, the Director of the *Mossad*, who reported directly to the Prime Minister. Many would say that he was, with the Defense Minister, Aaron Spielberg, the "core" of the war council. *Mossad* was the main entity in the Israeli intelligence community, along with *Aman*, responsible for military intelligence and *Shin Bet* whose duties covered internal security. Quite a few people have argued that *Mossad* was the most powerful secret service in the world, on the simple basis that intelligence for Israel has always been a matter of survival, not just another dimension of some general defense apparatus. The *Mossad* was responsible for a wide variety of activities including intelligence collection, covert operations, and counterterrorism, as well as bringing Jews to Israel from countries where the official *Aliyah* agencies cannot protect Jewish communities. Though it had become a bit more open in recent years, it was still a very discreet and secretive group; the only crack in the armor had been the decision to no longer keep the name of its leader a state secret.

With them, were Aaron Spielberg, Moshe Shamir, Minister of Foreign Affairs and Uri Caban, Minister of Intelligence. In addition to these cabinet ministers, five other people completed the group. Three were the top people in the Israeli Defense Forces: the first was Yitzhak Landner, the *Rav Aluf*, (the only member of the armed forces with the title of Lieutenant General), and the senior commander of the Israeli Defense Forces; the next two were the heads of the Air Force, Ehud Eshkol, and of the Navy, Yael Orbach. The remaining two were Ariel Landau's counterparties at *Aman* and *Shin Bet*.

To describe the meeting as tense would have been an understatement. It was not unusual for these "security conferences," as they were labelled internally, to be summoned. Usually, they were in response to skirmishes here or there, or to some pronouncement by or development in one of the most volatile or aggressive regional enemies of Israel. Yet, they were often more in the mode of "for information" sessions. This one definitely felt different; it had an aura of profound seriousness. The very short notice and the face of the Prime Minister when he came into the room said it loud and clear.

The meeting began with Prime Minister Benaroya stating that he had just made a secret roundtrip to the U.S. to meet Roger Caldwell at his Florida estate, at his invitation.

"I don't normally jump when I get that kind of call. But, this time, it was crystal clear that the only possible reply to his question was: 'how high, sir?'"

He went on discussing the Caldwell meeting, offering enough detail to make sure that everyone understood, but remaining vague enough to avoid getting lost in the weeds. He paused for a few seconds—as was very much in his style when presenting challenging assessments. He wanted to let his colleagues absorb the shock. And, as a solid, poker player, he also wanted to try and read the initial reactions on their faces. As he began discussing possible replies to Caldwell's request, he rejected the idea that Israel would refuse to participate in any action, adding: "Can't let down our closest ally! Anybody disagrees?"

His question garnered unanimous agreement: they had to support the U.S. He then outlined the next step for them along two different lines.

As he saw it, Israel could offer to be a lead player, on its own with assistance from the U.S. and only limited help from Saudi Arabia, if any was needed. Alternatively, Israel could conclude that there would be some help required from Saudi Arabia, and possibly Kuwait as mentioned by Caldwell. In which case, Israel would need to know whether their Arab neighbors were on board before going further.

Speaking first, Ariel Landau started with a simple listing of what he saw as the available options; he argued that he could only see four but was open to the notion that there were more. First, they could strike from the air; second, they could repeat the Stuxnet episode and use it to detonate Iran's enrichment locations. The Stuxnet worm had been created, allegedly, by Israel and the U.S., and introduced into computers, primarily in Iran. Analysts speculated that it was transmitted through thumb drives and infected tens of thousands of computers. In plain terms, the worm was able to burrow into operating systems and, unlike a virus, which is created to attack computer code, it was designed to take over systems. Once in place, the worm had taken over key instructions and caused several systems to malfunction. Rumors that were never confirmed by Iran were that the Stuxnet worm had targeted its uranium enrichment activities and caused damage to centrifuges by getting them to operate in the wrong condition, such as spinning too fast or not fast enough or operating at too high or too low temperatures. This was said to have caused minor explosions and mechanical breakdowns.

The third option Ariel mentioned was to engineer some cruise missile strike from the Gulf of Oman, while the fourth involved infiltrating special forces into the country and blowing up the enrichment facilities.

As he well expected, Ariel's simple list triggered a healthy discussion among the participants. Yael Orbach, the Commander-in-Chief of the Navy, immediately argued that the missile option was simply too dangerous. A cruise missile needs nearly an hour to fly from a ship off the coast of Oman to Qom or Natanz. Officially, Israel's only missiles cannot fly further than 320 miles; here the distance would be 600 miles or more. Plus, the fleet is north of the Strait of Bab al-Mandeb, and they would need to sail beyond it.

"I know we've done all that before, but it's something that can hardly be done surreptitiously."

Orbach added that, in addition to the obvious fact that it could not be done stealthily, the major problem with a ship-launched missile was that the ship instantly became a retaliatory target. Yitzhak Landner asked: "What about submarines?"

Yael conceded that it was a feasible option, though he viewed it as unadvisable: "You know the story, Yitzhak . . . Our submarines, the Dolphins, were known to have four 650-millimeter torpedo tubes when they were acquired. Nobody knows that we have refitted them. They can handle our secret cruise missiles."

Yael added for the benefit of the group that those had nuclear warheads and a one thousand-mile range. Turning to why he thought the option was not advisable, he said with a smile: "Guess who would immediately be suspect? Either Israel or the U.S. Who else if not one of the two of us? So, forget it being discreet and deniable."

The group nodded its agreement. In either or both cases, this seemed a poor bet at best. They went on to debate the notion that a particularly important issue for Israel was potential retaliatory strikes. The lesser the risk that the attack could be traced to Israel, the less aggressive and thus potentially deadly any strike could be designed to be. Ostensibly, as Aaron Spielberg, the Defense Minister, pointed out, there was always the *Iron Dome*, but it had its limitations.

He was referring to Israel's all-weather, air defense system, which was designed, with the help of the U.S., to protect the country against incoming rockets or artillery shells. It had proven its worth in recent times, when it managed to intercept a large number of rockets fired from Gaza or even from Lebanon. Unfortunately, though it might arguably be the world's most advanced missile defense system, it had only been ninety percent accurate. This meant that ten percent or so of the missiles might go through. The good news was that current belief as to the capabilities of the dome was wrong. It was believed that the dome could only handle projectiles launched from a relatively short distance, less than seventy miles. Aaron added: "As you all know, the Dome has been secretly enhanced; it could now intercept flying objects at altitudes as high as 30,000 feet and rockets fired from up to four hundred miles away."

He concluded with the observation that protection would still be good. Yet, the problem with the system, he explained, was that it blew up incoming missiles; an attack could therefore still injure the Israeli public if fragments of nuclear devices were to fall on populated areas.

"If they had access to nuclear bombs mounted on missiles!"

"Absolutely, Ariel. But remember, it does not need to be a high yield bomb. Anything with some nuclear element would be enough. Plus, if that was done through Hamas or Hezbollah, we couldn't even retaliate directly . . ."

They agreed that any missile solution would have to be the responsibility of the U.S. and concluded that it was therefore an unlikely option. President Caldwell had clearly said that any action would have to be short of an official "act of war" and plausibly deniable. An added consideration would be if the group thought that the President could not order such a strike without informing Congress under U.S. law, unless the whole plan was in response to a serious attack that had just occurred. Since it was ostensibly not the case at present, informing Congress would be a sure way of informing Iran of the incoming strikes.

Jesse then seemingly casually added: "Guess that rules out the air strike option as well."

Looking to Yitzhak Landner for support, Ehud Eshkol, the head of the Air Force, agreed. He outlined the two challenges which the option would involve: evading Iranian air defenses and the need to find a way to refuel the planes. He argued that the need to evade Iran's air defenses was not the pressing concern. The real issue was the need to refuel the planes, as they only have a range of a shade more than two thousand nautical miles. Iran's installations were about eight hundred and sixty miles from Israel: the jets should refuel on the way to or on the way back. He added: "Failing that, the crews would have too little room to maneuver in case of trouble."

Aaron Spielberg, the Defense Minister, asked whether the planes could take off from closer range, for instance the Red Sea, the Persian Gulf or the Gulf of Oman. Ehud agreed that a closer range would help, but that went straight to the question of outside help.

"We can do round trips from the Persian Gulf, but we couldn't do it from aircraft carriers; the ships would be sitting ducks, short of a whole armada going through the Strait. Imagine the U.S. Fifth Fleet coming through."

Aaron interrupted: "Good point . . . Any room for a strike from anywhere else?"

Ehud went back to his earlier thoughts: "It'd be tough from the Gulf of Oman, and I'm sure the Red Sea wouldn't work. Too far and too hard to get into or out of."

But he added that "the air raids would be feasible if the jets could land in and take off from Saudi Arabia." His conclusion was still that he agreed with Jesse: it was not a good route to consider because any action would have Israel's name written all over it, and also the name of Saudi Arabia if it had provided landing rights, adding: "There's no way we could organize a raid from Saudi Arabia without its consent. Brings us back to square one in terms of deniability."

Jesse brought the meeting to an end with a simple conclusion. It seemed to him that a special operations effort from within Iran was the only possible solution, assuming, as he did, that developing another computer worm would take too much time. The group agreed, which left Ariel with the task of planning and executing the move.

CHAPTER.03

General Landau's next priority was to meet with his protégé, Colonel Simon Rabinowitz.

Ariel was in his early fifties and relatively short in stature. His hairline had receded virtually all the way, leaving but a small crown of black and grey hair arranged in a semi-circle, going from one ear to the other around the back of his head. He wore black-rimmed, round glasses. He almost always dressed in civilian clothing, though with style, despite the fact that many Israeli officials tend to dump their ties in the summer because of the heat. In short, he did not look the part of a general, and might have been mistaken for the proverbial mad scientist or a Wall Street investment banker. Yet, people said that he had one of the most piercing minds and was noticed almost immediately by his superiors in whatever capacity he was employed. He had an informal nickname within the Cabinet: "Steel Trap." This referred to his mind being like a steel trap—nothing escaped.

Simon had come to work directly for Ariel a little more than five years earlier, after a very successful career in the field as a covert operative. Yet, he too, did not fit the classical image of the secret agent stereotyped by novelists, ranging from Ian Fleming's James Bond to Jean Bruce's OSS 117 and many others. He was neither suave nor debonair, and looked at times more like an accountant or a lawyer rather than someone about to shoot to kill or fight with a villain. In truth, he had not had many opportunities to fight and even fewer to kill, as covert operators from the *Mossad* were much more likely to outwit their opponent than fight with them in hand-to-hand combat. He still held a black belt in karate and in jiu-jitsu and had become an expert at *Krav Magra*. It is a self-defense system developed for the military in Israel. It consists of a wide combination of techniques sourced from a variety of combat sports ranging from judo to wrestling and boxing to grappling. It is known for its focus on real-world situations and its extremely efficient, brutal counterattacks.

This was where he had learned not only the skills that could be employed in combat, but also all the mental elements that allowed one fighter to beat another. He had learned that the key was never brute strength or technique alone; it was also having the right attitude, both toward training and life balance. This gave him that sort of calm assurance he needed when facing down some opposition. He was a happily married man and never had a reputation for seeking casual sex or for being terribly funny in marked contrast to the stereotypes in paperbacks or movies. He was known to be quite smart and extremely thorough and disciplined. He was a full six feet tall with an athletic build but, like his boss, had also already started losing his hair at the tender age of forty-one. He had a deep voice which could alternatively sound quite stern or charming, depending on the circumstances.

Simon had a bias which Ariel knew well. He hated risk because he hated to lose agents. He led two operations early in his new role under Ariel, each of which had led to the death of an agent. Though there was nothing in the plan that could remotely be faulted, Simon kept feeling that he could or should have done something to avoid the losses. He took them personally and insisted on being the one that visited the grieving spouse. One of the two agents that died was a woman, and he had spent time with her husband and young child. He always attended funeral services as well. Therefore, Ariel knew that he could have total confidence in Simon, when it came to planning.

Simon was totally dedicated to his job, though he reserved his highest emotional priority to his family. Yet, once his mind was set on a mission, he would not let go. His attention to detail and willingness to speak his mind were, in Ariel's view, rare qualities in a world largely populated with bureaucrats and politicians. Combining these technical skills with great empathy made him a truly unusual associate. In fact, though it had never been said in so many words, Ariel had the strong conviction that Simon was probably his most likely successor.

Ariel had somewhat of a special relationship with Simon; he was the one that plucked Simon from field missions to work directly on planning issues. Simon had a unique ability to think problems through to their logical conclusion. Ariel was sure that, this time, the planning that would be needed had to be even more detailed and precise. For this, Simon's intellectual rigor and discipline would be indispensable.

Ariel took Simon through the gist of the meeting in Jesse's office, starting with Jesse's trip to the U.S. and ending with the group's conclusion that the likely solution to discuss with President Caldwell involved a covert operation into Iran. He made the point that there was an unusual dimension: *Mossad* special forces would have to work with the Special Forces within the Air Force and the Navy, and possibly the U.S. or others. He asked whether that raised equipment issues or substantially extended the time they should plan for training. Simon was not definitive in his reply, but the message was clear: "Should be able to handle it . . ."

Then came the clincher: Ariel added that he needed Simon to give him a "yea" or "nay" on the feasibility of any plan designed to strike Iran's enrichment facilities within the next thirty-six hours or so. Ariel explained: "Jesse needs to get back to Caldwell by January 5 latest."

"Got it, Ariel. You can count on me."

CHAPTER.04

As soon as he heard from Jesse that Israel would be prepared to cooperate, Roger Caldwell summoned Jack Mitchell, his secretary of state, to the Oval Office. He used his cell phone to call Jack on his own cell phone. Contrary to the norm that has several other people in attendance, he had said that this had to be a one-on-one meeting. After having briefed him on the most recent developments, he asked him to meet with his opposite number in Saudi Arabia as soon as possible.

Jack understood that Israel was ready to consider helping the U.S., most likely through some form of covert operation within Iran; however, Jesse had made it clear to Caldwell that no such operation would be conceivable without Saudi help with respect to at least two dimensions: overflights and the use of some land base near or on the Persian Gulf. Caldwell had added that he was pleasantly surprised that Israel had beaten his deadline by one day, calling him a couple of days earlier, on January 4, bemoaning the fact that he had to wait a day to speak to Mitchell as he, Caldwell, was away from Washington: *"Not the stuff I'd discuss by phone, however scrambled."*

Abdul Al-Sudais, Saudi Arabia's Minister for Foreign Affairs, was a very well-known entity in the U.S. He had obtained international relations degrees from U.S. universities, the first from Tufts and the second from Georgetown. He had spent a good part of his career in or around the U.S. He was eventually named Saudi Ambassador to the U.S. A number of important events took place during his tenure, ranging from major arms procurement contracts to challenging developments in the region. He returned to Riyadh when he was eventually named Minister for Foreign Affairs. The steadiness and predictability of his approach had led the State Department to view him as a very reasonable individual and one willing to work with the U.S. It did not hurt that he was known to enjoy a close relationship with the Crown Prince. In short, he was very comfortable with the U.S., though he would always think Saudi Arabia first; but what else would one expect from a Saudi diplomat?

Mitchell had called Al-Sudais as soon as he left the Oval Office, knowing that he could still reach him before evening prayers. He had decided to possibly visit him in Riyadh on Saturday, as he knew full well that Friday would be out of the question. Though, technically, he knew that Saturday was a part of the two-day weekend in Saudi Arabia, he thought that: *Al-Sudais would be willing to meet with him. This would allow Jack to travel back to the States and arrive Saturday evening and thus be able to attend the Sunday Mass which Al-Sudais knew was his regular practice.*

Al-Sudais was surprised by Mitchell's call. Initially, he had thought that: *the call was to brief him on the circumstances of the U.S. drone strike which killed two high-ranking, Iranian officials in Bagdad.* One of them, the commander of its Quds Force, a division primarily responsible for extraterritorial military and clandestine operations, was widely perceived as the right-hand man of Iran's Supreme Leader. His death was considered a very serious blow to the regime. The other headed up an Iranian-backed group in Iraq and, though powerful, paled into insignificance when compared to the first. Mitchell indicated that the topic would likely come up, but more importantly that his need was for a much broader and arguably more serious conversation which President Caldwell had asked him to have urgently.

They had agreed to a meeting early on Saturday at the famous building housing the Ministry on An Namudhajiyah, a major artery in Riyadh. It was a twenty-minute ride and a bit more than six odd miles from the residence of the King, the Al Yamamah Palace. Designed by Henning Larsen, the Foreign Ministry building was a major landmark. It blended both the local and monumental styles of Islamic architecture and earned the Aga Khan Award for Architecture in 1989. Built in 1984, it resembled a white fortress carved out of a single piece of stone. From the top, it looked like an expanded triangle with two, large sides, featuring four rows of small square windows and a large entrance on each. The spectacular front of the building was set on a diagonal, with a large, majestic entrance door in the middle, flanked by two lower, semi-circular, tower-like structures on either side. Nine light wells distributed around the roof of the building ensured that virtually every part of the building had natural light inside.

Al-Sudais met Mitchell in the reception area of his top floor quarters and walked him to his office—well-appointed and very functional. Yet, it was devoid of any form of outright ostentation, other than the fact that it was quite large. Mitchell, who personally enjoyed Persian rugs, could not help but notice the fine carpets that were on the floor, particularly a wonderful cream and red Nain in front of his desk, and the deep blue and cream Isfahan that was in the sitting area. Al-Sudais pointed to the French Empire-style armchairs, with gilded, wood frames and red and green French tapestry as upholstery. He selected the chair to the left, allowing Mitchell to be seated to his right. Two cups of tea with a plate of local sweet delicacies discretely appeared and were placed between them. The male assistant who brought them carefully served the tea and left the room without more than a couple of words.

Mitchell started with a quick discussion of the drone strike that killed the two generals, not because it was an important agenda item, but because he knew that Al-Sudais expected him to mention it. He quickly moved on to the key topic—enlisting Saudi help to neutralize Iran's uranium enrichment facilities. Yet, rather than focusing on that question, which, after all, was the point, but was likely to trigger potentially adverse emotional reactions, he first discussed the belligerent activity of Iran and its proxies over the prior many months. He talked of the hijacking of tankers in and around the Strait of Hormuz, of the numerous rocket attacks on U.S. and Israeli forces in the region and finally spoke of the unprovoked attack on Saudi oil facilities. Through his discussion, Al-Sudais seemed to nod approvingly, although Mitchell had noted a much less visibly favorable reaction to the mention of rockets aimed at Israel. *Par for the course,* Jack thought to himself.

In the end, he had to come around to asking the key question: "Would Saudi Arabia be willing to help the U.S. deal with the problem posed by Iran in the region?"

As he heard Jack's question, however diplomatically couched, Al-Sudais almost at once sat more erect in his armchair and appeared taken aback: "You're not going to go to war, are you?"

Mitchell reassured him that the plan was not to conduct open activities, adding: "We want to find discrete and unattributable ways to disable or at least substantially impair Iran's nuclear enrichment activities."

As Jack put it, using his hands and arms to modulate the message, the desire was to make Iran realize that there was no point in continuing on the route they had taken. At the same time, he had to accept Al-Sudais immediate rejoinder that he was not convinced the Iranians would respond to anything subtle. Mitchell countered: "That's exactly our point . . ."

As he explained it further, the need was to strike a major blow, all the while doing it in a way that could not be traced in any credible way to any of the participants.

"What do you mean?"

"Honestly, the plan has not been developed in detail yet. That's up to *Mossad!*"

However, he explained that the main element would involve a set of covert special operations within Iran, which might involve either or both Israel and the U.S. For this to work, they would need a measure of cooperation from Saudi Arabia, most likely in the form of logistical assistance, and maybe more, but never extending to anything official either in the eyes of the world or even known or visible within the Kingdom. He added that some assistance might also be unofficially asked from Kuwait and would be equally discrete and anonymous.

Al-Sudais took a deep breath and stayed silent for what seemed like an eternity. Mitchell, as do all senior diplomats, knew that silence was at times necessary and thus let his Saudi counterpart sort out his thoughts without disturbing him. A minute or so later, Al-Sudais cracked a small smile. Mitchell took it as a good sign and smiled back. Al-Sudais offered a simple and encouraging message but was still broadly non-committal: "I can see certain angles, but I've got to do more thinking."

In short, he was saying he understood the general thrust and appreciated that no detail could be forthcoming at this point. Still, he wondered what next step Michell expected from him or from the Kingdom. Jack earnestly responded that some indication that there was indeed room for cooperation, even if Israel was involved, was a requirement for any form of planning to move forward. Al-Sudais replied: "I must ask for the Prime Minister's views before going any further . . ."

Though the King of Saudi Arabia is the *de jure* Prime Minister of the country, and had been since the 1964 coup, the Crown Prince had become, in the most recent past, the *de facto* Prime Minister. However, officially, the Crown Prince only held the title of Defense Minister, along with those of Chief of the Royal Court and of Chair of the Council for Economic and Development Affairs. The Crown Prince was known to be a very smart but, at times, impulsive individual. However, he was very much admired for his efforts to move the kingdom into the present century, for instance, by recently allowing women to drive. His image had suffered somewhat at the time of the assassination in Turkey of a U.S.-based, Saudi journalist critical of the royal rule. He had kept a low profile for a while, and now seemed to be regaining his power and his poise.

Mitchell told Al-Sudais that he fully expected him to have to consult internally. He stressed the highly sensitive nature of the issue: "Got to keep it all very close to the vest."

He added that President Caldwell would be happy to make a formal request, though he impressed on Al-Sudais the difficulty for the President to travel with the discretion required while the project was being developed. He added that there would have to be some official cover for him to come to the Kingdom, and that would conflict with the current sense of urgency, unless Saudi Arabia could think of one immediate concern. Al-Sudais seemed to say with a broad wave of his right arm that a trip by Caldwell would not be all that important. Mitchell added that time was of the essence, at least in terms of an initial agreement in principle, as quite a bit of planning would probably be required.

"Understood. May I have a few days?"

"Sure."

CHAPTER.05

Jack Mitchell had just talked to President Caldwell, and both had breathed a sigh of relief. They could not know it, but surely would have assumed, that Moshe Shamir had also talked to both Jesse Benaroya and Ariel Landau. Their reactions were similar to Caldwell's.

They all had just completed the final meeting of Hydra Defense, the code name that had been given to the joint effort to destroy as much of Iran's nuclear capabilities as possible without anyone stepping across the line of an attributable official war declaration. The name came from the Lernaean Hydra, a many-headed serpent in Greek mythology; it reflected the fact that the operation would involve a small coalition and several distinct actions. Attending were the four foreign ministers: Jack Mitchell for the U.S., Moshe Shamir for Israel, Abdul Al-Sudais for Saudi Arabia and Walid bin Mohammed Al-Saleh for Kuwait. As everyone spoke English, they had no need for translators; and they had not brought along any aides. They had chosen to meet on the jewel of the U.S. Fifth Fleet, a Nimitz class aircraft carrier, for several reasons. The most important was security and discretion, even if it required all Foreign Ministers to travel the last leg of their trip by helicopter. Also, there was the requirement that Israeli and Arabs were not to meet in each other's countries, given the absence of diplomatic relations. Finally, meeting in the U.S. would involve a big waste of time and greater risk of leaks. The only other candidate that received some consideration was Ramstein Air Force Base in Germany, but the ultimate discretion of the aircraft carrier won the day.

A lot of advance planning had taken place in a relatively short time among the four ministers. They wanted to develop a clear list of what could and could not be done from political points of view. That list would then be passed on to Ariel Landau and Simon Rabinowitz who would use it as parameters to plan an operation or to come back with the view that nothing was feasible within the constraints, in their considered opinion. The sooner that information was made available, the sooner plans could be developed, finalized and logistics organized. Simon had nevertheless been working on the assumption that things would work out as expected, i.e. that he would get what he needed, but he also had a number of contingencies for situations where the desired outcome would not materialize. The most crucial element was a base on the west side of the Persian Gulf, preferably in Saudi Arabia, but otherwise in Kuwait though the latter would raise the risk of loss of anonymity at some point.

As one could expect, the biggest challenge in their behind-the-scenes conversations had been Saudi Arabia, principally because of domestic politics. They simply could not afford to be seen as involved in something which would most likely be blamed on Israel, the U.S. or both. At the same time, they had been the object of an unprovoked attack on a part of their oil infrastructure, and, in the eyes of the world, would probably have been justified participating in an action which weakened Iran.

Eventually, Saudi Arabia agreed to offer the use of Khafji as a base, a small military installation on the coast of the Persian Gulf, less than ten miles from the southern Kuwaiti border and no more than sixty miles south of Kuwait City. They asked, however, that any aircraft or equipment landing there or transiting close enough to the base be absolutely unmarked: No trace of any Israeli origin. They agreed to allow the use of their airspace to and from the base. Furthermore, they even offered to give code names and numbers such that Saudi air-traffic control would recognize the aircraft but would not know who they were. This was a trick they utilized whenever they needed to fly members of the royal family who wanted to be truly incognito. Finally, they allowed the coalition to use their territorial waters on the west side of the Gulf, but only for submarines, again to ensure that no one would know of the Israeli connection.

Dealing with Kuwait had been easier, as they were in the room for only two reasons. First, Kuwait had eight U.S. military bases, the largest of which was Camp Arifjan, an Army installation that included elements of four of the five U.S. services: Air Force, Navy, Marine Corps and Coast Guard. Second, Camp Arifjan was located around forty miles from Khafji, the base offered by the Saudis. Access to the larger U.S. resources available in Kuwait if needed and the clear likelihood that there would be some use of Kuwait's air space made it a required partner. Further, they fully expected the Navy and Coast Guard forces to be on patrol in international waters during the whole of the mission. The risk of enlarging the group from three to four seemed worth the additional flexibility.

In short, neither Saudi Arabia nor Kuwait would play an active role in the overall operation, but they would be key, logistical, hidden partners.

The U.S. would also play a role, but it would be limited and stealthy. They would provide ongoing AWACS coverage before, during and even immediately after the operation in Iran. Equally important would be their efforts to reduce the ability of the Iranian revolutionary forces to disrupt traffic in the Strait of Hormuz, because, as they all knew, a substantial share of the exported oil produced in the Middle East transited through it.

The U.S. Navy would be using a new class of naval mines that had three important features. First, they could be dropped by submarines, rather than by airplanes. Second, they rested on the seafloor and were triggered to detonate when a metal-hulled ship passed over them, causing an alteration in the earth's magnetic field. Third, and most importantly, they were also remotely controlled, in that they could be activated or deactivated at will. This would be crucial both to ensure that any friendly ship that passed their location could be safe and that any unexploded mine, by the time the mission ended, could be safely detonated. They would be principally placed near Larak, Siri and Abu Musa, three islands strategically located in the Strait area. The U.S. Navy would be using an underwater drone, the Orca, to place them. The submarine alternatives might be too easily picked up by the Iranians, while dropping them from the air made no sense either. The plan was to dispatch one or two Orcas as soon as the mission started; they would need to be flown from the U.S. to the Fifth Fleet as soon as agreement was reached. The mines would remain deactivated until they were needed; the deactivation would avoid the need to send an official warning to any ship traveling through the Strait.

The U.S. would also play another important role. With the help of Israel which would provide the required missiles, U.S. operatives would fire at the nuclear fuel manufacturing center in Isfahan and the Arak reactor, probably from Iraq, but possibly as well from inside the Iranian territory. The Isfahan facility was the place where the Iranians took enriched uranium hydrochloride gas produced at Natanz and Fordow and made it into uranium pellets.

Israel, on its side, would focus on Fordow and Natanz with a team of four individuals who would carry out the work from within Iran. Their part of the overall mission would be called Operation Kovesh, named after a drone which would play a crucial role throughout their effort. They would need logistical assistance from the whole of the coalition, military assistance from the U.S., probably from Camp Arifjan or jets from the Fifth Fleet, if things did not unfold as expected; the team would also be expected to fly back into Khafji, after the completion of the mission. Parenthetically, Israel and the U.S. would conduct military exercises in the Mediterranean as a diversion, in the few days before the strike.

At the end of the meeting, Jack simply got up and saluted everyone: "Thank you all. This looks like one hell of a joint effort . . ."

CHAPTER.06

**MARCH 31
JERUSALEM**

The prior three months had been draining for Simon. He was responsible within *Mossad* for the activities whose name was a massive understatement: **disruption**. His group, probably the most secretive within an already very secretive organization, was generally in charge of activities which many would consider illegal. However, these activities still needed to be carried out in the interest of the State of Israel. They were thus considered within the spirit of Israel's Constitution: assassination of foreign leaders, sabotage of certain installations of which Israel did not approve, internet warfare and the like. His group did not appear on any organization chart—that anyone could procure.

Three months earlier, he had been charged with the most complex and ambitious assignment: dealing a massive blow to Iran's nuclear program and doing it in a way that could not be traced back to Israel. A month or so later, he had been told that both Saudi Arabia and Kuwait had agreed to offer some support, with the important proviso that nothing could ever been traced back to them. He also knew that the U.S. had promised AWACS support (Airborne Warning And Control System—a mobile, long-range radar surveillance and control center for air defense). The U.S. was also ready to help with two, so far unspecified covert operations, as well. These would not include people on the ground in Iran, or at least no people on the ground in Iran for any period longer than a few hours at most.

He had to consult a number of internal resources, particularly Marvin Goldstein. A veteran of the service, Marvin had an encyclopedic knowledge of the capabilities of each of the branches of the Israeli Defense Forces. He also knew exactly what was being planned for the future and even what research directions were emphasized and those which were not. At fifty, Marvin had worked with nearly all the key players in the service and his reputed friendship with Ariel opened many doors. He was of medium build and could not pass for a field operative: he did not look the part, with a bit of a pot belly and his almost professorial manners. But he knew his stuff better than anyone and had a mind that thrived on challenges. He loved innovation, even if this was going to stretch his capabilities nearly to the breaking point. He was a man of vision; his vision was focused on technology. His only well-known shortcoming was that he loved technology and more often than not would extend his explanations into levels of detail that many considered unnecessary. Yet, most people still gave him a pass on those, as he was so good at everything else.

Now, Simon was sitting in the Cabinet Room next to Jesse's office, presenting his plan to the so-called war cabinet. The Prime Minister's Office was located in Jerusalem, in the Government center on the same hill as the *Knesset*, dominating a part of Jerusalem's skyline. The Cabinet Room was quite large and could seat not only all the ministers, but about twice as many people again, on chairs arranged along three of the four walls. The long, rectangular table was made of light-colored wood, with inserts of brown leather. The armchairs for the people seated at the table were upholstered in the same leather as the one used for the table and had chromed, flat metallic frames. Jesse always sat in the middle of the table with Ariel Landau. Defense Minister Spielberg and Minister of Foreign Affairs Shamir were usually sitting one on each side of him and the other opposite. To his right was the one wall that did not offer any room for sitting, as it was the one that had a couple of large, flat screens and four smaller ones. These were typically used for slide presentations or for videoconferencing.

Simon started by clarifying that his presentation would solely be focused on the Israeli side of the action, Operation Kovesh, developed by the Hydra Defense group. He knew that other activities were planned by the U.S., in particular. He was sure that these would be covered by Ariel or someone else. Simon's group activities would concentrate on the two main enrichment plants. He added: "There are a couple of other sites, but they were still small and might be targets for the U.S."

The two plants they would attack were Fordow, north of Qom, and Natanz, south of Kashan. The strategy would involve blowing the facilities up from the outside at Natanz and from the inside at Fordow. He emphasized the need to strike both places at virtually the same time; any material delay between the two operations would increase the risks to the team which would, in his opinion, become unacceptable. A lack of perfect synchronization would also raise the risk to the mission: Iranian defenses might be up. He added that a couple of diversionary actions would be undertaken, with the help of the U.S. in the Mediterranean, to train the Iranians' focus on the "wrong thing" for a short while. He concluded that the mission was both quite complex and the various activities mutually dependent: "Never done anything quite that complex before . . ."

He would use one team, which would be based in Qom, both because it was close to both targets and because *Mossad* already had assets on the ground that were relevant to the plan, though they might also choose to have a base in Kashan. He expanded on the earlier decision to use a different approach in Fordow and Natanz. First, they had assets in Qom which would allow them to do something in Fordow that they could not replicate in Natanz, adding: "By the way, these assets are crucial: the natural topographical protection in Fordow is much greater than in Natanz. Fordow looks practically impregnable in terms of an outside hit; it's deep within a mountain, in the general area where the Iranians extract uranium ore."

Turning to Natanz, he conceded that it was also very well-guarded, but the topography was friendlier, as Simon added with a modest smile: "Protection for the installations is man-made rather than through a mountain range, so the breach could be instigated from the outside. Whatever was made by man, man can destroy . . ."

The field team would comprise four men. Two would play the role of German scientists working within the German nuclear industry—they were both excellent German speakers. Two would play the roles of overseas Iranian businessmen returning to the home country in the hope of starting a manufacturing business there. And, of course, they were both fluent in Farsi. The first stage in the plan was due to start within a week. The two so-called German scientists would be flying, in response to an official invitation from the chief technical engineer at Fordow, to Tehran to inspect those nuclear enrichment facilities. He added that this had been arranged through contacts with German nuclear suppliers and a deep-cover agent in Qom.

Turning to one of the touchiest parts of the exercise, he explained that they would stage the action from the west coast of the Persian Gulf, specifically at Khafji, a Saudi town eight miles south of the Kuwaiti border . . . Ariel interrupted Simon: "Isn't that the town that made a name for itself during the Desert Storm campaign when it marked the culmination of the coalition air campaign in 1991?"

"Precisely, Ariel. Khafji has a useful air base; it's not heavily used by the Saudi forces. However, they have army and air force troops stationed there. I expect it should provide all the infrastructure needed . . ."

Then, with a wide smile, Simon added: "And, that, with minimal dissemination of Saudi involvement."

This was where Simon would establish his command post during the actual operation. The plan involved the use of special purpose equipment which he was going to have Marvin discuss and a small squadron of fighter jets. These fighters really were principally meant for the eventual evacuation of the team, but they would be ready to swoop into Iran and defend the team, if it came under attack.

Simon then explained that the most challenging part of the planning had been with respect to the equipment and to the training that was required. There were three important equipment needs that required creativity: transportation and associated operational material; explosives in several forms; and something to bring equipment into Iran and evacuate the team once the missions were accomplished. Looking around the room, he asked whether more information was needed on the equipment front, adding that Marvin Goldstein was standing by outside the room if the Cabinet wanted to hear more. Seeing that the key players wanted to have more detail, he asked for Marvin to come in.

After the usual pleasantries and mutual congratulatory remarks, Marvin started with the discussion of the Natanz project, which would be the most difficult to execute from an equipment standpoint: "Got two problems. First, the proximity of Iranian troops. Second, the distances the team would need to cover in relatively open space. Plus, I bet that space is mine-protected."

A major challenge was to bring what would be needed into Iran and to transfer it onto the site. He said that the Service had a couple of "neat" pieces of equipment which would do the trick both in terms of transport of the material needed and to bore tunnels through which explosives would be dropped directly on top of the enrichment halls.

He then turned to the part of the project that he had enjoyed the most. The modification of the Kovesh drone, which would play a crucial role on at least two fronts. In passing, he noted that non-Hebrew speakers, therefore most people outside of the room, might not know that Kovesh was the Hebrew word for *conqueror*. The Kovesh had started life in the U.S. as a RQ-170. The RQ-170 was like a flying, triangle-shaped wing; it had no tail, and its engine took up the middle portion of the wing. The air intake for the jet was above the wing eighteen inches or so beyond the leading edge; the body of the engine made up a good part of the fuselage which protruded mostly above the wing. The RQ-170 became a Kovesh after a number of important modifications.

After these, the drone was no more than six feet tall and indeed looked like a flat wing-like snake that had just swallowed some big animal, now stuck in its belly. From the front, the only thing noticeable was the large air intake on top of a very thin and very wide wing. The whole belly of the beast was relatively flat as most of the fuselage was above rather than below the wing, except for a couple of small bulges where the cargo bays were built in. The wings themselves appeared to never end as the aircraft was about ten times larger than it was high. The frontal section of the drone, one of the ways it could be picked up by radar, was, therefore, truly minimal.

Turning to the modifications which Israel had made to the U.S. drone, Marvin first mentioned efforts to make the drone into a stealth aircraft. To achieve that property, the drone was painted in a darkish grey color and its external parts coated with stealth material; they had also developed notched landing gear doors and sharpened the leading edges of the wing; finally, and most important, was the move of the engine exhaust from below to above the wing. He explained the need to shield the exhaust of the turbofan engine that powered it from any instrument that could pick it up from below: certain radars could pick up heat, and any exhaust gases that escaped below the wing could be detected. They had also enlarged two bays that sat on either side of the engine, sort of fairings above the wing really, as they still had to preserve the almost flat shape of the underside to ensure stealth.

Marvin then moved on to yet another set of modifications that would adapt the Kovesh to the particular mission at hand. The big deal was that the Kovesh drones would be used to airlift the team out of Iran upon completion of their work. So, to allow the drones to ferry humans back from the mission, Marvin and his team had to reengineer a part of the aircraft. But they had neither the time nor the willingness to make major structural changes. They zeroed in on the idea that the two bays, the fairings on top of the wings of the Sentinel, which they kept on the "normal" drones, offered the ideal solution. Typically, these compartments house highly sensitive electronic equipment and some armament; but, in this mission, much of these would be surplus to requirements. So, they relocated the part of the electronics they needed to keep toward the fuselage, got rid of the armament and used the space thus freed up to create symmetrical pods. A human could slip into either of these pods easily. Each drone would be able to ferry two members of the team back to base, one on either side of the fuselage. They put a small window at the front of each pod to provide the occupants some forward vision, although it was still very limited, and Marvin noted: "Frankly, it's more to control claustrophobia."

He added that they also put a small video screen on the fuselage side of each compartment. These were connected to the drone's GPS system. This would allow the men to follow the progress to their destination. Also, they inserted oxygen equipment where their heads would be. That equipment would connect directly into the helmets they would be wearing. Those would be part of the cargo that would be ferried by the drones to Iran on their second trip, just before picking the men up. Finally, they mildly pressurized the compartments as the men would not have G-suits. Marvin mentioned a final detail with a smile: the engineers even provided a small depression at the tail end of each cavity to allow the men to maintain their feet in a vertical, downward facing position. This should make the trip more comfortable and reduce the risk of cramps anywhere along the legs and all the way to the hips. In fairness, he added it also allowed the designers to maintain a slightly narrower profile for the pods. He explained: "If their feet weren't facing down, they'd have to be off to the side and we'd have to find space for them."

Simon was conscious of the fact that the room was at its limits in terms of details and technobabble; impatience was increasingly visible on people's faces, except possibly for Ariel and Ehud who were directly concerned with the aircraft. He still wanted to add a couple of points. He explained that he had seen the "bird" and was surprised that it looked a lot bigger than he had imagined, adding: "A twenty-meter, twenty-two-yard, wingspan is a lot."

Second, looking inside the cargo bays and at the pods where the team would eventually ride, he found that there was more space than he had feared. Though the bulges underneath the wings were quite small, there was plenty of space in the cargo bays. Marvin had confirmed that they were easily large enough to hold everything the team needed. Third, he wanted to give formal credit to Marvin and his team for their attention to detail. He said he had looked at the inside of one of the pods in which a man would eventually be and saw plenty of cushioning on the bench and even noted that the bench had been designed so that it was a bit lower at the front and at the level of the ankles, and a bit higher at waist level. Seeing the quizzical reaction in the room, Marvin had interjected: "That's to maintain the normal angle of the body at the waist. It should be more comfortable and less tiring for the guys that way."

Jesse asked: "Looks great, guys, but . . . what's the role of these drones, except ferrying back the men? Simon? Marvin?"

"You mean the role of these drones earlier in this mission, right?"

"Right, Simon."

Marvin looked at Simon who batted his eyelids to let him know he should answer Jesse's question. So, he explained that they would fly in at the beginning of the mission and land with all the equipment at the base near Kashan. They would leave right away and fly back to the base in Saudi Arabia. Then, they would return to pick up all the four team members when they were done. He added that, on the second trip into Iran, they would ferry a couple of last-minute items that Simon did not want to risk being discovered or stolen on the ground in Iran. He was referring to ground-to-ground missiles, which *Mossad* had captured from Hezbollah.

■ ■ ■ ■ ■

Marvin was referring to a great, but still secret, *Mossad* success. A year or so earlier, *Mossad* had heard that Hezbollah was working with Syria to bring additional rockets into Southern Lebanon. Officially, the press reported that Israeli jets had bombed the convoy; and this was almost true. In reality, the mission had been quite a bit more complex. *Mossad* had managed to infiltrate the convoy and to place two men in it. They were in the last truck, one of them driving and the other sitting next to the driver, apparently ready to fire if attacked, in a setup which was replicated on all trucks. When a pre-arranged point in time was reached, the last truck in the convoy fell behind, allegedly with a flat tire that needed to be replaced—a small bit of explosive had been conveniently located on the wheel to ensure that the tire would deflate. The rest of the trucks had slowed down but kept going, and the tail escort overtook the stopped truck to stay with the rest of the convoy. The tail escort and the whole convoy expected the last truck to make up any lost time by driving a bit faster once the tire had been changed.

As soon as the convoy was a safe distance away from the "stranded truck," the wave of fighter jets had, as reported, descended and destroyed the whole group. Not reported, was the fact that, trailing the jets, a couple of helicopters landed right next to the last truck and loaded the ground-to-ground missiles and launchers it contained. As their colleagues were making the arms transfer, the two agents set explosives on the truck so that, after they boarded their helicopters and both aircrafts had flown a safe distance away, they could trigger an explosion, destroying the truck and making it seem as if it had been bombed from the sky as well. Hezbollah never knew that the last truck had not been destroyed in the same way as the others. And in the meantime, Israel had Iran-made missiles, with Iranian markings. Those were the missiles which Israel would use in the mission and provide to the U.S. for their share as well.

■ ■ ■ ■ ■

At this point, Simon judged that there was no need to go into any further detail, unless anyone in the group felt otherwise. So, he asked: "Any question?"

The room was initially silent. This was not the first briefing ever on the topic, as the group had been kept generally informed through the development of the plan and while the negotiations with the U.S., Saudi Arabia and Kuwait were proceeding. Certain members of the group, Ehud, for instance, certainly knew everything there was to know about the Kovesh, as did his boss Yitzhak Lander, the *Raj Aluf.* They should, therefore, not have been surprised. Yet, now that they could see the effort in its totality and view how the various pieces came together, they still had numerous questions, principally about the equipment and on the coordination of the effort, not forgetting logistics. Other members of the group had more general questions, principally focused on risks. Simon and Marvin handled them as expertly as they could and, in the end, Ariel brought the meeting to a close with a wave of his hand and a broad smile, offering a simple conclusion, "As you all know, no plan is perfect, but this one seems as close as we can get to perfect. Thanks all around."

CHAPTER.07

Simon sent an email to Minoo Rakhsha, fully assuming that it could well be read by the local Iranian authorities. He had the email sent from a Paris address which officially belonged to Minoo's second cousin, Adan. His father, Fardin, a cousin of Minoo's father, Cyrus, had moved to Paris during the Shah's regime; he had stayed there, marrying Catherine, a beautiful and charming French woman. Simon knew that the Iranian authorities considered Adan and Fardin neutral from a political standpoint. The email simply told Minoo that Catherine was seriously ill and would like to see her if at all possible. It also added that the family would reimburse her the cost of the ticket when she got to Paris, if it was too much for her. That was Simon's way of conveying a sense of urgency.

Minoo immediately understood Simon's message. She knew that she would not need to worry about meeting Catherine, Adan or Fardin. She knew that Fardin had died several years ago, and that Catherine and Adan had secretly relocated to Israel, under different identities. She still wondered what was up.

■ ■ ■ ■ ■

Minoo was currently a physics professor at Qom University of Technology. She was born in Paris, where Cyrus was studying engineering when he met Sophie Rosier, a fellow student and a stunning, French Jewish woman to boot. A true Persian and native of the Isfahan Province, Cyrus had left Iran as a young adult to study abroad, first in London, and then in Paris, for his advanced engineering work. He and his parents had agreed that the advanced education available in Iran, his home country, was not sufficient, given his drive and his intellectual faculties. He eventually married Sophie who quickly found herself pregnant; they decided to call their daughter Minoo, which, though a Persian name, appealed to Sophie as it sounded so much like 'Minou', the name of the cat she had so loved as a child. As is often the case with many Jews in France, Sophie did not practice her religion while at university, nor did she seem particularly focused on her ancestry and tradition. So, after having married Cyrus, Sophie accepted Islam as the family's official religion, though Cyrus himself did not attend the mosque with any more regularity than Sophie attended the synagogue prior to their being wed. Minoo had spent her early years in Paris, until Cyrus, who had, by then, been working as a production engineer for the French oil giant, Total, for at least four years, was posted back to Tehran. Minoo had no trouble moving to Tehran and agreed when her parents told her that she should not mention her Jewish ancestry.

■ ■ ■ ■ ■

When she received Simon's email, Minoo asked for and got permission from the University Rector to make that urgent trip on compassionate grounds. She booked herself on the next Iran Air flight, IR 733, from Tehran to Paris Orly. She dutifully sent an email back to "Cousin Adan" to let him know that she had made reservations and would arrive two days hence at 12:45, Paris time. She said she would be well rested as she knew the flight was rarely full; the Airbus 340-600 that flew the route rarely operated at more than 50% capacity. So, she said she hoped that she could stretch out a bit. Simon understood that he was expected to meet her at the airport, located less than fifteen miles south of Paris.

Simon wore what was for him a heavy disguise, but in fact had him look quite a bit like Adan, who was of about the same build. He was fairly sure that Minoo would not be followed; she was trusted by the authorities as her nuclear physics specialty was very much in demand in Iran. Though her course focused on relatively basic notions that fit the second-year students she taught, she had participated in other activities involving considerably more complex and advanced matters. She had done a couple of consulting projects jointly with other colleagues. She was convinced, probably quite rightly, that the fact she was a woman had prevented her from doing more than a small number of projects. Yet, a few of these projects came close to dealing with the nuclear activities of the State; she had to receive a security clearance for that. The authorities had never found out that she had Jewish roots and thus did not know that she really was still a Jewess, especially as she attended the mosque on Friday to fit with her assumed identity.

Though she was under no local suspicion, Simon thought that: *one was never too careful* and too, his ability to look like Adan would satisfy anyone who did not look too carefully. He had rented a Peugeot 308, which would be in keeping with the budget which Adan would have, were he still in France.

As per normal, operating procedures, they met at the official meeting point in the Orly South Terminal, pretty much in the center of the main floor. She had gone down to the baggage claim area to retrieve her one piece of checked luggage. Simon had positioned himself in a way that Minoo could not see him as she went to retrieve her luggage, yet he could check that she was not followed. After retrieving her luggage and going through customs, she took the lift up to the main floor. Simon had moved to the bottom of the two escalators coming down from the departure floor, which was the usual meeting point, not only for Mossad but for most of the traveling public. She walked a few yards from the lift and saw him. They hugged each other and exchanged a couple of kisses. They walked to the parking garage, climbed into his car and started driving toward Paris and its legendary, clogged, ring road.

"Simon, it's good to see you. What's up?"

Matter-of-factly, he simply replied, "We need to talk."

"Guessed that much. About what?"

He started with a general comment to the effect that they were embarking on a major "disruption" that was more sensitive than anything he had been involved in before: "We're talking of the "mother" of all disruptions."

Minoo was ostensibly surprised. She replied, "Is that why you would even consider wearing a disguise?"

"Absolutely."

He said that from then on, they should make triply sure that nobody follows any one of them. She was clearly excited and wanted to know more. Simon was partially dancing around the topic, as the question he had to ask was quite difficult, and both touchy and personal.

Minoo had been dating a very senior nuclear engineer working in Fordow. Farid Kashani was one of the two most senior engineers at the nuclear complex near Qom. In fact, he was the second-in-command in Fordow as well. His boss, Dr. Reza Pashtani, was viewed as the lead political appointee.

As an undercover Mossad agent, she had initially sought and met Farid because she knew she needed a contact inside the uranium enrichment community, in order to do her unofficial job. It had not been terribly difficult for Minoo initially to meet Farid because of her official job. A professor of nuclear physics at Qom University of Technology had every reason to seek a scientist whose background was in nuclear physics as well and who worked on a very practical challenge in that field to boot, a few miles away. She had initially managed to get herself introduced to Farid under this pretense: she would love to have him talk to her students.

She was an attractive brunette, of middle height and slim build. Her father, Cyrus, was an aristocratic looking individual whose family had been involved in medicine for three generations in the region of Isfahan; he was the black sheep of the family having gone into engineering. He didn't see that as "treason," but rather as a mere continuation of a family tradition. He defined that tradition as one of intellectual excellence rather than medicine. Before he prematurely grew old when he lost his wife, Sophie, he was tall and slim, with a dark head of hair that did not want to thin out and a full mustache. Minoo had taken her father's aristocratic demeanor and his piercing, almost eagle-like eyes, although she had inherited her mother's smaller build. She was quite a beautiful woman with dark eyes and an oval face which was often neatly framed by long, wavy, dark hair, which she occasionally wore in a bun.

When she met Farid, ostensibly to discuss the possible engagement to speak to her students, she could immediately see that he was not indifferent to her charm. At forty-one, he was six years older than she, but he did not really look his age. The one thing that she noted above everything else was his smile—perfect, shining, white teeth and darker lips to frame it. He did come to speak to her class, though they had agreed that he would be quite vague as to what his actual professional duties were. He would just admit to working for the government research effort on the development of nuclear energy to help the country.

Over the ensuing months and year, they had become quite close, though, in the Islamic Iranian Republic, any of the thoughts which might immediately come to the minds of people living in a freer environment had to be banished. Finding time together and in a quiet environment that they could live their growing passion was already hard enough. Living together would simply be out of the question. This had not prevented them from becoming intimate and having sex, usually in either of their apartments, after a dinner or an evening together. They had, however, never spent a full night together. It always had to look as if they had been visiting, and they had been careful that the evening should never extend too far into the night. They were both a bit frustrated because they had to maintain these appearances. Farid, however, had not felt ready to propose to Minoo and the lack of an immediate family for both—Cyrus, Minoo's Dad was their only local relative—made that even harder; he had no one in whom he could really confide and seek reassurance that he was doing the right thing. Minoo could not take the initiative, although she had considered it a few times. She felt she was ready. But, was he?

Having let Minoo tell the history of her relationship—some or even most of which he already knew—Simon had to pop the question: "Would he be willing to help if you asked?"

"Depends what you mean by help," she replied matter-of-factly.

"We'd love to have more detailed information on the Iranian enrichment operations?"

With that point, Minoo had a solid hunch of what was coming, but she was still taken a bit aback. She thought for a minute and argued that the response to Simon's question could not be straightforward. She started: "On the one hand, Farid . . ."

Simon interrupted . . . "Farid?"

"Yes, Farid, Dr. Farid Kashani . . . My boyfriend . . . Farid is his name . . ."

"Oh. Sorry . . ."

She continued but could not avoid telling the story behind Farid's family name. Many Iranians started having a family name only about a century ago. So, with origins in Kashan, a town seventy miles southeast of Qom and famous for its rugs and small industry, the family simply took a name that said they were from there—thus Kashani.

Returning to her earlier conversation, she said that Farid would certainly answer if she only asked a couple of innocuous questions.

In fact, she admitted that he had already told her a few things, which Simon would know of, as she had already shared with the Service. On the other hand, she said that she had to be extremely careful: "He doesn't know that I'm Jewish and that I've got a second line of work besides the university, if you catch my drift."

"OK—so he doesn't know that you work for the Mossad."

"Absolutely not," was her response, with a tone sounding surprised that Simon would even ask.

Simon's voice then registered a more somber note. He turned to Minoo, as much as he could, as he was still driving, and said that the real question was whether she would be willing to ask him questions that might eventually involve him in her unofficial activities. She could not disguise her surprise—not that she felt she needed to—and argued that Farid would be bound to wonder why she appeared to be grilling him. The hardest truth had yet to come, but she felt she had to be on the level. She then added, "I'm really not sure I want to involve him in my unofficial activities as you nicely call them—at least not yet."

Simon had to admit that this was reasonable. He added that, in normal circumstances, this would be the end of the conversation. However, he reminded her of what he had said a few minutes earlier; this is a very unusual and crucial mission. He had to have all relevant hands on deck and suggested that Minoo might have to tell him more than she had told him so far. Minoo understood the quandary but argued that this was where things became difficult and dangerous. They became difficult because she did not want to arouse suspicions. And, it could be dangerous because there might be a point at which his love would not be strong enough to prevent him from denouncing her.

She started thinking out loud, adding that one thing made that less likely—he had told her that he was not terribly happy with some of what they're being asked to do . . . So, he had ostensibly taken some risk in sharing that because she could denounce him for that, as well. Taking the logic a step further, she recalled that he had also mentioned that he thought that his work was scientifically exciting but a big waste of money in a country where people did not have all or even most of all of what they needed. He had always supported the use of nuclear power as a source of energy but was only going along with the rest, because he felt then that his finger was effectively caught in the gears.

"Where does that lead you?"

"Well . . . I'm sure he's not supporting the military part of the effort. But there's a helluva big step from discontent to what could be viewed as treason."

Simon nodded. She added, with tears welling up in her eyes, "In Iran, treason takes you straight to the gallows."

Simon realized that a pause was needed. The conversation had not gone as well as he had hoped but was very much in line with what he feared. He switched gears on Minoo, asking whether she would ever consider relocating.

"And what else?"

Simon worked to calm her. He asked how Farid felt with respect to Germany, where he had gone a few times to visit with suppliers, as his job was to focus on the equipment side of the plant activity and more specifically on how the process could be made more efficient. She noted that he had been there less recently. Though Germany was where a lot of the equipment was manufactured, a lot of that manufacturing activity had to be brought to Iran, because of the sanctions. Returning to Farid, she said that he usually came back from Germany with a smile on his face, adding, "He talks of the freedom there, of how much he'd like to show me the country and what it has to offer."

With a wink and a smile, she added, "But he's usually not so enthusiastic about the weather."

Simon was going to keep on that line of questions, when she told him that he was barking up the wrong tree. She explained: "Farid's not the sole issue. My Dad's still in Iran. Couldn't leave him."

■ ■ ■ ■ ■

Minoo did not mention her mother because she had sadly died two years earlier. She died of a form of blood cancer, a lymphosarcoma, which the family came to believe was due to her work in the nuclear field, and as well to the radiation exposure she probably had received there. Minoo never had any siblings. Her mother became pregnant again once they were back in Qom but had lost the baby and had been told that she should not try again. Cyrus became a changed man when Sophie died. He elected to take early retirement though that meant that he would have to be happy with a lower, though still comfortable lifestyle. He was by then near the top of the civil service hierarchy in the energy sector. His hair which was plentiful turned grey almost overnight, except for his bushy eyebrows and mustache which both remained pitch-black. While he had stood erect in an almost aristocratic bearing, he was now partially stooped. Minoo felt he was often lost in his thoughts, and, though a very affectionate father, he was also quite proud; he simply refused to discuss the past. He would shut up like a clam whenever Minoo tried to make him feel better by mentioning happier times. Yet, in the recent past, it seemed he had mellowed a bit. Minoo had been delighted; she immediately mentioned to Farid that her father had seemed willing to open up anew and to recount both the good and the bad times.

■ ■ ■ ■ ■

"Your Dad's not an issue, Minoo. We'd take care of him, too. Would he agree to leave? After all, since the death of your mother, who else does he have in Iran? Plus, given his stints in France and the U.K., it's not as if he's never lived anywhere beside Qom, right?"

Minoo calmed down a bit. She accepted that his interests had shifted, with a passion developing for ancient history in general and, in particular, for the civilizations of the Middle East and the way they were affected by the numerous trade routes that crisscrossed the region. She also readily agreed that this had nothing to do with living in Qom.

Shifting gears again, Simon then asked about Farid—would he be prepared to leave? Minoo thought a minute and concluded in her own mind that he did not seem to have much keeping him in Iran. She did not know of any direct family; his parents were both dead and he had never talked of any brother or sister. There might be a cousin or someone like that, but she pointed to the fact that he had never had her meet anyone he introduced as family.

Suddenly, Minoo decided to turn the tables on Simon.

"What in the world are you planning, Simon?

Simon conceded that he had seen the question coming. Unfortunately, at that point, as he put it, there was little that he could tell. Yet, he would trust her with two important elements. First, they were totally committed to do everything they could to ensure a minimal number of civilian casualties, adding that, for him, that means zero if at all possible. Second, whatever they did, she would be warned first and have ample time to flee.

She figuratively jumped up in her seat and said: "This is big, very big . . . Simon, are we going to war?"

Simon stressed that there was no intention to start a war. The point would be to do things such that they could not be traced to Israel. So, the only risk for Minoo was if she got caught between now and then, which was all the more reason to be more careful than usual.

He continued, "We booked you for a couple of nights at the Hotel Regina, on Rue de Rivoli, almost across from the Tuileries Garden. There's a lot of shopping around there, under the arcades and further on . . ."

He added that, in fairness, shopping there was quite touristy: from copper or plastic Eifel towers to the well-known jewelers of the Place

Vendome, and anything in-between . . . He said, "I won't be staying at the Regina for obvious security reasons."

He gave her a new iPhone, adding, "You can communicate with me any time you wish. My number is on quick dial under "Simon." Feel free to call Farid, but don't use this phone. Use your Iranian phone if it works here. Better yet, use the internet in the hotel . . ."

They agreed to have dinner that evening, with Simon picking her up at 19:00. Minoo had to remind him that he still had not given her the address of Catherine, the relative she was supposed to have flown to Paris to visit. Simon kicked himself for having forgotten and mentioned the old apartment; Mossad took it over when Catherine left but kept it under her name. They rarely used it, other than as a mailbox, but it did have two fully, functional bedrooms; they did not use them for visiting agents because they did not want to take any risks, but the option remained in a true emergency. He reminded her that the apartment was near the St Augustin Church, Rue de La Boetie, which went from Place St Augustin to the Champs Elysées.

After a pleasant dinner at Le Soufflé, a restaurant specializing in all sorts of sweet or savory soufflés, they walked back the half a mile to Minoo's hotel. There, Simon took a taxi to his own hotel. Once in his room, he composed a message to Ariel. He had been musing on it ever since he dropped Minoo off: "The plan for Fordow is not a done deal yet."

Ominously, he added: "Gonna think of an alternative, just in case . . ."

CHAPTER.08

Simon had a lot of work to do before he could present his plan to the war cabinet, which, in his mind, he had scheduled for late March or early April. His first task had been to select the team that would carry out the mission. Today, he was meeting Ariel in his office to get his approval on his choices. He took his boss through the steps he had followed, recounting as much of his various meetings as necessary but avoiding all rabbit holes.

He first had to pick a leader and he had settled on David Heller. David was one of the most respected members of the *Mossad* Special Forces and the agent with whom Simon felt the most comfortable working. He had been in the service a number of years and always seemed to love his job. Simon had a particular appreciation for him, as he saw David as someone who was prepared to give his all to any mission that was entrusted to him. Doing his best was a crucial driver for him. A jovial individual, he was a true athlete, and this was obvious even if he wore a suit, which he hardly ever did. He was six feet tall and broad shouldered; yet, he was not like certain American football players who seemed to have no neck because of over-developed trapeze muscles. David was elegant and well-proportioned, tipping the scales at around 195 pounds. He had come to Simon's office wearing khaki slacks and a blazer, with an open neck shirt in a light shade of blue. Simon began, "I need you to assemble a team to blow up the two main,

Iranian, nuclear enrichment centers."

"Come again . . . Are you serious?"

Simon's face became more severe and his voice deeper, and he simply replied, "Absolutely."

When he first discussed his plan with David, Simon felt pretty sure that everything was workable and that all contingencies had been or could be addressed. He had therefore felt he was ready to present the preliminary outline to Ariel, Jesse and the war cabinet. However, experience had taught him that it was always a good thing to have another set of eyes look at a plan and critique it if required. David pointed out a couple of interesting points, validating Simon's belief that you could always learn from others, even when they report to you.

■ ■ ■ ■ ■

The first mission he had entrusted to David was to assemble a team. A few days later, David came back with three names. He outlined his selection criteria, just to be on the safe side. He wanted to make sure his assumptions made sense and to verify that he had not missed an important point.

David started by saying that he viewed the biggest challenge to be the combination of technical and linguistic skills. He argued that all the guys on the extended list had some of the stuff that was needed and might be able to learn the rest. The one thing that characterized his choices was that they all had the basic skills he was looking for, including the crucial language capabilities.

For the Fordow team, the two men he selected were Daniel Himmel and Nathan Ruhring. They were both matched from a weight standpoint, at about 180 pounds and both about six feet tall, though Daniel looked marginally taller than Nathan. They had both been with the service for more than ten years. Daniel came from the Army and Nathan from the Air Force. They had solid technical skills; they were both engineers by training. Daniel's engineering degree partially dealt with nuclear topics, but it was principally focused on electrical and mechanical issues. Nathan had only limited knowledge of atomic physics or anything in the field, but he had studied materials science. They were both fluent German speakers.

David went on telling Daniel's story saying he was married, with no children. His wife was still in the army, a young captain. He was thirty-four and had been in the service for twelve years. He came back to Israel from Germany where his family retreated, after the communist takeover of East Germany. He was halfway through his engineering degree when he arrived. He enrolled in *Sayeret Yahalom*, the IDF special engineering unit that handles missions such as precision demolition, with the use of pinpoint explosives or commando and counterterrorism, among others. In other words, as David added, "He's almost custom-made for our needs. He's participated in ten important covert operations. All but two of them involved the acquisition of "information" as we like to say . . ."

"Love your euphemism for spying."

Chuckling, David continued and mentioned that Daniel's last two assignments had him working on location as part of an action team, including breaking into an office building and into a secured area. In both instances, he had to carry weapons, for self-defense purposes. It turned out he didn't have to use them, but he was ready, willing, and able, and his file said he was an excellent shot, particularly with a handgun. He added, "According to the notes in his file, Daniel is very meticulous, especially during training. He pays great attention to detail and keeps his cool. His major weakness? He can try too hard and he'll need to learn that, at times, the mission may be compromised and that's it."

Turning to Nathan, David mentioned that the story was broadly similar, but with a few interesting twists and turns. He came to Israel from Russia. But his family didn't make it. So, he was by himself and his parents were believed deceased. He had one brother and a sister, but the service only knew of his brother, who was in Israel, too. He worked in the philanthropic field. Nobody knew where his sister was, and Nathan did not believe she was dead.

"That could be a weakness, if he were ever captured."

David conceded the point but mentioned that he came to Israel when he was young enough to be in high school, so he's been schooled here. He went through high school on a pre-*Atidim* scholarship and joined *Atidim* in the IDF after graduation. *Atidim* is a program that encourages bright, high-school graduates to postpone their enlistment in military service and study for an academic degree, often in the scientific field. Both pre-*Atidim* and *Atidim* gave him the financial aid he badly needed. Then, he enrolled in the Air Force (as per his *Atidim* contract) and did very well. He actually got his wings, but on multi-propeller-powered reconnaissance planes. He chose to learn German because that was the language his family spoke at home when he was young in Tbilisi. He had been in the service only ten years and was a year younger than Daniel. He had also been principally employed in information acquisition but had participated in three live missions where he carried and had to use his weapons, at least once. He was a bit of a ladies' man and still unmarried. No known steady girlfriend.

"Is that another weakness?"

"Cuts both ways."

David added that it had not been one in the past but accepted that one never really knows. He still chose him because, as he put it: "We're comfortable as he doesn't seem to carry it to the extreme of trying to have sex with anyone who's got a pulse."

"OK, so what about your team, David?"

David joked that Simon already knew everything about him, so he turned to introducing Mike Robert, who was, in fact, Michel Robert. He came to Israel from France when he was seventeen years old, about fifteen years ago, when his parents emigrated. He completed his high school studies in Paris. His parents waited until he passed his *baccalaureate* exams to move. David added that this meant that he was pretty smart, since he had received the French equivalent of his high school degree at seventeen, about a year younger than most of his classmates. He had an older brother who taught mathematics in Tel Aviv. He was moderately studious, and his studies were not brilliant, except when the topic fascinated him. David added, "He's a lot like me. Neither of us has a great degree. My engineering qualification is pretty basic, and his degree is in foreign languages. But he's got a lot of hands-on experience. Also, he's got a natural talent for all things mechanical. I hear that he once took apart and rebuilt an old, Lotus Elan sports car in his parent's garage. I thought that could be great in Natanz."

In response to Simon's obvious question about whether David or Mike spoke Farsi, David replied that Mike was fluent in Farsi, together with English, Hebrew and French, with bits and pieces of Spanish and Italian. He added that as for himself, he started learning Farsi a few years ago on the side when it became obvious to him that Iran was becoming one of Israel's most important intelligence targets. Though he would not rate himself as highly as Mike on Farsi, he was sure that he could be mistaken for a native speaker, particularly one who has been out of the mother country for quite a while. Simon concluded, "Well, one down, many to go . . . We've got our team."

David injected the necessary note of caution: "We've given it our best shot . . . Time will tell."

CHAPTER.09

JANUARY 23
ATHENS

Simon had organized to meet Amir Mashhad in Athens. Amir was another manager at the Fordow plant; he worked quite close to Farid, though Farid, of course, did not know of Amir's connections to the *Mossad*. Additionally, Amir's job was both considerably less technical and lower down the totem pole than Farid's; he managed the physical plant.

A solid man in his early forties, Amir had become a part of the *Mossad,* after he suffered a personal tragedy. His wife had been killed by the Revolutionary Guards while being interrogated. It turned out that it had all been a massive mistake on the part of the Guard, as Nina, his wife, had done nothing wrong, nor did she have any questionable connections. It was a nasty case of badly mistaken identities. Amir had, until then, been a faithful, if not totally enthusiastic, supporter of the regime. In his own mind, he was first and foremost an Iranian. He did not mind the prior regime of the Shah, though it certainly did not send many crumbs down as low as he stood. He was well-aware that some corruption prevailed under the Shah but felt that it did not affect people like him. He enjoyed the relative freedom that people enjoyed then, and certainly did not mind seeing his country become more open to the more modern Western culture. At the same time, he did not mind the revolution either, He had been a devout Muslim and could see that the Western culture that he initially readily applauded was leading to a number of excesses and quite a bit of decay, particularly within the generation behind his. He also hoped that it would help poor sods like him. Yet, he did object to the brutality of the repression, but almost managed to convince himself that it was needed in view of the visible corruption in both financial and moral realms.

The murder of Nina, as there was no other way of describing it, changed everything. He was inconsolable as she was the love of his life; she had not yet borne him any children, and this not for lack of trying as he would readily admit. Not having a child was still difficult for him. He knew she was white as snow and could not understand how anyone could have gotten things so wrong. How could they come to kill her for no reason at all? He had concluded that leaders and their minions were so arrogant and convinced of their own righteousness that they felt they could do anything.

He became very bitter vis-à-vis the revolution, and his bitterness only increased with time, as the loss of his wife weighed more and more on him. At first, he did not show his bitterness because the revolution that took his wife's life could just as swiftly take his own life. Additionally, he really needed his job and was sure that a miscreant, as he would certainly then be labeled, did not belong in a top-secret plant. Though no one actually directly apologized to him, he received a couple of unexpected promotions, which moved him from responsibility for all janitorial functions at Fordow to the much bigger role of a facilities manager. He was grateful for the extra responsibilities and income but did not feel thankful for what he had come to believe were signs that the regime had probably realized that they had made a mistake and wanted to atone for it in some way without openly admitting their guilt.

A few months after Nina's murder, about a year ago or so, Amir met an individual who turned out to be very kind to him. He was not involved in the plant, but they met at a dinner party organized by one of Amir's friends. He seemed genuinely interested in Amir's story, particularly in his personal tragedy. He quickly introduced Amir to his sister who, he had said, lived abroad, but might settle back in Iran. She was not married, he said, and would enjoy meeting someone as kind and thoughtful as Amir.

When Amir met her, she had said her name was Afri Nahan and that she had recently returned to Iran, her native country; she had lived throughout a good part of the "old" Middle East, as she called it, but still held onto her Iranian passport. She was in her late thirties and was strikingly beautiful, with long, dark and wavy hair, and a tanned, oval face with almond-shaped, dark brown eyes. Her teeth were perfectly arranged and extra white, giving her an enchanting smile, which she knew how to vary, from alluring to downright irresistible. She looked physically trim and wore clothing on that first unofficial date which, though sufficiently modest for a Muslim country, framed and displayed her charms to her advantage. Her body looked firm and almost athletic, and it was challenging for Amir to take his eyes off her cleavage.

With Nina's death only a few months before, Amir had until then refrained from any non-professional relationship with women, out of love for his dear, departed wife. This time, though, he felt tingling all over his body and in his mind when he met Afri. She was so fine, so calm, and so full of charm that he just could not resist. Nothing happened at first, in part because there was at least one unnecessary witness—Afri's alleged brother. Eventually, he faded into the background, and they started a long-distance relationship, as she said she lived in Tehran. Yet, she made every effort to come to Qom often, officially to visit libraries. Somehow, there never was an invitation for him to come to Tehran, which is only just about an hour away by car; they thus only met in Qom. She said that her archeological research took her to a lot of places in the Middle East, and Amir thought *that explained perfectly why she seemed so often away from Iran.* In truth, despite the excuses about visiting libraries, Afri was coming to Qom to meet with Amir who was quite transparent as to his intentions.

Amir did not know, however, that Afri was in fact named Sarah Miller and was a *Mossad* agent. And so was the individual, unrelated to Sarah, who had introduced her to him. Amir could not know that the *Mossad* had gotten wind of Nina's assassination and had selected him because the murder of his wife made him an ideal potential source and in view of his responsibilities at the plant.

Afri, aka Sarah, convinced Amir that he could avenge Nina's murder if he was prepared to help her. She did not initially say why she might need that help, but the love Amir felt for both Nina and Afri got the better of him. He started providing the odd piece of information. Initially, her questions related to things which seemed totally innocuous, but over time, they became more pointed. Afri always appeared to be interested in finding out whatever she could about the layout and the intricacies of the Fordow plant. What was it that was really happening there? How did it really function? Were there as many centrifuges as sometimes reported?

At one point, she had even asked about the rumor that the Iranians had modified the standard centrifuge cascade design by pairing cascades in a tandem fashion. In short, the second in a pair received the waste from the other as its feed, while its own waste was fed back to the first at whichever stage would minimize isotopic mixing. Practically, this was supposed to improve efficiency and rumor had it that Dr. Farid Kashani was a very important driver behind the concept, its design and its implementation. The rumor was that Fordow had two such tandem pairs among the cascades at the plant. Afri was happy to report to Tel Aviv that Amir confirmed that two of the cascades did look a bit different, though he was unable to say anything definitive about technical specifications. She said he also confirmed that Dr. Kashani was indeed credited with the idea and seemed to have led the effort. He also implied that, though not the boss, Dr. Kashani was viewed as the top scientist at the plant.

Convinced that he was really going to help, Afri had eventually become more open with Amir and had mentioned to him that she was really working part-time for a foreign regional government, although she had refrained from telling him she was an agent or that she was Jewish. That would have to come later, she felt.

A few months passed and she felt she could tell him that the foreign country was, in fact, Israel, and that she was a secret agent. He agreed to help her more formally. That's the point when Amir was given a direct access to certain people outside of Iran and even provided with the secret light flash communication tool with its external miniature receiver, and a computer tablet, with the appropriate application for sending and decoding messages. That tablet also had a voice activation feature that allowed the owner to dictate messages rather than having to type them. Amir had become a junior *Mossad* agent himself, with Afri as his principal handler.

Simon and Sarah met Amir in the International Arrival Hall of Athens's airport and immediately drove away. They had decided that Simon would meet Amir and talk to him in the car to minimize the risk of detection. Simon and Sarah had booked a rental car in Afri's name to have as much privacy as possible, though driving into or around Athens can be hairy at times. With Mount Hymettus located directly between the airport and the city, they had to drive north first and then turn south and west. They elected not to use the freeway, but rather to use highway 89, as traffic would go slower and would require less concentration. That the drive was a bit more scenic was the cherry on top of the cake. The plan was for Amir to spend a short weekend there, arriving Friday mid-morning and returning to Qom Saturday evening. Amir would then fly back to Tehran with Sarah; they would drive to Qom together afterwards.

"Amir, we're going to need more than your usual help," Simon started.

As Sarah was driving and he was seated next to her with Amir riding in the back seat, he turned toward him as much as the seatbelt would allow. Amir looked startled but kept his composure. Simon then directly asked whether he could help provide access to the plant to a couple of their people. In response to the obvious "why?" Simon simply said that they were going to walk along all the cascades in the two halls. He also added that he would rather not tell him more now, simply to protect him. Amir thanked him but added that this was bound to mean they were planning to attack the facilities, adding: "I can't think of any other legitimate reason."

"Could be."

"What will happen to me, then . . . ?"

Sarah replied that they could relocate to some other country and live a quiet life there. Amir was now truly completely shaken. He could only say that Iran was his country and that he could not find work anywhere else. Trying to calm him, Sarah replied, "Trust us, if we say you'll get a job, you will. And, we'll be together, my love."

Simon was watching this and asking himself whether Sarah was a great actor or had really fallen for Amir. He made a mental note to ask her, because that is something which the service should know. *Why is it that my female agents often fall in love with their charges?* he thought to himself, with Minoo and Sarah in mind. Amir, who was completely smitten, agreed to do whatever she asked, although he said that he would need a lot of help.

Thinking of the meeting later in his office, he realized that this was the interview that helped him finalize the Fordow plan. It would involve two waves. First, Farid would help by allowing the team to visit the plant in a semi-official capacity. That was obviously dependent upon Farid agreeing to cooperate—with or without knowing why. Simon knew that point was still far from settled. Simon was indeed convinced that direct intelligence would likely be necessary at some point, unless Sarah and Amir were able to get a lot more done than expected or Minoo somehow managed a miracle with respect to

Farid. Second, in due course, the team would return to Iran, probably surreptitiously, but that did not have to be the case. Circumstances would dictate. They would set up the explosives and eventually trigger them, with Amir's help, hopefully after Farid, Minoo and her father had been able to leave Iran; Sarah would have to leave earlier, together with any other agent that might possibly be identified, starting with her alleged brother.

In many ways, the plan sounded so simple. Yet, Simon knew full well that it had a number of unsettled moving pieces. Any hole caused by lack of success with Farid or Amir and the whole thing would collapse in a heap.

CHAPTER.10

JANUARY 28
QOM

Sarah found herself in Qom to visit Amir again. Their distant affair was then well over six months old and seemed to be getting better by the week. As always, he was delighted to see her and kissed her passionately, after they reunited and were in a place that was discreet enough. As usual, she had rented a car at Tehran Airport and driven the seventy-five odd miles from Eslam Shahr to the Al Zahra hotel where she always stayed in Qom. She loved the fact that the hotel was quite small, with only nine guest rooms. Its location was unique, just around the corner from the Shrine of Fatimah al-Masumah, one of the holiest sites in Shiite Islam. One could argue that the small size of the hotel made her more visible, less anonymous. At the same time, she very much believed in the principle that the best place to hide was in plain sight. She didn't mind it if the management of the hotel knew her. She was a pretty, darn good archeologist, and she was doing research. In fact, she occasionally showed this or that picture to the desk clerk, who always seemed impressed by her passion. She really liked what she was doing, and it showed; Simon in fact always marveled at the fact that she was so good at dealing with what, after all, was only a cover, though she had indeed studied archeology at university.

She maintained a place in Tehran under the cover of being a researcher and writer on ancient history based there. It was a small one-bedroom flat, but she did not use it regularly. She traveled a fair amount, both within and outside of Iran. Archeology and ancient history were topics which were not taboo in Iran, except maybe when it came to issues that related to episodes which involved Israel or Jews. This provided her with a great deal of freedom of movement, particularly as she always seemed to need to visit one site or another or consult some unusual document in some library. The fact that these various places were always in close proximity to Iranian military or scientific centers had never dawned on anyone. Iran had a number of interesting sites, as did the whole region which had been ground zero for much of civilization. After all, Christianity had gone to India via Iran and the surrounding areas. Also, archeologists found some of the oldest traces of Hinduism in next-door Pakistan, with spillover effects in the whole region. In fact, Sarah liked to regale Persian audiences with the story that they contributed to India being named India. In ancient times, the river that flowed through Pakistan used to be called the Sindu River. Yet, because Persians have trouble pronouncing the letter "s," they started calling it the Indus River, from which the names Hindus and India originated. It always played well to local pride and served to confirm her status as a very knowledgeable researcher.

With her main mission being to develop Amir as a source and the affair blossoming in the last several months, she had become a bit more sedentary than when she first arrived in Iran. Her travels within Iran outside of Qom had become much rarer, although, "surprisingly," she had needed to travel abroad more. That this was needed for her to report on progress with Amir was obviously not something which the Iranians needed to know. She was no longer looking for potential sources, she had then started to "run" one.

She and Amir went for a walk which was her *modus operandi* when she needed to ask Amir a favor, just to be sure they were not overheard. Though there were risks still, she felt it gave her more control over the environment. She knew there would be strangers around, but they would need to make a visible effort to follow their conversation and that might uncover them. She always carried with her a mini receiver, in her handbag, which was designed to emit small "beeps" when they were within close-enough proximity of microphones. Ostensibly, that did not protect her from those long-distance microphones, but she assumed that Iran was not readily using them, unless they already had serious suspicions and were conducting a formal surveillance.

"Amir, I need two bits of information from you."

"OK, what my love?"

First, she needed him to confirm the layout of the two enrichment halls in the plan.

"I know we've discussed that a number of times, but I need quite specific info . . ."

In fact, she added, the best would be if he could help her draw a map of the inside of the plant, and in particular to verify the actual number and arrangement of the centrifuges. She was deliberately, as she often did, misleading him a bit. She knew very well that there were supposed to be eight cascades of one hundred seventy-four centrifuges in each of the two halls. In fact, that information was all over the internet and had been disclosed in a report by the International Atomic Energy Agency. But, feigning not to know what she did know would allow her to tell if Amir was truthful or not when he reported on the information. She did not have long to wait and was delighted to hear him tell the truth.

Amir simply replied

"Some of this is public knowledge, my dear . . ."

"Really?"

He went on to tell her that there were eight cascades in each hall, and they have one hundred seventy-four machines each. In fact, there are a couple of experimental cascades, much shorter and smaller in the second hall. He admitted that he had never counted them but would guess that there were no more than fifty centrifuges. He promised to come back with an exact number. He noted that Iran, officially, had said that there are 2,710 centrifuges, but the number is obviously wrong arguing, "Just adding up the conventional cascades gets you to more than that."

He added that he did not know if the newer shorter cascades were public information but guessed they were not.

Sarah asked whether he would be ready to draw a rough floor plan of the place later that day. He replied he did not know but could always try. She turned to the second question. She said that she had done a bit of digging on the internet to get a sense of what centrifuges looked like. She had seen a few pictures, but there seemed to be so many types that she was lost. She said she would like him to take a few discreet pictures of a few centrifuges within a cascade to see first what they looked like. Also, she would like to see how adjacent centrifuges were tethered to the ground.

Amir replied that he could try but argued that he had to be very careful.

"Taking pictures isn't something I'd normally do."

However, he said that he sometimes went back to the plant late in the evening and then usually would be the only living soul there. He explained that he did that to inspect the plant and make sure everything was in order. He added that he could also look carefully at those things that interested Afri and give her an oral report. Sarah said that would be great, but pictures would allow her to see all the details. Further, it would help her avoid a lot of back-and-forth with questions . . .

Amir countered that her coming back to Qom more often was not a bad thing. She smiled and said that she could see where his mind was going. But the mission took first priority. So, she went back to the issue of photos and asked for pictures of both ends of a cascade and for shots which would allow one to see how the various cascades were linked to one another. She asked when he could have the pictures.

"I'll try and get them tomorrow morning as I do my usual

inspection of the place. How long are you staying this time?"

She replied she was planning to return to Tehran the next day in the afternoon, but added she was sure she could extend her stay by another day. She lied that she would need to cancel a couple of meetings in Tehran but noted that it wouldn't be the end of the world. She observed that the hotel in Qom did not seem terribly busy, so keeping her room should not be a problem, and neither should there be an issue with the rental car.

She switched gears on him: "Should we find ourselves a good place for dinner now? Then we can go back to the hotel and slip discreetly upstairs for a bit of "private time," she said so coyly that even an outside observer wouldn't have wondered whether this was feigned affection.

They spent another wonderful evening in Sarah's room. Amir was now known to the desk clerk who preferred not to see anything. As a good Muslim woman, she could not condone what looked very much like fornication, as she was sure that the two were not married. But Afri Nahan was a good customer and should be offered the full "hospitality" of the hotel. Plus, the clerk loved the occasional pictures of sites she would probably never see, but had heard of, in school or even at the mosque.

Sarah did not have to wait terribly long. By midday, Amir sent her a message to let her know that he could have dinner with her that evening. She immediately understood that to mean that he had the pictures. *Now, what they will show is the question*, she thought to herself.

As planned, Amir arrived at 6:30 p.m. at the Al Zahra hotel and called Sarah from the phone in the lobby. Within minutes, she was down, and they started walking towards Amir's car. While he was driving, he handed over his cell phone to let her see the photos. She looked at them and guessed out loud that each centrifuge is about a foot in diameter in total. Amir corrected her: "Yes. If anything, it's a bit less than that – call it ten to twelve inches. But I'm sure I can take a more precise measurement, if you give me a bit more time to wait for the right moment."

"Great idea. let's do it. Let me know by flashlight when you have more precise measurements.

■ ■ ■ ■ ■

Mossad had been one of the leaders in the development of a laser, light-based, communication system that is virtually undetectable. That was the flashlight to which Sarah was referring. It consists of equipment which can be linked to a simple computer or handheld computer-like device such as a modern phone or even a computer tablet.

The agent sending a message would compose that message on the computer or on the phone—most often through the voice activation feature—and then have the system encode and transform that message into high intensity light pulses. These pulses would then be aggregated into a single signal or at most a few flashes which would be sent, via a high-intensity light beam, in mere milliseconds, to a satellite. The flashlight-like emitting device only needed to be set on a windowsill or on the ground; it would detect the actual position of the satellite and thus the direction in which the laser must be flashed.

The device looked like any small modern pocket flashlight: a plastic cylinder with a slightly flared front end and a short black strap attached to the back end so that whoever used it could secure it to his wrist; at the front end, the unit seemed to have two types of bulbs. First, there was a white LED crown around the periphery; it lit up when the on-off switch was activated, as one would expect from a regular flashlight. Second, in the center of that crown, there was what looked like the top of a traditional light bulb surrounded by a narrow metallic ring. In fact, this was the source for the high-intensity light beam. To transform the unit from a classic flashlight to the secret device, the agent would have to complete two steps designed to ensure that no unauthorized person could use it. First, the agent would pull gently and rotate a crown located at the back end of the device in a sequence of five clockwise or counter-clockwise moves, with four different rotation angles in each direction: ninety, one hundred and eighty, two hundred and seventy and three hundred and sixty degrees; this was a conceptual equivalent of the combination locks on traditional safes in existence prior to the digital age. Then, the agent would pull on the strap until he or she felt a click and then would twist the rear crown counter-clockwise 90 degrees, all the while pushing the on-off switch to the on position. At this point, the metallic ring inside the LED crown would disappear and the center bulb assembly telescoped out of the device about an inch, revealing what looked like the top of a normal bulb which was, in fact, almost a full bubble. This allowed the light source within the bubble to rotate almost two hundred and forty degrees in all three directions, searching for the most direct line to the satellite. The fact that there had to be a direct line of sight between the instrument and the satellite was indeed the only absolute requirement for the device to function.

Once it had received the message, the satellite would re-send it to its desired destination; there, a similar piece of equipment would decode and transfer the message onto another simple computer or smart phone. Indoor fixed locations, such as the *Mossad* office or the Israeli residences of those agents living there, often had a small receiver on the outside wall or window frame of the house, apartment or office complex that allowed the satellite to know the exact direction in which it should shine the laser beam; this receiver was in direct contact with the preferred computer, tablet or smart phone. Though, conceivably, one might notice the flash of light as it was sent, the enemy would need the appropriate equipment to figure out what the message was. Further, unless someone was under constant surveillance, the odds of looking in the right direction and at the right spot to catch the flash were pretty poor. The real loose end in the whole security chain was with the external receiver for agents in the field. Typically, the tool was still fixed to a structure, but it had to be hidden; so, rather than a window frame, most agents hid it on a roof or near a smokestack, for instance. The equipment was small enough that it would normally escape detection unless the agent was already under suspicion or burned; but the risk remained. In those very few cases when an agent was under suspicion and the equipment was found, headquarters would simply send a coded instruction to the receiver that would use a small ampoule that broke open to release acid to destroy the elements of the equipment that would have intelligence value or could be used by some intruder to send fake signals.

It was always a bit more of a challenge when agents were in temporary quarters as they did not always have access to an external receiver. They had to place their light emitting unit, which also functioned as a receiver, in a way such that they could get replies to their own messages. Depending upon where they were, agents could place them on a windowsill as well, or on the dashboard of a car or on any surface where the unit would be stable while it was receiving. Agents typically first tried to locate the satellite by holding the unit in their hands and then positioned the device appropriately; they then retracted the center bulb assembly into the device to minimize the risk of detection.

■ ■ ■ ■ ■

Sarah went back to the pictures and said that it looked to her like there were roughly three centrifuges per four feet. So, if a cascade has one hundred seventy-four centrifuges, the whole lot should span about two hundred thirty feet. Adding some space at the front and the end of each cascade as she could see on the pictures led her to conclude that the whole area was about two hundred fifty feet long. Amir showed some surprise: "Amazing, Afri."

"Why?"

"The hall IS about two hundred fifty feet long; that's a fact."

Sarah smiled and added that it was just a lucky guess. They agreed that it had to mean that there were about ten feet or so at each end of the cascades. Amir could not answer the question about the width of the halls, other than noting that they were different, but argued that there was space on either side of the cascades as they stood currently. He thought *they could nearly double the size of the installation.* They kept going back and forth into minute details, including the way each centrifuge was mounted. Afri noted: "Each centrifuge seems to be mounted on a small base; it looks like it's made of metal, with an empty space underneath . . ."

"Yeah, absolutely right. By the way, that's an important part of the design, or so I've been told when I asked . . ."

"Why did you ask . . . ?"

Amir's reply was so disarming: "It's not easy to keep the space underneath clean. I wanted to know if that was critical. You can't believe how much dirt can accumulate there, particularly as there are electrical cables going through the space."

Amir went on to explain that he was told the machines rotated at speeds up to 100,000 revolutions per minute; so, they had to be absolutely vertical to keep spinning without disintegrating. He added that each centrifuge was comprised of two cylinders. One spun and the other was a container that preserved almost perfect vacuum, to allow them to spin so fast. The elevated base was there to make sure the whole assembly was absolutely vertical, which required the base to be absolutely horizontal. He explained that he had seen a few that had an extra washer or two on one of the four corner screws fixing the base to the concrete. In response to the question of the size of the space below the platform, he said that he had never measured it, but would assume around three to four inches, maybe one or two more. He agreed that he should get a precise number.

Amir agreed to send the picture to Sarah via the flash system and listened with a great deal of attention when Sarah added, "Also, make absolutely sure to erase them from your phone. That would be VERY compromising if found."

With this, they arrived at Amir's flat. He told Afri that he had prepared some food before going to the office that morning. The apartment looked nice and comfortable, although, the first time she visited, Afri noted that it could use a woman's touch. It was a two-bedroom flat, although the second bedroom had been converted into a computer and TV room at some point. Afri never asked whether this was something that Nina had arranged or if it was done after her death; Amir never volunteered anything of how that came to be. The living room was not large and contained a dining area which could hardly seat more than six. In fact, the dark brown dining table only had four chairs set around it. It was connected to the relatively modern kitchen by a window in the wall separating them, to simplify serving since dishes could be passed through the opening. The walls of the living room were painted in a light beige color, but they turned dark green in the dining area. The change in color helped distinguish the two spaces. The living room furniture was comfortable, although a bit on the heavy side; upholstered furniture had visible dark brown wooden frames, which made them look somewhat out of fashion. The bedroom's central feature was a low chest of drawers that was literally covered with picture frames, most of them showing Nina, with or without Amir. Afri had noticed that there was only one rug in the whole apartment, and it was small and placed in the bedroom; it had to be Amir's prayer rug. Amir suggested, "Why don't we just warm the food up and have a nice, quiet dinner?"

She smiled her agreement. He was beaming.

When she got back to the hotel, Sarah was delighted. She spent a wonderful evening with Amir; some of it in the dining room and the food had actually been quite tasty. Most of it had been spent in his bedroom which had been quite nice as well. Still, there were a couple of issues which she wouldn't discuss but were troubling her. As usual, she asked Amir to drive her back to the hotel. No self-respecting, single, Muslim woman could be caught staying overnight in a man's apartment. Despite wanting her to stay, Amir understood this very well. His protestations were chiefly to try and delay her inevitable departure and to give himself a chance to dream of when they "could make this official," as he said.

"Your wife has not been gone long enough for this to be something we can discuss yet" was her simple, but disarming reply.

She decided not to transfer the photos immediately onto the hard drive of her laptop. She felt that it would be best to leave Iran and be in Israel before they were transferred; in fact, they should never make it onto the laptop with which she travelled. She carried a number of thumb drives in her computer bag, officially because that's how she kept her various research projects distinct from one another. This latest one could easily be lost amid the others. There obviously was a risk if the authorities had any real suspicions; they could choose to scan all of them. But she had been careful to save all pictures under innocuous names.

■ ■ ■ ■ ■

Also, *Mossad* had thankfully tinkered a bit with the normal design of a thumb drive. Her default display for any of them was a list of file names rather than an icon which would be much easier to read. Also, the drives were partitioned into "official" and "unofficial" sections with the unofficial part of the drive appearing only after the appropriate password had been typed into one of the files in the official section of the drive. Even if someone accessed the file where the password had to be entered, there was no prompt asking for the password. It was one of the thousands of words in that file, and she had to right-click on it. Yet she knew, however, that making a list of pictures into a series of icons and having access to password protected and hidden storage spaces were only a few mouse steps away. So, if someone started a real search of her computer paraphernalia, that someone would find things she wasn't supposed to have. But she discounted that risk. After all, if somebody had serious enough suspicions to start a search, it really did not matter whether they were on the computer or on a thumb drive. But, without suspicion, the odds were much more in her favor if there were several possible things for an enterprising customs officer who might want to do some random checking, before he stumbled onto the stuff she did not want him to find. Even then she might have a chance of steering him to a thumb drive she knew to be innocuous.

■ ■ ■ ■ ■

She did what little work she knew she had to do, confirming her flight to Istanbul and sending a few messages "to headquarters."

When she completed her bookings on the internet before going to bed the prior night, she had felt lucky that she could get a seat on the first flight out. She had booked herself on a flight from Tehran to Istanbul on Turkish Airlines. She knew she would still need to get her ticket at the airport, as Iran did not allow sophisticated internet access to its own people yet, but she could at least make the reservations. From there, she could fly to Tel Aviv. In fact, the two reservations were totally distinct and under different names. There was absolutely no way she would ever fly directly to Israel even if she could, which in fact she could not, as there are no direct flights between Iran and Israel. However, she tended to alternate the cities which she used as waypoints and the airlines she took. In general, her options were Turkish Airlines or one of the Gulf States airlines, as there were also no direct flights between Iran and Jordan. She did not even check to see if there were options via Lebanon or Syria. Even if there were, she assumed the second leg of the trip would likely not exist.

She used her light flash tool set discreetly on the open windowsill of her room to send a message to headquarters. The surface was flat enough that the unit should be able to find the direct line of sight to the satellite. When she put the laser tool on her windowsill, she thought to herself: *I hope the satellite faces this way, because, if it doesn't or it's in the shadow of the hotel, I'm gonna have to get to the car, which would look very odd at this time of night. If that's the case, I'll just send the message tomorrow from the roadside. That'll be safe, too.*

Fortunately, a line of sight was available, and the message was sent. She had asked headquarters to book her on a flight from Istanbul to Tel Aviv that could connect with her flight from Tehran. She told them she was on TK879 into Istanbul and that she had very good news.

She undressed looking at herself in the mirror and was evidently satisfied with what she saw. She was incredibly trim, with stomach muscles visible if she bent slightly forward. Her hair was long, dark and quite wavy. She seemed quite happy with the slightly concave lower back and firm buttocks. She liked her breasts that curved a bit upward toward the nipples, almost in an arrogant pose, as if saying to the potential lover *"are you ready for me?"* They were firm despite being larger than one would expect for an athletic young woman with small buttocks. In a country known for cosmetic surgery, one would probably assume that these were the best breasts she could buy. But they were hers and had not been touched up. Her nipples were erect, but this was not due to sexual arousal as much as to the fact that the temperature in the room was a bit too cold. So, she went to the thermostat to raise it a couple of degrees, all the while thinking: *"You know, you're a pretty attractive lady. Who's the real man whom you'll marry? Amir . . . ? Not sure. He's so sensitive, but is he that way because of what he feels for me or because he thinks I'm Nina, somehow reincarnated? Also, he's really not so great in bed. He's well-built and means well but has no staying power. Could I stay with a man who has me fake orgasms at least every second or third time we sleep together? Time will tell."*

She then took a short shower, washed her face removing what little makeup she wore and brushed her hair and her teeth. For once, she was ready to crash into bed without needing to read anything. Also, she decided she was too tired to look for her nightgown and simply went to bed and slept naked.

Her flight from Tehran was scheduled to leave at 8:10 am. She knew that this meant that she would not get much sleep tonight, but the alternative was to take a flight at 3:55 in the afternoon and that would not get her to Tel Aviv until nearly midnight. Calculating backwards from when she wanted to be at the Imam Khomeini airport, ready to board her plane, she had figured she had to get up at 4:00 a.m. and to leave Qom no later than 5:00 a.m., and preferably earlier. To get up at that hour to get ready would still leave plenty of time, if needed, to read any message she might have received from headquarters or from Amir. She didn't, however, expect any message from him, having left him barely half an hour earlier and knowing she would be leaving the hotel before he would be up the next morning. *But you never know,* she thought.

She had figured an hour-and-a-half drive from Qom to the airport, including filling up and returning the rental car. She didn't want to be too early at immigration and customs to minimize the risk that someone with little to do would decide to search her belongings with more care than necessary. But she knew that she had to be there at least ninety minutes before flight time. Headquarters had told her that her flight from Istanbul was TK 786 which gave her nearly a two-and-a-half-hour layover at Ataturk Airport. That gave her enough wiggle room in case of any delays in the flight from Tehran. Yet, she would arrive in Tel Aviv just after 2:00 p.m., which gave her plenty of time to go to the office.

The next morning, feeling only partially rested, she went through the routine she had mentally checked the night before and, when ready, left for the Khomeini Airport. As instructed by Simon recently, she conducted a series of safety checks after passing through customs and security at Tehran Airport and when boarding the aircraft. When paying close attention to security procedures, she could not help but feel they were so rudimentary when compared to Ben Gurion Airport in Tel Aviv. There, even when one was not traveling on El Al, she knew that the questions she was asked were so comprehensive and even insightful. She kept thinking that they were not looking for nail clippers here, as contrasted with certain other airports in other countries. *These guys were looking for terrorists*, she thought. The questions they asked truly tested who she might be. Though the process there was much less relaxed than in many Western countries, it was much less frustrating than being asked stupid questions, ostensibly written by lawyers to protect airlines in case of an attack rather than the traveling public. Here, in Tehran, the questions were pretty standard and would not catch a terrorist except if he were totally braindead. She could not help but ask herself: "Do they really want to catch terrorists when they leave? Bet they export more of them than they import . . ."

She had been asked to check whether the crew would allow her to disembark the plane on the pretense that she had lost something in the gate area. Once the aircraft doors were closed, she also noted that the crew did not seem to be doing a physical passenger count. The plane took off and she fell asleep, effectively finishing her night. She felt she had the Amir situation under control and that they were moving apace.

CHAPTER.11

**APRIL 6
QOM**

Drs. Dieter Hinterland and Nikolaus Reinhardt, aka Daniel Himmel and Nathan Ruhring arrived at nearly 1 a.m. on Lufthansa's flight 600, directly from Frankfurt. Immigration formalities had been made relatively smooth thanks to the letter the German visitors had from Dr. Farid Kashani. The invitation almost carried the force of a letter from a top government officer. The questions the immigration officers asked were fairly routine; yet, Dan and Nate both thought to themselves how comical the situation was that they were answering in German-accented English to questions asked by officials who spoke Farsi-accented English. With barely more than overnight bags as their only luggage, custom's inspection went even faster, and they found themselves suddenly in the international arrival's hall.

They were met in the arrival hall by Minoo and Farid, as one would expect. Dan and Nate had sent photos of themselves to Farid when they had gladly accepted his invitation to visit. These reflected their new identities which Simon had suggested were necessary. Arguing that the two of them were going to operate in an open environment for a while, both on this visit and the next one, he told them he did not want them to have to worry about being tracked in the future. He did not want the Iranians to know their real names or to have clear pictures of their faces. He had added that, in the end, the Iranians were bound to think that the two scientists had something to do with the explosion they wanted to trigger. Given the fact that Iran had never hesitated to go after their enemies abroad, having them with the wrong pictures should provide an additional layer of protection.

They had adopted names which kept their original initials as is usual protocol in the trade and wore minimal disguises. While both were naturally dark-haired and clean-shaven, they sported lighter and longer than usual hair. Both had elected to comb their hair in a way that hid some of their foreheads; that was meant to make fuzzier one of the characteristic features of many faces. They were also wearing glasses, Dan opting for dark, circular frames, while Nathan chose tortoise shell, colored frames, with extended, octagonal lenses. In truth, the idea of wearing glasses as a disguise had come from Marvin. Ostensibly, it would change their appearance, but that was not the main goal, as anyone who can manipulate Adobe Photoshop could easily recreate a face without them. What was "really cool," as Marvin had said, was that it would also allow them to use the latest camera-in-lens gadget that *Mossad* had developed. They had adapted the Google technology to their needs and improved on it while they were at it; they had added an important recording and data storage feature. Both men had grown facial hair as an added precaution; Dan wore a thin, straight mustache, while Nathan elected to grow a goatee; they both had subtly dyed their new facial hair to match their lighter hair color. Finally, *Mossad* had refined a Botox-like injection process that made their lips look fuller, though the effect of the treatment only lasted for a few days to a week at most.

Armed with these pictures, Minoo and Farid had no difficulty recognizing them among the small crowd of disembarking German tourists, all the more so as they had chosen to wear formal business suits. Additionally, they wore bow ties rather than regular ties for good measure, eschewing the simple "open-neck shirt" look that so many seasoned travelers choose; comfort was often the key when spending more than a couple of hours or so in an airplane. Minoo and Farid greeted their guests somewhat formally and proceeded directly to the parking lot. They drove the seventy miles from the airport to Qom in Farid's official Peugeot Pars, a locally made version of the French carmaker's old 405. They kept their conversation very general during the ride, always fearing that the car might be bugged. This was a habit which Minoo had taught Farid who had then marveled at how a physics professor might have such a spy-like mind. Minoo had laughed at the suggestion that she might have anything to do with a spy.

The carrot they had concocted to capture the attention and imagination of Farid was the idea that they had developed something called self-lubricating micro-carbon fiber. As the trip was being planned, Minoo had told Farid that a consulting firm she knew, from research they had done and shared with her, had two of its scientists looking for an invitation to Iran. They mentioned they had found a better way to balance the rotation axis of nuclear centrifuges and needed a contact in Iran. They specialized in exotic materials. Farid was immediately interested because he knew that Iran had been working on a next generation of assemblies which would allow them to enrich uranium to a higher concentration and more quickly. Anything that could make the process more efficient would be great. His government bosses would be even more impressed by him if he was the one coming up with an important element of the new solution. He had already received plenty of commendation for the parallel set up that was being tested on the small set of centrifuges at Fordow. This could really mean being put on the fast track for promotion.

Farid immediately agreed to help without displaying any suspicion as to Minoo's intentions. She had indeed not told him anything beyond the basic lie about the reason for their trip. He was a bit surprised when Minoo told him that the two professors were willing to travel at relatively short notice. She said that something told her they felt Iran could be a great new client; she added, "They're the sellers . . . So, the client is king."

The clincher was her rationale that the fact they were selling technology rather than an actual piece of equipment made life a lot more convenient for them and cut their lead times. The embargo would be a lot easier to circumvent with electronic files of blueprints than some actual piece of machinery that would be much harder to ship discreetly.

During the training phase of the process, in Tel Aviv, they had spent a full couple of days with real nuclear and materials scientists who had helped them understand what they needed to know. They had also spent at least another two days on their own reading the material that they had been given to bring them up to speed on nuclear enrichment equipment and basic nuclear physics. Nathan's degree in materials engineering certainly had come in handy. The Tel Aviv experts had focused on three main topics. First, they discussed the actual design and installation of gas centrifuges, their key parts, the roles they each played as well as their strengths and weaknesses. Second, they had drilled down on the way the rotation axes were secured and given them many statistics on what was needed in parts that rotate at ninety to one hundred thousand revolutions per minute. Third, they had speculated on what might reduce whatever friction still exists; it occurs principally in the needle bearing connecting the axis to the electric motor powering it at the lower end of the assembly; the other, upper end of the axis is maintained in place by a magnetic bearing that ensures that the axis remains absolutely vertical, and yet generates minimal friction or even wear.

Certainly, they did not understand all of it, but the session had involved both an initial learning stage and, most importantly, a question and answer phase during which the scientists would ask questions they would expect Farid or his colleagues to ask. Together, they had worked on Nate's original idea and had concocted a process where a lubricating material, such as a combination of congealed oil and grease would be made into fibers that had the mix enclosed into some sort of casing. That casing would be heat resistant enough to remain intact at the high temperatures used to bind the carbon fibers with resins to make carbon fiber composites. They could repeat that process two or three times, such that there were several layers of casing and lubricating material. The number of layers really would be dictated by the acceptable diameter of the fiber. When combining these lubricating fibers into the mix, the resulting product could become self-lubricating. As the product made from these fibers was used, gradual wear would break down the sheathing around the oil and grease mix, releasing lubricants for the product, in this case, a needle bearing. Ostensibly, they all knew that the material did not exist nor were they even sure it could be made. However, a couple of the scientists credited Nathan with a great idea and said they would test it. So, they all agreed that there was enough logic to the idea. They had worked to make sure that Nathan and Daniel would have enough insights to know when they could give a plausible answer and when they should simply reply that they did not know, or that more research was needed.

Farid had booked rooms for his visitors at the Melal Hotel, on Tohid Boulevard in Qom. He had picked it because the hotel had charm, being in what looked like an old palace rather than a modern structure like many of the other luxury business hotels in the city. Also, though in the center of the city, it was in a perfect location to drive to Fordow. When they were out of the car in front of the hotel, Farid said in an almost official tone: "Gentlemen, you must be dead tired. Why don't you turn in? I'll pick you up at 8:30 a.m. to drive you to the plant. We'll be able to talk about the equipment you want to discuss with me while we drive."

"That would be nice . . . But you should know we're not talking of equipment; just a new material?"

"You're right. My mistake . . ."

He went on to explain that he planned to give them a tour of the facilities and hoped there would be an opportunity to introduce them to a couple of colleagues. He said that Minoo—whom he called Doctor Rakhsha—told him that their return flight did not leave until 2:50 a.m. two days hence. He said to them he or someone else at the plant would find a way to get them to the airport in plenty of time.

"Many thanks, Doctor Kashani. Doctor Reinhardt and I are delighted to be here for the next few hours and hope that this initial contact can be fruitful. Doctor Rakhsha, it was very nice meeting you."

"Same here, Professors . . ."

Daniel had been quite careful to maintain the full decorum that would be used by two visiting German consultants. Simon had indeed told both Nate and Daniel in their briefing that Farid was still not fully aware of any part of Minoo's unofficial role.

The next morning, Daniel and Nathan met for breakfast and made it a point to act as German as possible. They ordered a breakfast that differed from typical Iranian fare. They knew not to expect any pork products, so ham, prosciutto, sausages or salami were definitely out. In many ways, they were grateful that Islam prohibited these foods: as Germans, they would have been expected to have them, but that would have conflicted with their Jewish traditions. Yet, they were still surprised to see a buffet that included a variety of cheeses, fruits and breads; it even had a hot meatball dish, which they assumed, correctly as it turned out, was lamb-based, and which they found quite tasty. They kept conversing in German and addressing each other as "Doctor" or "Professor Doctor" to make sure that anyone that looked at them would be in no doubt that both were serious German businessmen.

Farid arrived at 8:30 as promised. Dan made a mental note that he looked a bit tired. He remembered that he had picked them up after one in the morning, dropped them at the hotel at 2:00 and probably did not sleep for longer than four or five hours. *I guess he's not used to that*, he thought to himself. He could not know that Farid and Minoo had not been able to resist spending a bit more time together.

The drive to Fordow comprised two, distinct segments. First, they drove through the Holy City of Qom which was already bustling at this hour, though the hotel being on Tohid Boulevard was a big help. Tohid Boulevard was indeed a main road that was a straight shot to the ring road about two and a half miles away. Once on the ring road, they would drive for about four miles, eventually veering onto highway 71, a bypass road to Highway 7 which they would take as soon as they could. Highway 7 was the main thoroughfare that linked Tehran to Qom and further south. After driving twelve miles on Highway 7, they turned right onto a road that seemed to take them south and west, but suddenly veered onto a smaller yet very well marked two-lane highway, with plenty of road lighting, ostensibly for night traffic, seemingly the whole length of it, or at least along the part they had travelled to that point. Daniel noted that the road seemed to point mostly east, but a bit north as well. Bearing in mind their eventual destination, one of Iran's two largest nuclear enrichment plants, he thought to himself: *Not surprising that this small road is in such good condition and designed with so much care . . . Wonder how they explained that to the locals.*

Nathan's watch helped him estimate that they had initially climbed about three to four hundred feet as they hit the second of two, major, left curves. After that, they appeared to be going back down into a valley. The entrance to the Fordow facility was in fact about five hundred feet below that initial crest. In all, they suspected they had travelled a good ten miles from Highway 7. He made a note to himself that the distances were more significant "in real life" than when they were simply looking at them on a map. He thought to himself: *It is going to be stressful to say the least to drive all that way back after we have done the work inside . . . What if they want to ambush us?*

Dan noted that the plant was very well dissimulated, as it seemed to be in a valley surrounded by what looked like mostly barren hillsides. He wondered whether they had guard posts around the hills, as that would be the most efficient way to provide advance notice to the guards at the main entrance to the plant. He kept looking but could not see anything obvious. He made a mental note to discuss this with Nathan when they were alone. He noticed that there were a number of secondary roads on both sides of the mountain road. He focused his attention primarily on the right side of the road. On the return trip, he was able to deduce that these roads were about a couple of miles before the main entrance to the overall complex. He had quickly concluded that they should avoid the left-hand side of the road as the two or three pathways he noticed seemed to be leading either to a small village or an isolated farmhouse. He mentally noted a couple of places thinking *they would make perfect hiding places for any car or truck we decide to rent. Amir will simply need to get us the last two miles into the actual complex.*

They turned right into the well-laid-out drive that went past a first gate toward the complex. For some reason, it had been left open and there did not seem to be any guard. Dan and Nate noted this might be indicating some lax security procedures, while Dan added this to the note he already had in his memory bank that he had not seen any trace of guards on any of the surrounding hills. He thought that *either the Iranians were very good at hiding things, or they were incredibly arrogant.*

A few hundred feet later, they reached a large roundabout with four exits; all four roads seemed quite well-maintained and one of them appeared to be leading toward a mountain crest they could see in the distance. A number of buildings—they guessed there were between fifteen and twenty—occupied the land around the roundabout; Dan and Nate assumed they were military barracks or offices. Farid took the second exit at the roundabout and very quickly arrived at what Dan thought must be the main gate to the facility; there was a distinct guard house and Farid had to show his credentials before the gate was opened. They thought to themselves that *the first gate, the one that had been left opened, was probably redundant, but still wondered why the Iranians even bothered keeping it; they want to maintain some uncertainty* was all that Nathan could conclude in his mind, a thought he later shared with Dan. They drove uphill about a mile and a half along a straight road before they found themselves in front of the entrance to the actual facility; they passed through another gate to enter the area; that gate was also duly manned. Dan revised his earlier thought and concluded that *their security philosophy must be driven by massive control within the plant and its immediate facility rather than outside.* So, he had to conclude, *they were not arrogant; they were simply inefficient.*

The facility then directly in front of them did not look impressive. *It's really all carved into the mountain,* Nathan thought, as he knew that there was a great deal that should otherwise be visible, based on the satellite pictures he had seen of Natanz. They could only see one single-story building beyond the guardhouse and to the right. Everything else was rough, barren landscape, very much like the land they had seen on either side of the road from the main gate to the one they just passed. The mountain top facing them was at least two to three hundred feet higher than the ground on which they stood and thus probably five to six hundred feet above the main gate. Straight ahead of them, they could see a couple of tunnels with well-paved roads, with yet another gate controlling access to the right ramp. Dan wondered why the other tunnel appeared to have free access. Two to three hundred feet to their right, another pair of tunnels appeared to go into another part of the mountain and only one of them, the right one again, had a gate controlling access. Further right was the large, whitish, single-story building with an overhanging roof they had seen a minute earlier; it appeared to be at least a couple of hundred feet long and most likely housed offices.

Dan noted that both sets of tunnels appeared to be protected by another fence. The fence surrounded a relatively small area that could not be more than fifteen hundred square feet in the case of the first set of tunnels. The second fenced area was much larger, as it encompassed both the space around the tunnels and the office building. He immediately thought that *these sets of tunnels had to be the accesses to the enrichment halls*; he assumed that *the reason why only one of the access ramps was gated in both cases had to be because there was a one-way traffic pattern inside the mountain*. The logical explanation probably was that the tunnels were not wide enough to allow large trucks to pass one another. He assumed that *these trucks brought in the unenriched uranium gas and took delivery of the enriched product that would then be sent to Isfahan for the production of nuclear fuel*. He would eventually be proven correct in that assumption.

This led them to conclude that *Simon's plan was right on target, IF they could get the inside help, they needed. They could not do the job on their own*. Both would have much preferred not having to rely on insiders, "*just like Mike and Dave at Natanz*." They trusted each other but did not have the same level of trust to what they called "semi-outsiders," though, in fairness, Amir was a *Mossad* agent. They would need someone to drive them into and out of the complex. They could not get in on their own unless they could fly in and remain undetected. Dan had noted that several patrols appeared to be continuously making rounds. He felt he had seen at least four different groups of soldiers, if not five, along the road from the first to the second guarded gatehouse. The patrols would have ten times the chance to catch and kill them if they tried to sneak in, though he noted that he could not see what was behind the mountain crest above. He thought that *there might be a viable entry or exit, which they would need to check at some point*.

Farid turned right when he arrived at the first pair of tunnels and drove past the second pair to stop in front of the office building; Dan noted two small trees, one on either side of what had to be the main door, thinking: *this will help with radio equipment*. He also asked himself whether there was a tunnel access from the office building to the enrichment halls.

During the drive, Nathan and Daniel had offered enough cursory information on their new technology to wet Farid's appetite, but not enough that they would be exposed for their lack of real detailed scientific knowledge. Farid seemed to buy into their game; though he appeared surprised that they did not have the answer to a couple of questions that he seemed to think weren't really all that complex. Dan thought to himself that *Minoo would need to work her magic and possibly come clean for Farid to be able to provide them with the appropriate cover if there was a next trip.*

Farid had made sure that they received appropriate badges when they went through the first guarded gate; this had given them a couple of minutes to look discreetly into the set up there. They both concluded that forcing through the gate without getting killed would be nearly impossible. The guardhouse was not very large, but it had at least two rooms. The first, in the front was where the guards on duty would sit, as it faced the road; the other, in the back, seemed to be where some sort of broader video surveillance was centered. Nathan noticed a number of what looked like television screens through a connecting door the guards had left open. They concluded the Iranians must have security cameras in several places; they would need to make sure they understood that set-up.

Farid had parked his car a short distance from the door. Nathan was inexplicably a bit slow getting out the car, but, after what seemed like a few, long seconds, he joined them as they entered the office building. They were immediately taken to modest changing rooms where they simply donned a white gown over their street clothes. They were also provided with masks, which they were not expected to wear, but were to carry in case an emergency developed while they were in either enrichment hall.

Generally, total nuclear protection is not needed, despite the pictures which one frequently sees, and which depict nuclear scientists wearing masks and head covers. The uranium hexafluoride gas that flows through the centrifuges has an initial low concentration. It only becomes dangerous toward the end of any cascade when it has been sufficiently enriched, often to around 5% uranium 235. Yet, the circuits are sufficiently hermetically sealed that only an accident, where a seal fails or a pipe develops a leak, would create a situation that would warrant wearing protective clothing. There would almost always be enough time to put the masks on, except in the case of an explosion where a mask might not serve much of a purpose anyway. Yet, official procedures called for visitors to wear protective clothing and have gas masks readily accessible; so, Farid followed the normal protocol.

He then took them to meet a few of his colleagues in a large conference room. Though Farid's colleagues asked a few questions, Nathan and Dan found them both much simpler and general than anything which Farid had thrown at them during the drive. Ostensibly, within the team, only the people at the top were allowed to ask the difficult questions. In that, they were lucky that Farid's alter ego, Dr. Reza Pashtani, happened not to be there the day of their visit.

They noticed someone who, Farid told them, was in charge of facilities and maintenance; he seemed particularly focused on them. They assumed it was Amir but were very careful not to let anyone realize they might know him. They wondered why he seemed to be paying as much attention to them as he was. Nathan thought to himself: *If he's legit, he should know that he shouldn't focus on us . . . I'm gonna have to watch this guy.* He conceded that the individual's interest might simply be "professional" and nothing else, but he filed in his own mind the obvious question: *what if he is not a straight arrow?*

Farid elected to escort and guide them himself through the installation. They walked down one story indicating that there was more to the building than met the eye: part of it was underground and Dan immediately concluded that access to the enrichment halls would be through direct underground tunnels, answering his earlier internal question. Being alone with Farid made it so much easier for

Dan and Nate to take turns speaking to him as they scoped out the place, making detailed mental notes and measurements that would allow them, when back in Tel Aviv, to create a reasonable small-scale replica of the two halls. They both wore watches that, though they appeared absolutely run-of-the-mill normal, could in fact carry out measurements of the halls, principally in terms of length and width, and of the geography of the various installations relative to one another: a sort of a multipurpose sophisticated Fitbit. Also, their glasses were equipped with mini cameras whose pictures were stored in microchips located in the frames. The plan was that they would both have enough memory in those chips that they would have a complete movie of the entire visit. Measuring the time spent walking between two points would allow the specialists to double check the measurements made by their watches.

As they walked with Farid toward the first enrichment hall, they were surprised that the tunnel leading from the office building to the enrichment halls required them to pass through a relatively open area. The tunnel from the office building to the enrichment facilities indeed proceeded in a rather straight line for what they thought was probably three to four hundred feet from the exit of the office building; then, they reached a small underground plaza, which looked like what it was—a cave dug into a mountain. No effort had been made even to create a proper ceiling. They were told that this was where the loading and unloading of trucks was taking place, as they brought plain, gasified uranium into the complex and took enriched gas to facilities where it was transformed into nuclear fuel. Given the floor plan of the plaza, they could see that there was indeed little room to spare; the initial assumption that the truck circuit had to be a one-way affair seemed totally appropriate. On their right was a double door which opened into the first enrichment hall.

Entering the hall, they saw a room that was uneven in shape, but still more rectangular than anything else. The walls were covered in some sort of plaster and there was a proper ceiling, which incorporated aeration vents. Dan and Nate both had the same thought: *"Where is the air eventually forced out . . . ?"*

This would determine what secondary effects there might be, if the explosion they were planning led to some enriched uranium gas being released into the atmosphere. They asked Farid about the air circulation system. He said that it was simple in "normal circumstances," adding: "Would become more complex if there was a radiation leak. Then all sorts of filters come into play . . ."

They realized that Farid's explanation told them next to nothing, but did not feel the need to press, thinking "Amir will answer the question if we need a detailed answer . . ."

They were able to verify the manner in which the centrifuges were secured to the floor. Farid indeed spent some time focusing on the constraints under which needle bearings had to operate in order to allow high rotating speeds: this was where the "new material" could help. They also were able to inspect the actual distance between any two centrifuges and the way the rows were laid out. This last element was particularly important to the decision as to where the explosives should be placed and how they should be accessed. Additionally, knowing as they did how the plan was supposed to play out, Nate noted that the rows appeared to be a bit nearer to one another than expected. He felt that they would need to be careful as they walked between two rows to avoid knocking anything out of place: that could trigger an alarm and kill the mission.

Exiting from the hall back into the plaza, they found the continuation of the tunnel no more than a hundred feet from the double door. It now veered slightly to the left and, after what they assumed to be around eight hundred feet, reached another small underground plaza that looked exactly like the first one, or at least as exactly similar as one could expect from caves dug into the rock. Truck traffic was again to their left and the second enrichment hall to their right, deeper into the mountain. It looked very much like the first one, except for two, additional, smaller cascades. Farid simply said that they were an experimental setup but did not reveal any of their special features. Nathan noticed that the piping between two adjacent centrifuges appeared more convoluted.

They had mentally noted all the distances but were comforted by the thought that *their watches would tell them more precisely once they could process the data they were accumulating.* They decided that the overall dimensions of the halls were probably generally accurate; yet, there was more space at both ends than anticipated since the centrifuges appeared closer together than expected. It was not obvious to them how that affected the plan, but this was another element that would have to be revisited.

They observed that both halls and the tunnel system seemed to be covered by an internal video surveillance system. Nathan was wondering whether this might be the same system being fed to the screens he had seen in the guardhouse at the main entrance. *This was an important question,* he thought, *as it would determine the likely speed of any response to a security breach.* He made a note in his mind: *Another loose end we need to tighten up . . .*

So, they concluded that Amir should stay in his office where he could safely monitor the corridors, the underground plazas and thus the accesses to both halls. For this to work and Amir to be able to warn them in the case of an emergency, they would need a simple communication system. The system would need to allow Amir to differentiate between the two of them such that he warned the one in most danger first. Logic suggested that a simple three-way radio system might be the best alternative, but this would be up to Marvin to decide. The question they needed to address was how Amir could be seeing real-time activity while anyone else monitoring the halls and plazas would not see them depositing their explosives. Dan remembered a mission where he had dealt with the same problem and thought that *the same approach would be feasible: a feed from a player showing a video of the hall in normal circumstances could be substituted for the live feed for the duration of their work. This would mean that Amir would have to shoot the first videos and that he would need equipment to feed that back into the surveillance system.*

The good news was that radio reception appeared quite good throughout the space. Before leaving Farid's car, and going into the complex, Nate, who was riding in the back seat, had left a small radio-signal emitting device; this is what had delayed his following Dan and Farid into the building. That allowed him to test how that signal was received while they were inside. He now felt that he received the signal throughout the visit with a strong enough intensity for the purpose they had in mind. The signal's strength never fell below 50%; this was both unexpected and more than enough. Discussing this later with Dan, they concluded that a device placed even closer to the entrance, but still on the same general vector would do even better. They would have to work with the lab to decide how to trade the strength of the signal against the risk that the emitter could be detected.

Their first impressions, as they later discussed them on the flight back to Frankfurt, were that there was a real need to revisit the plan with Simon. The primary concern, or rather the concern that was the most driven by assessable facts, was that the distances between the two halls were somewhat longer than originally expected. The plan that they would both work each hall together simply no longer seemed to make as much sense given the distance between the halls—too much time wasted in transit. The layout made them think that they should probably each be responsible for one hall rather than working together as a team for both. However, having each of them responsible for one hall had an important drawback: having whoever was responsible for the second hall transiting through the second plaza alone, with no gun cover, did not seem terribly appealing. Secondarily, they drew up their list of "loose ends" for Simon's benefit.

Nathan could not help himself. He added: "I'm not convinced by Amir if he was indeed the individual whom we saw focus on us during the earlier "general briefing."

His mind was nearly made up; he was unsure whether he was truly reliable, adding: "There's something I really don't like here."

Daniel countered: "I understand, but why not give Simon and thus Amir the benefit of the doubt?"

Nathan kept harping back on the fact that Amir would have their lives in his hands: "I want to be able to trust him 100% and I am nowhere near that . . ."

They agreed that they should mention Nathan's misgivings to Simon.

CHAPTER.12

MAY 5
DUBAI, TEHRAN AND KASHAN

David and Mike arrived in Dubai as planned, from Tel Aviv via Istanbul, and waited calmly for their next flight. They had to go through immigration, as they needed to check in for their next flight, from Dubai to Tehran, as Dubai residents going on a business trip to Iran. They did not leave the airport, but simply went from the arrival to the departure level, praying that no one would change workstations from one floor to the next. David had argued: "This is a huge airport. Minimal risk."

They could not help being a bit tense as they presented their passports to border control. The passports were the work of talented *Mossad* agents who not only reproduced UAE passports perfectly but had to create a travel history to demonstrate that David and Mike had both lived in Dubai for the last five years and travelled to various places where their "customers" would have been expected to be. This meant having a number of entry and exit stamps, from the Emirates as well as several other countries, principally in the region.

Ominously, the passport control officer was focusing on these and asked a few questions on a couple of the trips the stamps indicated they had taken. The usual "Why did you go to Kuwait?" "Why did you not go back for six months?" And the like. However, in fairness, it was not all that unusual for residents of the UAE to travel extensively; he had to have realized that there was "nothing there" if he was trying to catch them out. Plus, a queue was forming in front of his booth. So, he proceeded to stamp each passport, right next to prior stamps. After they were out of earing range, David and Mike commented that this last stamp would make their entry into Iran that much easier.

They walked back into the almost grandiose international concourse, with all its exclusive shops and even the well-known luxury car lottery drawing stands. As they had some time to kill, they decided to walk into the Premier lounge so that they could get something decent to drink, though, at that time in the morning, they were thinking decent coffee rather than hard liquor, which is served at the airport despite Dubai being a Muslim state. Eventually, they left the lounge, walked calmly to their gate and boarded their plane. The flight from Dubai was totally uneventful. They landed at Imam Khomeini International Airport on schedule at 9:35 a.m.

Mike's premonition that entry into Iran would not be hard had proven a bit optimistic. At immigration, they walked to the visa counter, together. They told the officer that they were partners in a small manufacturing operation. They wanted to add capacity to their Dubai plant, but do it in a place where costs would not be as high as Dubai, or the Emirates more broadly. Their margins in the Emirates were, they said, low. They could not afford to expand there. They describe the purpose of their trip as a scouting effort; they were looking for alternative plant locations. And, since they were both Iranians by birth, Iran was a logical candidate.

"How big will the plant be?" the immigration officer asked. Mike replied: "At his point, we've got to start small: fifty to one hundred people at most. But it can grow. We employ over 1,000 people in the Emirates."

"Where are you looking . . . ?" This time, it was David's turn to answer: "We're thinking that the region around Kashan could be great. That's where I'm from originally. It'd be nice to go back where I grew up."

"When did you leave Iran . . . ?"

"I was only four or five years old," David replied. "I can't remember much, but I know that this was where home was."

So far, the questions were pretty simple, and totally expected. The curve ball came when the officer asked about all the trips they had taken out of and into the UAE. Mike thought to himself: *Why does he even bother? That was the job of the UAE immigration officer . . .*

But the officer was insisting on having them explain what their business interests really were in all these places. More importantly, it led him to question why they would only request a tourist visa. He explained to them that, as they had to know, a tourist visa only allowed them to come in as tourists. They could not enter into any transaction but could make plans. He went on and asked: "What will you do if you find the ideal location?"

Though this was a fair question, it was one they had not rehearsed. Ostensibly, they had no intention of making a firm decision. Nevertheless, they kicked themselves for not anticipating it. David, as the leader, eventually offered a disarming answer: "Great question, Officer. I guess we just assumed we would need multiple trips. Plus, as you know, we cannot get a business visa unless we have a contact in Iran that could vouch for us. So, we hoped to make enough progress that we could be in the position of having contacts in Iran next time, and, for our next trip, apply for a business visa in Dubai . . ."

This seemed to satisfy the agent who gave them both a visa for 10 days.

Armed with those visas, they completed their immigration procedures with ease. Collecting their luggage was also easy; the time they had spent at the visa counter had given plenty of opportunity to luggage handlers to deliver their two suitcases. The customs officer gave a cursory look at their declarations and asked to see Mike's tablet computer. The officer asked Mike to switch it on and then off and waved them through. They made their way to the car rental agency where they asked for the largest SUV they had. Fortunately, a white Toyota Land Cruiser was available. Otherwise, they would have been stuck with a Morattab Series IV, a local, simplified clone of a Land Rover. The clerk did say that they didn't see too many of these Toyotas. They were in high demand from people doing serious exploring.

"That's exactly what we're going to do" Mike replied, in perfectly accented Farsi.

Once in the car, they set out for Kashan, about one hundred ten miles due south as the crow flies, but a good one hundred thirty-mile drive. They could stay on divided highways all the way. With the one hundred and twenty kilometers (about seventy-five miles) per hour speed limit in force on a divided highway in Iran, they figured the trip would take about two hours, allowing for the time to get onto the highway at the airport and a slowdown at the Kashan exit. The highway indeed allowed them to bypass Qom completely and thus to avoid the ring road and its lower speed limit. They switched from Highway #7 to Highway #71, forty miles north of Kashan. Highway #7 then took a more southwesterly direction and thus led them away from their intended destination. They did not stop in Kashan and went straight to the air strip that the satellite had indicated. Mike turned his tablet GPS on and guided David, who was driving.

A couple of miles south of Kashan, they took the first available exit and drove toward Amir Kabir Industrial Town. That this might reinforce their story should anyone be watching them was simply a lucky bonus. Amir Kabir was three miles ahead on the left, but they continued on for another two miles and found a small, divided highway, with bushes in the middle; it was on their left and appeared to be the road they were supposed to take. David, who was driving, exclaimed: "Holy Shit."

Mike perked up and his heart sank too. The airstrip which the satellite had identified and which they had selected to base their attack on Natanz was in fact Kashan's airport.

"Disused facility, my foot," was the only thing Mike could say . . .

CHAPTER.13

Simon, David and Marvin agreed to meet at the *Mossad* Special Operations Lab on Palmachim Airbase, twenty-six miles southwest of Ben Gurion Airport, due south of Tel Aviv. One of the issues which Simon knew he would have to address, and resolve, was the need to transport heavy equipment across difficult terrain. Marvin had promised an ingenious solution that required minimal modifications to a tool they had just developed—a heli-drone. Simon watched with a smile on his face David's reactions and Marvin's responses to his questions: "A what?"

"A heli-drone, David?"

"What's that?

"A remote-controlled helicopter . . . But, not a toy my friend!"

"Sounds ingenious . . . Gotta see it . . ."

They walked to the building from which most of the drones in service in Israel are remote-controlled. It looked very generic from the outside, but the inside was incredibly impressive. It was a two-story building, with the second floor reserved for offices and resting rooms for pilots; the first floor was the major control center. It was about one hundred yards long and about half that wide. The end closest to the main door had a couple of offices, one on either side of the receptionist area. As they walked into the main hall, they could see that there were two conference rooms at the far end of the hall, one quite large and the other much smaller, with an emergency exit between them. Other than that, the room was the fully open plan, with eight rows of individual cubicles, each of which was a control station for one drone. Each cubicle had enough space for three operators to sit in it. There were a few empty cubicles, suggesting some room for expansion. Typically, each day, operators would work two three-and-a-half-hour shifts, separated by an hour of rest. That rest was crucial to keep them totally focused, very much like the practice for air traffic controllers who would be exposed to similar intense stress, possibly even more in places where there was a lot of activity.

Marvin took them to the cubicle that controlled the heli-drone they were going to demonstrate. It was in the far left-hand corner of the room.

"This will allow whatever you guys do to be as discreet and confidential as possible."

"Good thinking, Marvin," was all Simon could say.

They were amazed to see that the right-hand side of the cubicle looked exactly like the cockpit of any helicopter they had seen. They noted three computer screens in front of the two pilots; each was showing the pilots what they would see if they were actually sitting in the cockpit of the drone, if it had one. The dashboard, which created something like a Y with the vertical bar of the Y jutting between the two pilots, had two smaller screens in front of each pilot; these provided the normal attitude and navigational data. There was a large screen between them on which all the operational information needed was displayed—remaining fuel level and fuel flow, for instance. On the left-hand side of the cubicle, there was another workstation; it was reserved for a support officer who would be responsible for dealing with any issue that either pilot could not or should not handle.

"Meet Captains Albert Schoenberg and Barack Leven," Marvin

started, adding: "Captain Schoenberg and Captain Leven, meet Colonel Simon Rabinowitz."

With only a bare minimum of initial pleasantries, the two pilots went about the task at hand. They explained how they worked and demonstrated it with the heli-drone which Simon and David had been told was right behind the building. The telltale sign that the drone was indeed there was that they could see the building in which they were standing appear on the pilots' screens as soon as they had ignited the drone's systems. The pilots had the heli-drone take off and execute a number of maneuvers to show how versatile and flexible it was. They demonstrated that they could do anything any pilot would want to do in a real helicopter: take off straight up, hover, slide left and right and even descend in a tight spiral.

The pilots landed the heli-drone right behind the building again and switched its engine off. The pilot sitting on the right in the cubicle, the first officer so to speak, Captain Schoenberg, offered to accompany the three visitors to see the drone close up. He took what looked like a regular computer tablet with him: "I'll demonstrate the remote operating capabilities that could be used by an agent in the field."

They walked out of the building and the heli-drone was sitting on the tarmac. The first thing they noticed was how small the whole contraption was: probably no more than twenty feet long and ten feet high. It, indeed, looked like a small helicopter, with a large, horizontal rotor at the front and a much smaller one at the end of a triangular steel assembly affixed to the main body of the aircraft. Under the engine, which was located immediately below the main rotor, there was a large bay for ferrying cargo or equipment. This particular model actually had a crane that could be seen when the doors to the lower belly of the drone swung open; the two retracting landing gears were just long enough to allow two cargo doors hiding the crane to open longitudinally without hitting the ground. The front end of the aircraft was much smaller than usual; not surprising since there was no need for a cockpit. Marvin explained that the forward space was occupied by electronic equipment and the largest of the two gas tanks. A smaller tank was located at the base of the tail assembly, . . . "for balance," Marvin added. He pointed to the two, 360-degree, infrared cameras, both facing downward, one under the nose and the other right ahead of the rear rotor. He also pointed out the camera at the front of the aircraft which fed the screens of the remote pilots and showed them what a pilot would see; it was equipped with a zoom lens, with a wide-angle setting and could thus provide a wide range of vision in both horizontal and vertical directions. Marvin made the point that the infrared cameras were meant for surveillance, both in flight and when the heli-drone was parked: "With these, we can always monitor what happens around it, even when it's on the ground at some remote location."

The heli-drone was painted a matte gun gray. Marvin explained that the paint had certain radar-evading capabilities but added that it would be an exaggeration to claim that it was a totally stealthy aircraft. He joked that its small size played at least as much of a role in its being difficult to detect as the stealth paint. Marvin also pointed to a number of small, blue boxes distributed around the structure of the drone; he explained that they were explosive devices. They could be triggered remotely to ensure that the drone would not be traceable to Israel. To emphasize the point, he added that when they were last tested, no one could find a single piece of the drone larger than fifteen cubic centimeters, or basically a cube less than one inch in any dimension. In short, never enough to carry any complete marking or allow any analysis, other than the nature of the metal, which was not a state secret.

Albert showed Marvin, Simon and David that he was typing an instruction on his tablet. He was asking Barack, his teammate, to start the engine. He added: "I could also speak the instruction directly into the tablet . . ."

Simon, who had initially objected to the noise of a helicopter for the critical role the drone was to play in the mission, had to eat his words. He had to admit that the drone was indeed much quieter than any helicopter he had ever heard. David was furiously nodding his agreement. Marvin credited a different approach to the management of exhaust gases. Simon knew enough not to ask for more . . .

Albert then took over the commands from Barack and had the heli-drone take off and hover a few yards overhead. He then launched into a series of maneuvers similar to those that they had controlled from the inside. The aircraft was indeed quite versatile. He invited David to hold the tablet and worked with him to demonstrate how he could control the drone. The screen on the tablet simply showed a joystick on the right side. It moved in the direction the craft was to travel on a level plane; the longer the travel on the joystick, the faster the heli-drone speed would be. It also showed another joystick, on the left, which controlled the altitude of the drone. Combining the two would allow the operator to move freely in a three-dimensional space. David noted that the tablet did not show a forward-looking picture of what a pilot might see. Albert explained that clicking on a green button at the top left of the screen allowed the remote pilot to see that screen. Dragging one's fingers on the picture would control its size, although it was limited by the need to keep seeing the joysticks. Albert added: "You can even zoom the picture if you press the yellow button above the right joystick and move the joystick toward more or less zooming."

David asked what that did to the normal function of the right joystick—the forward speed of the drone. Albert replied that, in an inspection mode, the speed of the drone is maintained at the last speed selected by the remote pilot.

"Inspection mode?"

"Yes, David. The system assumes you are inspecting something whenever you switch the screen to video and do any kind of zooming."

"Pretty cool. Any way to override?"

"Unfortunately, not at this time."

Going back to his demonstration, Albert added that you did not have to be a helicopter pilot to handle this drone. You simply told it where you wanted it to go and how fast or slow—the software would do the rest. He switched to another important point, which, as time would later tell, would be used in the mission. The tablet required the operator's right thumb to remain applied to the key in the lower middle section of the screen. He explained that it told the home pilots, those sitting here at the base, that the remote operator was in control. He added that the home pilots would take over the operation as soon as the remote operator removed their thumb—or any other finger you care to use—from the key. Right on cue, Albert removed his thumb from the key and in a split second, Barack had taken over the controls and was gently landing the drone in front of them; a flashing red light with a buzzer in the cubicle had told him that he was in control. Albert added: "Can't miss it . . . even if you are not focused on the screen 24/7. The red flash and the buzzer do it . . ."

Retaking control of the heli-drone, Albert then demonstrated the use of the crane; it had to be maneuvered with the left hand. The right hand was keeping local control of the drone and having it hover. Marvin had brought a couple of bulky packages which the drone picked up and deposited a few yards away. The same principle applied to this control as to the two other joysticks: the more amplitude in the moves on the screen, the faster the movement of the crane in reality.

He invited David to try. Initially, the heli-drone's flight was quite unstable . . . David motioned to Albert that he wanted him to take over the controls. David clearly was not ready to operate it, thinking: *Funny how things always look simple when others are well-trained to do them . . .*

Simon offered: "Marvin, this is really awesome. Judging by David's performance, he and Mike will need to practice . . . But this is a gem. Well-done."

Marvin was beaming. He could not help switching into technobabble and adding that the good news was that they did not need to make any changes to the drone, except that they would need a couple of external gas tanks to get it to Iran and back.

CHAPTER.14

David and Mike decided that their initial disappointment with the so-called disused airport had to be overcome. They could see that the road was well-maintained and that whatever was there was signaled as a bona fide airport. They decided that they had no option but to keep driving toward it, as originally planned. David took that small, divided highway and proceeded to drive toward three structures in the distance on the southwest side of what looked like the sole runway. Though the installation did look like a bona fide airport, Mike suddenly said, "Wait a minute . . . I can't see any traffic . . . There aren't many people around that airport."

David agreed and ventured the guess that, though it certainly did not look like a disused airstrip, it still did not look particularly busy, asking: "Shouldn't there be more people milling around if the airport was truly active?"

Mike conceded the point, but casually noted that it could have become principally used for military purposes: "That would explain the lack of people traffic . . ."

They kept driving and quickly came alongside a group of six small one-story buildings that looked like barracks, or a small garrison. David noted: "Could well be right, my friend . . ."

The news seemed to be getting worse. David summed it up, "First, it's a formal airport and second it's guarded by the military. Damn, this ain't good news . . . Can it get any worse?"

Mike could only agree. Having debated the prudence of their immediate plan, they still decided that they had to look more closely. *The only way to find out*, David thought, *was for them to go check out the barracks*, as he called them. They turned right, lowered their windows and agreed that, if stopped, they were to plead they had gotten lost looking for the airport. As they passed the first three barracks, they noted a total absence of activity: no light, no sound, no one standing or sitting on a doorstep, just dust, a lot of dust, as they drove by. This did seem to suggest that the area was indeed deserted. David stopped the truck. Both of them alighted and started walking in the direction of the fourth barrack. It was just ahead of them, on their left.

Suddenly, a noise came from around the fifth or sixth barrack, no more than a couple of hundred feet from them: the sound of metal hitting stones. They stopped in their tracks, each wondering how they would explain the fact that they had gotten out of the truck. They moved slowly in the direction of the sound, somewhat unhappy with themselves at being there, totally unarmed. David was the first to see the two dogs running after each other . . . They had kicked down a metal drum, probably used as an outside garbage container. Mike simply said: "How stupid of us."

"I know . . . But, tell you what, still want to look these over more closely," David replied.

They went around each of the next three barracks, testing front doors and windows. They found the doors unlocked and the windows closed. The inside of the barracks looked dirty, full of dust, as if they had not been used in some time. Rudimentary, probably military furniture was still there; kitchens seemed operational—however minimally equipped. They had to conclude that they seemed not to be in current use, probably abandoned for a while, but not years. They retraced their steps and similarly inspected the first three buildings. Same results. They concluded, as a "preliminary effort" they called it, that the place was indeed deserted. However, they thought *they should keep looking carefully at that area each time they were driving to or from the airport, just to make sure and avoid an unpleasant surprise.*

They turned around and drove back to the road into the airport. Further ahead, there were indeed the few, small buildings they initially noticed. One of them looked like a small terminal, or a nice hangar; it could be either, as there were precious few windows that they could see from where they were. Hardly more than a quarter mile to the right, they saw a single, bigger hangar, with a small structure in front. They eventually concluded that this "complex" probably was the terminal building; the other one they had seen earlier had to be something else, probably a nice hangar. Tell-tell signs on this larger one such as a few more windows, a couple of doors opening to the front and some parking space in front gave the game away in their views. They could not see anything seemingly alive in either of the two buildings but decided that they would focus on the second hangar nearer the right end of the runway. Their spirits rose when they saw that they could drive to the hangar without being disturbed or even noticed. They scouted the area, ready with a story that they were looking for a facility to ship machinery or raw materials into the plant should they encounter someone. They saw no one. In short, the place looked completely deserted, yet . . .

Mike looked at his tablet which had a satellite connection to the Internet. He was looking for flights that might have Kashan as their origin or destination. He did not find any. He should have known that. The team back in Tel Aviv had done exactly the same exercise, to be sure, before they had picked the place. He did find flights for an airport about thirty miles to the north called Mahmudabad. A quick, google search told them what they needed. The old Kashan airport had been superseded by a newer one, Mahmudabad. So, the team in Tel Aviv might have indeed gotten it right; this was a disused airport. They still decided to let Simon know, just in case . . .

They focused on the hangar as they noted the large piece of tarmac in front. It could allow the drones to come close to the structure, which could, in turn, serve as their depot. Additionally, there was space where they could hide both behind and off to the side where, even if someone came to one of the other buildings, they would be reasonably hidden.

They decided that the plan still appeared to make sense, but they had to make sure the place was truly deserted. They agreed that they should take turns staying on site for the next twenty-four hours to ensure that they had observed a full twenty-four-hour cycle. A good leader, David offered to take the first three-hour watch, then it would be Mike's turn to come and take over. He added that he had his flashlight tool, so he could get in touch with David any time. He elected to hide in the "terminal" to keep the heat down. There were two large rooms, which he correctly assumed were, respectively, where ticketing and luggage handling had been. There was, however, no trace of any remaining equipment.

CHAPTER.15

MAY 5
KASHAN

After leaving David and the airport, Mike drove back to Kashan and started looking for the two places they had identified on the internet as possible apartment rentals. He immediately dismissed the first one. It was smack in the middle of town, which might have been good, but offered absolutely no privacy. The parking area was visible to all, and the buildings around it were all of same height and quite close to one another. With the plan calling for night operations at Natanz, there was too much risk that someone might notice the odd hours kept by the two tenants. Even if that someone did not instantly call the police, the risk was too big. Also, Mike thought that *someone might climb the large tree at the back of the building and find a way to get into any flat that faced that way, including theirs. I don't want them to find anything they're not supposed to find here,* he thought to himself adding *and I don't want either of us having to sweep the flat each time we leave.*

The second place was, in fact, more convenient as it was barely a half-mile from the southeastern end of town and had much easier access to Highway 71. Also, the building looked a bit more secure. It was more modern, though that did not mean much in traditional, old Kashan. Parking was on the ground floor, under the building, which was built up above ground as was, at times, the case there. This was ostensibly to promote air circulation under the building and keep it cooler. They could load or unload the car without being noticed. There was no elevator, obviously, but he saw that as a plus. No elevator meant that no one could sneak up on them, as they were climbing back to the apartment. And with only one staircase, anyone going up or down would have to be using it. There was no place to hide or surprise. If either or both of them were doing anything they felt was sensitive in the garage, the one keeping watch only had to stand at the foot of the stairs. The only other access would be the ramp into the parking, but you could see the ramp as well from the foot of the stairs.

Mike agreed to a week's rental with the agent who showed him the small flat. It had two small bedrooms and something the agent called a bathroom. A shower closet might have been more accurate, as there was hardly enough space in it for the shower and a sink that looked terribly lonely in the corner, just left of the door. There was a separate toilet, not an unusual thing in Iran; and there was a bidet right next to it, for the ritual cleaning that Muslims had to perform, after going to the bathroom. The kitchen was equally rudimentary, but it would do. The bedrooms were so small that there was hardly any space around what looked like a double bed in each. The main point for Mike was that there appeared to be decent curtains on the main windows; this would effectively stop any peeping toms. He obviously was not worried about sexual deviants but about people who might look into the flat from across the small square.

Once the apartment question was settled, Mike went grocery shopping for the absolute minimum they would need: food items and toiletries. He did not find ground coffee beans but bought tea and powdered coffee. That would have to do. The food he bought was simple and required little or no cooking. He had noted that kitchen utensils in the flat were also rare and old. Yet, between a couple of saucepans and one frying pan, he felt they had what they would need to cook eggs, chicken or lamb meatballs and local vegetables and rice. Almost next door to the food market, he found a shop to buy toothpaste, shaving cream, something they called aftershave and a bar of unscented soap. But he had to go to two different shops to find bottled water. Initially, the shop he had chosen was in the local district of town; no luck. He concluded that the locals did not worry about drinking the local water. They had made their intestinal peace with the bugs and bacteria of the region.

Driving due north from the apartment on Baba Afzal Street, he passed a beautiful, rectangular plaza, measuring at least four hundred fifty feet by two hundred fifty, with a green space in the middle that looked almost like traditional French gardens. He turned right on Motasham Street and left at the next major intersection, Abazar Street. This eventually led him directly to the old Kashan Bazar, Akhavan, on the left, after the roundabout at Amirieh. The contrast was striking between the well-tended, one-story structures, with gardens in front and back, and a vacant space used as a parking lot but not sealed with asphalt. It looked more like any abandoned property in any big city anywhere in the world. He found what he needed at the bazar. There was much more choice in the range of goods available: still and sparkling bottled water, a few more food items that he hadn't found locally and a few, sweet, dry pastries, all of which he added to his stock.

As he was driving around town and back to the flat, he concluded that the town was a tale of two cities: one was well-tended, traditional and yet nicely maintained; it was where people worked. The other, where people actually tended to live, looked old despite being more modern. In fact, at times, it seemed almost decrepit.

He kept monitoring his tablet and flashlight tool but did not hear from David. He sent him a quick update. In truth, he was more interested in knowing that all was right at the airport than in reporting to his boss. David promptly replied to his flash message: "Thanks for the update; just saw one car go by in the last sixty minutes or so. No sign of life at the main terminal, either, at least none as of yet."

Mike went back to the apartment. He unloaded his purchases and, while there, decided to take a short snooze. He remarked that the beds were at least as uncomfortable as they looked, although possibly even more so. *We're going to have to be really weary to sleep here. But that's no different from many other missions,* he thought to himself.

He was in fact truly surprised when his alarm woke him up an hour later. He must have slept better than he thought he would. He took a quick shower and changed into more comfortable, less closely fitting clothing. He felt the pleasure of being clean, which was enhanced by the minty tinge that remained from the shaving cream and the strong scent of the aftershave, which he concluded probably was almost all alcohol, with a hint of some nondescript perfume.

"Helicopter just landed . . ."

David's message startled Mike. What could this be? Another message came back before Mike had the time to reply to the first: "Took off. Vehicle leaving the airport. Can't see where it's going."

"You all right?"

"Yes! All happened at the other end of the runway . . . Need to figure out what it is. Sending a message to Simon. We may need better AWACS coverage . . ."

"Stay safe."

He had already decided to start early for the airport, but David's message gave the idea a much higher sense of urgency. He needed to snoop around in the area between Amir Kabir and the airport. With Amir Kabir an industrial town, having him taking a walk in the neighborhood would be perfectly understandable and fitting with their cover. This would also allow him to ask a few questions of the locals. He wanted to play dumb and ask questions that someone with his cover could ask. What's it like to work here? How easy is it to find a job here? What's that airport there? Ostensibly, the last question was the one that he was most interested in, but he could not be obvious, and it had to be buried among others.

He found out several interesting things, which he made a note to share with David as soon as he could. The town was sorely lacking work, so that there were plenty of people who might work for them. Since David and he were really not looking for workers, in contrast with their cover roles, that was bad news. There would be plenty of people doing nothing. They could well be in the wrong place at the wrong time. People were principally involved in farming and the tourist trade, with the rest busy with religion. But there had been fewer tourists of late. Nobody wanted to tell a stranger why tourism was down. But he guessed, though he did not openly discuss any of it, that the combination of international sanctions and domestic saber rattling could not possibly help. There were, however, plenty of small farmers and the cover that they had was perfect. Officially, they were thinking of assembling rototillers, tools like small agricultural tractors, except that they had only two wheels. At times, they were called walking tractors because the farmer walked behind them, guiding and controlling them with handlebars that looked like those found on a large motorcycle.

He was told that he should consider spending a bit of time exploring the base of the mountain chain on the east side of the valley. It was very nice, and temperatures dropped quite quickly as you went up in altitude. The hills on that side were lower than the mountains to the west, but they were also more easily accessible. He immediately thought *of the heli-drone and the need to find a hiding place*. He confirmed that people did not go there much.

Returning to the airport, he found David who was a bit bored, though the unexpected helicopter landing certainly justified the decision to keep watch there.

"A car in three hours isn't really much, but one helicopter is one too many," was all he could conclude.

Mike brought him up to speed on his activity, starting with the observation that a car in three hours was just what he would have expected, or even hoped for.

He turned to explaining that he had scouted around the south end of Amir Kabir and chatted with a few people. He said he had avoided anyone who was alone and only talked to groups of two or three.

The big news, he said, was that this airport was virtually never used. The people to whom he talked had said that there used to be a few commercial flights, but they stopped a while back; nobody could remember when they did. He said he asked about the other airport, Mahmudabad, but mostly drew blank stares. He concluded that the people to whom he talked were not regular users of airplanes. An interesting point, he added, was that people said they hear jets or helicopters from time to time, but they thought "they were military, not commercial." Mike concluded

"Looks more and more like an active military site . . ."

David handed over to Mike the role of staying at the airport to watch for anything suspect. In the meantime, he said that he was going to do his own snooping but would obviously avoid the areas Mike had already visited. As he put it: "The Land Cruiser is not terribly discreet, and there can't be that many of them around here."

Mike suggested a trip across the valley on the other side of the runway if he had the courage: "You might find a hiding place for the heli-drone there."

Changing topics, Mike confirmed that the walking tractor cover was ideal, given the fact that their farms were poor and small; they needed help cultivating their fields, but no one around here could afford a real tractor. He added: "Their donkeys and oxen are screaming for some relief."

Mike gave David the keys to the flat and driving instructions but told him not to have high expectations for the flat. David took the Land Cruiser back to Kashan, returning to Hwy 71 at Amir Kabir; he drove on and eventually reached the first roundabout after having entered Kashan. There, rather than turning left to go further into town, he kept going straight and veered right about 1,000 feet further on, in the direction of the hills. He did not feel the need to rest quite yet and was not anxious to see the flat after Mike's description. He wanted to scout the surroundings a bit. The first twenty-five miles or so on the road to Kaghazi were sealed, but it gradually turned to dirt as he kept driving southeast. About ten miles on, he found a space which he thought *would be ideal for the heli-drone to be hidden while not in use at Natanz.*

There didn't seem to be another living soul anywhere. Not even the sound of sheep or goats who might have been looking for food in the area. Walking the last few hundred yards, he found a relatively flat spot. It was sufficiently isolated that it could not be seen from afar, but it was wide enough that, with the drone parked in its center, its camera with night vision capabilities would be able to pick up any approaching sign of life early enough to start the engine and take off without being captured. In fact, *the only way it could be captured,* David thought to himself, *would be if someone came looking for it, knowing it was there, approached it surreptitiously and shot at it from afar.* He noted the spot on his tablet GPS and flashed its coordinates to the heli-drone home pilots for future reference.

He decided to drive back to Kashan using a different route. He had noted on the satellite pictures that there appeared to be buildings and maybe businesses on the east side of 71, south and east of the furthest tip of the runway. He felt it would be good to get a sense of what they were. More importantly, he wanted to know what one could and could not see from there. The sound of the police siren startled him. Reflexively, he looked in the rear-view mirror and confirmed that a police car was behind him and asking him to stop. *What else now?* he thought.

It turned out to be a routine identity control, and the general explanation which he and Mike had agreed they would use was seemingly convincing. He was delighted to note that his Farsi had seemed totally up to the task. Continuing his exploration, he found a number of small farms. They appeared well-tended although he guessed that the quality of the soil and the lack of water probably made farming there a very tough business. He observed that they came quite close to the southern end of the runway. He made a note that any air approach should avoid that area. There was plenty of airspace to the north and east where there seemed to be nary a soul. There was no point taking unnecessary risk. Farmers listen to nature. So, *"avoiding unnecessary noise is key,"* he thought out loud. At the same time, he was happy that the embankment of the highway made it almost impossible to see anything happening at or near the hangar. He concluded: "If they see something, it has to be because they're looking for it . . . And that'd mean they know there's something to look for."

With this, it was time for him to stop by the flat in Kashan, take a shower, change and eat something before he took the next shift from Mike.

CHAPTER.16

While planning and training were about finished, Simon felt he needed to speak to both Sarah and Minoo to tie up the last, loose ends. The eventual success of the mission depended in no small part on them.

First, he sent a coded message to Sarah to suggest that they should meet. They agreed to rendezvous in Istanbul which was convenient, because there were direct flights between Istanbul and Tehran or Tel Aviv, plus it fit well with her cover. She arrived right on time at 9:30 a.m. Simon was not due to arrive until 9:55 a.m. They had agreed that she would meet him at the gate and play the role of the girlfriend waiting for him. They exchanged a big hug and a believable kiss and started to walk through the concourse as they were chatting, to avoid drawing attention.

He told her than Dan and Nate had been in Fordow the prior week and that all went very well. It confirmed virtually everything Amir had said. Sarah smiled. He did have a piece of news that was more difficult to communicate. *She should know,* they thought, *they had met Amir, though they were not introduced to him face to face.* So, from his point of view, Amir probably only thought *he met two German scientists who did not really look like Dan or Nate as he might have known them.* In short, Simon had to tell Sarah that: "They felt his behavior seemed suspect, if it was him."

"Suspect?"

"Yes, he appeared to be watching them with a great deal of attention . . . Does he know?"

"Absolutely not." Sarah added, "What's the problem?"

"They simply said that he was much more focused on them than the other people they met."

Sarah was puzzled. She thought for a while and then, almost as if she had been hit with a bolt of lightning she blurted out: "Can't explain it if it was not him. But, if it was him, what's suspect about a secret agent looking attentively at a couple of new people visiting the plant?"

"Good point, Sarah!"

Simon conceded he could see how she would get to that conclusion. He simply added that she should hold her guard up. He told her that one element of the plan needed a change. They felt the distance between the two halls was too long for them to work together in both halls. It would be best if they were each responsible for one hall. But it raised an issue. It created a surveillance camera problem. Amir would have to watch two halls and the various corridors to make sure the guys were not disturbed. Simon postulated that he would not have the time or the attention to do that and to control the cameras. He concluded: "When the guys are at work, Amir will need to broadcast a fake signal into the overall surveillance system . . ."

"A fake signal?"

"Well, fake, yes, in the sense that the signal would be a "picture"— no, a 'movie'—of something actually happening in the halls, but not at the exact moment they're there."

In short, he explained, they needed a pre-recorded video, a video of the signal from the cameras in normal circumstances and at the same time of the night that they planned on doing their jobs.

"He'll need to synchronize the recording to the actual time when the guys are in the halls. This eliminates the risk that someone sees a clock in the field of view that shows a time that's obviously wrong."

Amir would need to record a video of the halls one or two days earlier, picking a time window that would be the same as when the guys planned on being in the halls. Then, Amir would short circuit the real cameras and play the recording into the surveillance system while the guys were actually in the hall. The recording needed to cover a long enough timespan and would have to keep the same rotation of views that would normally be broadcast into the guards' system.

In response to Sarah's query, Simon handed her a list of questions he had scribbled with respect to the monitoring system. How many cameras or how many screens? How was it set-up? Where were the screens monitored? He added that Nathan and Dan said there were security screens in the backroom of the guardhouse at the main entrance. Was this where the monitoring took place for the whole complex? Or was there another system monitoring just the halls and surrounding areas? Wherever they did the monitoring, did the guards have as many screens as security cameras or fewer screens or even just one screen? If only one, was it a single or a split screen?

Then, he suggested a specific plan of action. First, Sarah should use her secure communication equipment to find out the number of cameras, the kind of connectors between the cameras and the system and what ability Amir had or did not have to control what the guards could see. Then, assuming that one could tinker with what they could see, Sarah would need to connect with logistics in Tel Aviv. Simon handed her a ticket in her name for a roundtrip to Tel Aviv, saying that he assumed she already had her return ticket to Tehran. He added: "As usual, it's booked in Sarah Miller's name, so no one can connect the two reservations. That's really crucial this time since you're doing both flights on Turkish Airlines."

"Totally understood . . ."

Simon continued, "Here's Sarah Miller's passport. You're on TK 788, leaving today at 6:10 p.m., which gets you into Tel Aviv a couple of hours later. Don't forget to send Sarah's passport back to the usual address in Tel Aviv."

Simon was referring to a safe house mail drop which *Mossad* maintained in Tel Aviv. Staffed with only one person, it was not expensive and still gave them a way to receive packages discreetly. He also was following a standard procedure for an agent working in another country, under an assumed name. The agent never travelled to his or her country of current residence with their actual passport; only the passport in the cover name would be used. Yet, since that agent could not come into Israel under the assumed name, a game of passport exchange kept taking place. Somewhat convoluted and complicated but essential to agent safety. He added: "Let us know what you want on the usual thumb drive for you to take back to Tehran."

"I'll send an email to Station T before boarding the next flight."

Simon went on with the logistical issues: "Fine, they'll get the thumb drive back to you as usual, in the hotel where you'll spend the night before you return to Tehran. Marvin Goldstein will be expecting your call to tell him about the camera situation and whatever else you can find out from Amir that's relevant to what he needs to do . . ."

"OK"

"Assuming there's nothing impossible, he'll have all the equipment you need when you get to the airport. Hopefully, your layover here and the flight to Israel will give Marvin enough time to work his magic in the lab. When you get there, you won't even need to leave the airport; he'll meet you right after immigration and customs."

Once the purely business issues were out of the way, they decided to have lunch, since her flight to Tel Aviv did not leave for several hours. A couple of hours later, he escorted her to her gate and moved on to his next appointment.

CHAPTER.17

Having satisfied themselves as much as they could that the plan was still workable, Mike and Dave needed to work on the details of their upcoming activities. Highest on the list was the final selection of their approach to the Natanz plant. Obviously, a lot of analysis had taken place in Tel Aviv, based on detailed satellite photography. Yet, as all agents know, however first class any photographic image is, it cannot replace the actual feeling that comes when one is on the spot.

Their detailed surveys had taught them that the complex was heavily guarded and very well protected. It comprised three, different zones. The first was roughly 3,000 feet wide by 3,500 feet long and was where the barracks of the Revolutionary Guard, a few administrative buildings and the two enrichment halls were located. To the east of that zone, a smaller area about 1,000 feet wide by 3,500 feet long contained other minor structures. These combined zones were surrounded on three sides by a third one, a no-man's-land that varied between 1,000 and 1,500 feet in width. An internal road circled both this protection zone and the overall complex. The east side of the entire area was bordered by the road linking Saleh Abad and Abouzeidabad.

The team had quickly concluded that the only realistic access to the complex was from the North. The National Revolutionary Guard base occupied the southern end of the space and they had all agreed that there was no point tempting fate, ruling out even trying the southern route of access. While they had briefly considered the option, it became obvious that, for it to be feasible, they would need some complicit source within the plan to provide them cover. In fact, Sarah had tried to get closer to an individual working in the plant, whom she could "run" alongside Amir in Fordow, but the route rapidly came to a dead end and, as Sarah had then thought: *Better find out about it earlier rather than later . . .*

Once access via the southern end of the complex was ruled out, the northern end was the only realistic alternative. Ostensibly, it would be no slam dunk, and require additional equipment, but as Simon had agreed, "You gotta do what you gotta do."

The fence at the northern end of the complex was quite impressive, particularly as one could not have a clean approach given the no-man's-land that stood between it and the semi-desertic area all around. Further, they correctly assumed that the no-man's-land was protected by land mines. This was the point where the decision was made that they view their approach to the plant as a two-step process. First, they should find a camp a few hundred feet further to the north and the east of the no-man's-land on the other side of the Amir Kabir Freeway, in the direction of Chaleh Qareh. That "camp" would allow them to store both the vehicle they were going to rent and some non-essential equipment. It had to be innocuous, as well-protected by topography or vegetation as possible, and yet accessible by car. Second, from that camp, they would be able to stage forays into the complex.

The nearest staging area they found seemed both sufficiently isolated to minimize the risk of being found out or disrupted, yet close enough to the actual halls. The place looked just like the rest of the desert surrounding the plant. There were a few trees nearby, two main clumps in fact. They would provide additional cover, if it were ever needed. The main attraction of the place was that it stood about six or seven feet below the area between it and the plant in the distance, at the bottom of a small gulley. This would hide anything that was there from anyone driving on the road. Mike had cynically noted: "The only way you can see it is if approaching the plant by air from that direction."

To which Dave had simply replied, "And there is no reason to come from there . . . Nothing for miles."

Mike, however, noted that they would probably need to smooth out a bump on the dirt path approaching the camp, as it could come into play when the Land Cruiser was fully loaded: "We sure as hell don't want to get stuck . . ."

CHAPTER.18

Minoo was due to land at 5:55 p.m. on TK 871. Simon had suggested that this trip would officially be a gift to her from her father, so that she could have a couple of days of R&R. Farid had initially thought that a bit odd, but she managed to convince him that she needed to change scenery, however briefly. Simon had arranged to meet her at her gate, prior to her moving on to immigration and customs. A car would be waiting to take her to her hotel after their visit.

After the usual greetings and small talk, they turned to the reason why Simon wanted to see Minoo. He wanted a face-to-face update on where they were on the relocation issue. When he said "they" he meant the three of them, that is her father, Farid and herself.

She started to cry. Simon understood the emotion and tried to help her, but, at the same time, this was late in the game. He needed to know. Minoo explained to Simon that this probably had been her toughest assignment. Simon nodded his understanding.

She began with Farid. There was a lot of news on that front. Simon raised his eyebrows and waited expectantly. She explained that when she returned from an earlier trip, she had found Farid waiting for her at the airport. She noticed that he had brought a small bouquet of flowers. They had kissed discreetly and gone straight to Farid's Peugeot in the parking lot. She had noted that he seemed particularly excited, more so than what she would have expected after such a short trip on her part. They got into the car, took the time for a longer, more passionate kiss. His hand had gone and touched her near the top of her thighs, and she had shivered. (Then, realizing that she was perhaps being too detailed in her description; she returned to the essential.) They exited the lot, but just after he paid the fee, Farid blurted out: "You won't believe this, but I talked to your Dad while you were gone."

Her mind started to race, wondering if he had discovered something.

"I asked for his blessing . . . and he gave it to me. So, now I can officially ask whether you'll marry me. Sorry the setting isn't more romantic. Just can't wait."

Minoo was overwhelmed with emotion and started to cry. Farid seemed a bit caught in the middle. He would have taken her into his arms to calm her down, but he was driving. And in Iran, it would not have been safe for him to stop the car on the side of the highway to console her. So, he extended his right arm and touched her gently on the left cheek, running the palm of his hands up and down the side of her face and partially through her hair.

Simon leaned forward to listen more intently. Minoo explained that, when she had regained her composure, she had turned to Farid and told him that there were a couple of things he needed to know about her and her past. She joked that they nearly had an accident, as Farid, betraying fear, momentarily lost control of the car; it veered a full meter to the left before he brought it back under control. Fortunately, there was neither traffic nor police to witness the event. But, she confessed, this was when she had to tell him that she was more than a simple professor at Qom University, and, more importantly, that she was working on something that required them to leave the country, to relocate. She had not yet told him about *Mossad*, but she had simply asked him to trust her. Tears welled up again in her eyes when she recalled that she felt that she almost lost Farid there and then, minutes after becoming engaged. Farid indeed was upset that she would not tell him any of the details and yet was asking him to completely upend his life.

In the end, after much back and forth, Minoo and Farid had agreed to have a quick and simple bite in Qom in her apartment. She stopped there, leaving the rest to Simon's fertile imagination. But she confirmed that, in the end, she thought *that Farid and she were ready to relocate.* Simon breathed a sigh of relief and asked the obvious question: "Does that mean your father is OK with it too?"

"It does, . . . but wasn't easy."

Minoo explained that when she first visited her father and mentioned that they needed to talk, he had mistakenly assumed the topic was of her engagement. After a bit of father-daughter small talk, he had asked if they had set a date, and her answer started the rest of the conversation: "In truth, we haven't yet, but we may have set a country."

"What are you talking about?"

"Well, we agreed that all three of us would leave Iran as quickly as possible."

"Are you serious, Minoo?"

This was when she explained to her father all that she had told Farid and continued with the details she would withhold from Farid, until they were all safely out of Iran.

"Papa, I don't have one, but two jobs. One of them you know; I'm a university physics teacher. The other is I work for the Government of Israel."

"You? My Minoo? An Israeli spy . . . ?"

She nodded that she was a spy in a way but really didn't think of it in those terms. Returning to the main point, their departure, she explained that *Mossad* would help them. They would find accommodations for them; they would provide financial help, until she and Farid could get decent and enjoyable jobs. As far as he, Cyrus, was concerned, *Mossad* would pay the retirement income he would forfeit. They would all be given new identities. In other words, *Mossad* would take care of everything and make sure that they could start new lives. She added that the only thing they needed to do was to get tickets, which *Mossad* would reimburse later in some foreign location. Officially, they would be going on some holiday or professional visit; it did not matter which. The key was that they would be leaving Iran and officially planning to come back a week or two later.

She conceded to Simon that her father's initial reaction had been mixed at best, but he eventually was persuaded. In the end, being close to his daughter was more important than anything else. They turned to practicalities, such as what to do with some of his dearest belongings, which included his treasured rugs. She had told him that her "friends," as she called *Mossad*, would help them. She knew they could not move everything, if only because it would be too obvious.

"You don't take all your personal belongings when you go on a two-week holiday."

But she was certain they could handle a couple of suitcases and items that could be carried away without a moving van. The final question he asked almost ruined it, or rather her answer to it. Cyrus had indeed asked: "So, when do you want me to leave?"

"I think you should leave before the end of next week."

"Whoa. What's the hurry? Why so soon? Are you crazy?"

Minoo had replied in an almost pleading tone: "Papa, I can't tell you now, I'm just asking you to trust me. It's important and it's for your own safety."

Simon interrupted at that time with profuse congratulations. He told Minoo that he could easily imagine how difficult the whole episode must have been. He added that it had to have been incredibly traumatic on her father and Farid as well. She replied that it had indeed been all of that and more. She volunteered that the hardest part was that she had to play her father and Farid almost a bit against each other. She had to pretend that the other was further than he actually was in accepting the need to relocate. Simon nodded with a frown and asked what her next steps were. She matter-of-factly replied that they had to gather whatever money they had, buy gold with most of it as it was easier to travel with, plan the itineraries so that everybody left Tehran alone but reunited in Paris as soon as possible, and buy the tickets. Her father and Farid would go on separate holidays to different destinations, while she would try to have her ticket sponsored by the University, on the pretense that she was going to attend a conference at the CERN in Geneva, adding, "It's probably easier for me to get a pass for a conference than for a holiday."

■ ■ ■ ■ ■

She could not resist expanding on the CERN and Simon let her go through her spiel as he felt she deserved that "psychological bonus." The CERN (Conseil Européen pour la Recherche Nucléaire) is the European Organization for Nuclear Research which earned Nobel prizes in physics in 1984 and 1992. Its main role is to provide the high-speed, particle accelerators and the related infrastructure needed for high-energy physics research. Its most recent claim to fame was the confirmation in July 2012 that the Higgs Boson that had been postulated since 1964 indeed most probably existed. The Higgs particle had initially been offered as a theoretical necessity to the standard model of physics; it was needed to explain the fact that certain particles have some physical mass when their interactions should require them not to have any. The CERN had undertaken to develop the Large Hadron Collider; it consists of a twenty-seven-kilometer ring of superconducting magnets, with a number of accelerating structures to boost the energy of the particles along the way. The whole structure is underground in an area that comprises both French and Swiss territory, near Geneva. The accelerator allowed the CERN to confirm the existence of the Higgs particle by generating millions of collisions between particles, in a way that allowed them to recreate what scientists thought might have happened when the Big Bang created the universe.

Any nuclear physics scientist would love to have a chance to work on one of the numerous teams within that organization, if not for life, as least for long enough to meet the leading lights in the field and soak up enough of their knowledge.

■ ■ ■ ■ ■

She paused and realized that Simon needed to get to his departure gate. So, they said good-bye and Minoo went on to meet her driver. Simon felt a lot lighter and got himself ready to board his plane back to Tel Aviv. He slept through a good part of the flight, not knowing in the end if it was true fatigue or the psychological relief from the good news; he was gaining confidence that the so-called "Farid end" of the plan was coming together, but cautioned himself: "It ain't over until the fat lady sings . . ."

CHAPTER.19

APRIL 30
QOM

As she woke up, Minoo as usual looked at her tablet to see if she had any important messages. There was one from Simon. It simply said: "Ready. Set. . . ."

Minoo called Farid to tell him that the countdown had started. They needed to get ready—in a hurry. But, totally shifting gears without warning, she mentioned that she needed to talk to her rector right away to get permission to go to Geneva. Farid was a bit startled by the abrupt change of subjects but did not question it, at least did not ask about it at that time.

Minoo walked into the rector's office, after having first called to see if he was available: "Sorry to bother you, Doctor Amid. I just received an invitation to attend a briefing at the CERN on their Higgs Boson experiments . . ."

He was surprised and said he was impressed, but Minoo told him not to be impressed. She said that she did not get the invitation because someone somehow picked her name on a list of eminent personalities. The rector's body language was saying that she was too modest, but he did not interrupt. She explained that one of the researchers on the team was a friend with whom she studied at Jussieu, the University in Paris. The friend thought that it would be the chance of a lifetime for Minoo and so got her invited. Minoo offered to pay for the trip out of her own pocket and to take vacation days if need be. The rector asked when she had to be there, and Minoo replied that the conference started on May 4th, in four days. He seemed surprised at the short notice, but in the end told her that it should be a business trip but added with a smile: ". . . but I can't afford first class."

She thanked him profusely and then drove directly to her father's flat. She felt bad that she had to trick the rector whom she liked and appreciated but, in the end, thought to herself, *you gotta do what you gotta do.* They had already done most of the packing. It had been simpler than she had expected once they knew they could have the two extra suitcases, and they could take his three favorite carpets along. The Qom silk carpet had been in the sitting area for ever. The Isfahan was in the bedroom next to the right side of the bed; it was a very fine Seirafian and bore the master's signature. Finally, he also had a cream and blue Nain which, though arguably a bit too large for the purpose, had been his prayer rug ever since they'd lived in Iran. Minoo had used the small bit of space in one of the two suitcases to take photos and a few small gifts from her parents. One of them was a carved, inlaid, wooden box in which she stashed all the photos she could fit.

She immediately looked for a flight to Paris for her father; she preferred Iran Air. She felt she needed to book the cheapest flight to be believable; a retired senior civil servant was not going to fly first class on a holiday. She also wanted the flight to be direct and, if possible, non-stop as Cyrus would probably not rest much during the flight. She was delighted to see that Iran Air, which flew only twice a week to Paris, had a reasonably priced seat on the next day's flight. This was perfect, since the next available flight was three days out. She booked the flight and sent an email to Adan in Paris to make sure that someone would be there to meet her father when he arrived at Orly. She told Cyrus that he needed to go to the Iran Air office to get his paper ticket.

With the flight leaving at 9:00 the next morning, Minoo knew she could take him to the airport and still be back at the University for her class before she, too, took off. She said goodbye to him and promised to pick him up at 6:00 a.m.

She drove home and was happy to see that Farid had not arrived yet, but it was not long before he rang the bell. They kissed passionately.

■ ■ ■ ■ ■

It reminded her of their formal engagement and the evening that followed. Farid had given her a ring and popped the question formally. She had looked at the ring and loved it. It was small solitaire diamond encased in finely worked yellow gold lace, on top of a simple yellow gold band. They were standing in the hallway without anyone able to spy on them. They were kissing, with their hands looking to see which one could undress the other the fastest. They reached the bedroom down to their underwear and socks. They kept kissing as they fell onto the bed. She asked him to allow her a minute in the bathroom. She had traveled the whole day and felt the need to wash up. While she was there, he finished undressing.

He revealed a body that was quite athletic for someone who worked at a desk most of the time. There did not seem to be more than an ounce of fat here or there and the only thing that might hide his muscles was dark hair that covered most of his front and even some of his back, principally just below his neck. He slipped between the sheets.

She emerged from the bathroom, totally naked; he marveled at her beauty, looking at her more intently than he normally would. Her build was indeed relatively small, but her body was perfectly proportioned. She had let her dark hair down and it fell below her shoulder level. On the left side, it hid her breast, but the right breast was firm, with a dark nipple which was already betraying her high level of sexual arousal. Her stomach was absolutely flat, with no trace of fat. He could not see it, as she was walking toward him, but her backside was also nicely proportioned and firm. Her skin was light olive color. She did not have much by way of tan marks because the swimsuits that she would wear while in Iran covered much of her torso. The rest of the evening was spent in a sexual and sensual whirlwind.

■ ■ ■ ■ ■

Returning to reality and the moment at hand, Minoo had real trouble hiding her excitement, for two reasons. One, she was leaving with her father and her fiancé and would be able to start a new life. Second, the project on which she had been working so diligently for Israel was about to become reality and avenge the many years of frustrations she had had with the Iranian government and the Mullahs. She told Farid that her father was leaving for Paris the next day and that they both would need to leave Iran no later than on May third—two days later.

The suddenness of the news and the fact that departure was imminent hit Farid like a sucker punch. He almost lost it. He asked for more information, probably knowing full well that he still would not get the full story. She tried the "trust me" routine: "Remember, everything will become crystal clear when we're together in Paris. Until then, I'm asking you to trust me . . ."

But, this time, it fell on deaf ears, even with the extra encouragement about Paris. Minoo realized that she needed to calm him and to tell him more. She understood his frustration at being kept in the dark. Though she was sure that Farid loved her, she could see that living in the male-dominated culture of Islam and Iran was making it especially hard for Farid. Above all, she needed to keep everything under control and progressing smoothly; she needed to take some risk.

"What can I tell you to make you more comfortable?"

"For a start," Farid replied with a measure of repressed anger she had not seen before, "what is this all about? Why do we need to leave? What's the hurry? Do you get my drift?"

Minoo was not prepared to lose the love of her life. And it was clear in her mind that the plan was not going to work without any believable answers to Farid's questions. She took a big breath and, looking Farid straight into his beautiful, brown eyes she said: "What if I told you that terrorists are going to attack Fordow?"

Farid was floored: "What? Are you kidding?"

"Unfortunately not. You heard me . . . That's right. I found out that some attack is planned. I am not totally sure of the details, but I have been warned that you, Papa and I should be as far away from here as we could."

Farid could not believe his ears. Part of him wondered how she could remain so calm as she was saying this. Another wondered how she knew; still another wondered what he should do; should he inform Reza? Should he call Security at the plant? He was still pondering his options when Minoo came closer to him and told him: "Don't worry. I've been told that people won't get hurt. I've been told that the goal of the terrorists is simply to stop or at least slow down the development of a nuclear bomb . . ."

This last piece of information shook him out of his confusion. He repeated "Nuclear bomb." "Nuclear bomb." Though he obviously knew what the program's goals were, this may have been the first time that it hit him that he was working on the creation of a nuclear weapon. Until then, he had mentally been able to distance himself from the ultimate aim of the program and concentrate his energy on technical and engineering issues—the classical conflict between short-term and long-term goals. At the same time, what about his loyalty to his country?

"Where do they come from?"

"Who?"

"The terrorists."

"Not totally sure, but there's a hint they're homegrown . . ." She knew she was now lying and simply passing on the disinformation that was part of the plan. She hated it. Again, she burst out in tears.

Farid seemed to be losing his anger and hugged her close. Minoo said, "Farid, I really love you. Can you believe I am caught in a bind? Will you trust me now?"

Farid nodded. Her tears turned into real sobs. He hugged her tighter. Eventually, she calmed down enough to pursue her original line of thought. She told him that there were a couple of "small things" she needed to do now. Farid straightened up. She asked him again not to get mad and to understand that she was simply doing what she had to do, repeating: "Please, do not ask why . . . My life is in danger."

This caught Farid's attention. She said that they needed to take care of a number of "small things." She said that Amir had invited the two German doctors back. They needed the invitation for their visa, and they would arrive on May fifth, at 2:55 p.m., the day she and Farid should be leaving. She added it would be nice if he could meet the Germans at the airport when they arrived. He seemed completely confused. His face was betraying surprise mixed with some renewed anger. His voice went up a few decibels and even turned a bit higher: "But, you told me I'm leaving."

He continued, "Wait, listen to what you're saying. Amir is sending the invitation. But he's not going to meet them at the airport. I'm NOT sending the invitation—in fact, I'm leaving—but I'm the one that has to be at the airport. This makes no sense, Minoo . . ."

Farid could not finish the sentence. He had become speechless with an air of complete disbelief. Minoo noticed, with a bit of hope that he appeared less angry. She said she understood the confusion, adding, falsely, that she was confused as well.

He tried again to articulate his case: "I can see why someone outside the plant might believe this story, but it's simply not believable to an insider. Amir's a great guy, but he's not a scientist. I'm not sure he'd be able to tell the difference between two types of centrifuges. I'm almost sure he couldn't tell the difference between metallic and carbon fiber needle bearings; and, by the way, that's what they're talking about—a special new type of carbon fiber which requires less external lubrication. So, I'll say it again: I hope you know what you're doing, because this is the first time since I've known you that you're not making sense."

For a moment, it looked as if he might lose it, again. Minoo was worried because she had told Simon that he had agreed to leave, and he had. But now, he might be changing his mind, both about the trip and her. Visibly, he was struggling very hard to keep his calm; he did not want to lose the love of his life in a fight at a time that looked so critical to her. How could he be sure that this would not destroy the entire relationship? At the same time, she was making no sense; more to the point, what little sense she might be making was disquieting. In fact, how did she know what she said she knew? Why would her life be in danger? What had she gotten herself into? Interestingly, at that time at least, he did not ask himself about her love for him. Nor did he even consider what this all might mean for him . . .

CHAPTER.20

MAY 5
KHAFJI

Simon and Marvin arrived at Khafji, together with their staff and equipment; they all flew in on a C-130 Hercules cargo plane. Though the facilities were exactly what they wanted, the environment was spartan to say the least. The Saudis had asked them to find ways to sleep in the planes or in the small barracks that had been made available; they wanted to avoid any mixing between the Israelis and anyone else on the base. They even had to bring their own food to be totally self-contained. Simon had arranged a small command post in the first room on the left as you entered the barracks. There was electricity, a good internet connection, direct communication lines to the satellite and thus direct, free and secure lines to wherever was needed, Tel Aviv and Jerusalem included. Marvin had taken the other desk in the room. That gave them the ability to manage all that had to be managed together.

Simon's initial reaction to the news on the airstrip from David and Mike had been one of real concern. He had asked them to keep him posted at least once per watch. The news of the helicopter that had landed and then took off a couple of minutes later really troubled him. They needed to find out what it was. Where was the car leaving the airport going? And why David had not seen it arrive? He was hoping that the strip, though technically not abandoned, was probably still the correct choice, silently adding in his own mind: *And that's a good thing because we don't have a plan B.*

He made a mental note this was definitely a planning mistake on his part. He called Ehud, the Head of the Air Force, and asked him to look into the possibility of having more AWACS coverage. Ehud said he would *liaise* with the Americans.

Simon called Marvin on his satellite phone, as Marvin was near the hangar where all the equipment preparation was taking place. He told him that they were almost ready to go with the first Kovesh wave. The Koveshes should be fueled and loaded, tethered and ready to go.

■ ■ ■ ■ ■

Back on February 16, when he first saw the Koveshes at the Palmachim Base, Simon had listened to what he could only refer to in hindsight as another of Marvin's lectures. He had indulged Marvin and patiently labored through that one, because it concerned the way the Koveshes would be launched. Because of fuel limitations, Marvin had explained that the drones would be launched from one of the two C-130 Hercules which IDF (Israeli Defense Forces) used as cargo planes and *Mossad* had planned to have on this mission. He conceded that although this was not the easiest thing in the world to do, it did not constitute rocket science. Offering an example, he noted: "Making drones or other smaller craft able to fly off a C-130 isn't terribly difficult in theory."

He was pointing to the fact that NASA had used a modified Boeing 747 to ferry the Space Shuttle from landing sites to its base at the Kennedy Space Center in Florida, ever since the shuttle program started. He further noted that any modifications required would be made to the mother aircraft, not to the drones. He added that the engineering of the Hercules was a much better-known field than tinkering with the drones. As usual, diving into too much detail, he said that an important issue had been that the wingspan of the C-130 was 130 feet, which was a tough constraint, as each drone was exactly 65 feet wide, noting: "Two times 65 is 130. So, we'll need to attach them a bit further out than the center of the wing of the Hercules on each side, probably at least three feet, to minimize the risk of them touching when they're launched."

He continued with the explanation: as the two drones would be six feet away wingtip to wingtip, the pilots would initiate turns in opposite directions as soon as they had cleared the tail of the mother aircraft. He had accepted that this could test the strength of the wings of the Hercules, cynically noting that NASA did not have this problem with the shuttle, as it was affixed on top of the main fuselage of the 747, explaining; "They have only one shuttle, but we have two Koveshes."

Simon had immediately understood that the one element that made the plan feasible was that the C-130 was an incredibly sturdy aircraft. This would make the modifications that much easier. The wings of the alternative, the Boeing 707 that Israel also used as cargo plane, might be stronger, but the wingspan was, in fact, a bit narrower. In the end, Marvin simply said: "The real reason to use the C-130 is that it has short landing strip capabilities which the 707 doesn't. It can even land on dirt runways or, as I think I told you once already, on an aircraft carrier. And it can take off from any of these, too. That's an added plus."

Simon had asked what the benefit of launching from the air did. Marvin explained that it saves fuel on the inbound journey and would give them plenty of room for evasive maneuvers on the return trip if they ever needed it. The C-130 would climb to its 33,000 feet maximum ceiling, flying wide circles over the base to stay in friendly airspace. It would launch the drones from there. The drones would first climb to 50,000 feet, their own ceiling. The goal of having the drones use as little fuel as possible on their onward flight to Iran required them to use as little power as possible as well. He had to explain that aircrafts of all types have a so-called glide ratio that was driven by their aerodynamic characteristics, such as the shape of the wing and the ratio of wing surface to the weight of the aircraft, adding in passing that the glide ratio was the forward distance traveled divided by the vertical distance an aircraft descended, when gliding without any power: "Kovesh has a glide ratio of thirty-two versus at best fifteen for commercial planes . . . Can glide more than twice as long as a commercial airliner."

Marvin explained to Simon that their plan was thus to take advantage of that higher glide ratio to trade fuel efficiency versus speed for the inbound trip. They would use only twenty-five percent of their fuel reserves to reach Kashan This would leave them with seventy-five percent for the return trip where they had to take off and climb as quickly as possible to evade radar. He added that they would still have about a twenty-five percent fuel reserve for the odd contingency.

Simon had immediately seen what he had thought was a flaw.

"Why have them climb to their ceiling early on . . . Won't that use more fuel since they would be heaviest then?"

Marvin had admitted that the maneuver would cost more fuel than if they didn't climb initially. But the other side of the coin was that the higher they flew, the harder it was to pick them out of the sky. And the place they would be most likely to be picked out on the trip to Kashan would be while crossing into Iranian territory from the Persian Gulf. He added, in passing, that they would also be most vulnerable on arrival back to Khafji. So, accepting that they could not do anything about the arrival, he argued that they were left with the need to have them cross into Iran much higher than under normal circumstances. His final point was that the drones would need to be careful to maintain some distance between each other to minimize the risk that their combined profile might be captured by Iranian radar.

■ ■ ■ ■ ■

Now, Simon was on the base with all the equipment. His team was in Iran, ready to start work. In short, it was time for the action to start, although he would have argued that, for him, the action had started three months ago. Marvin asked: "Simon, do you want to inspect the loading of the Koveshes and their launch?"

"Yeah, would really like it."

"I'm in the hangar. Join me."

He walked quickly the five hundred meters that separated the barracks from the hangar. He waved to the personnel tending the five F-15D jets that would ferry them out at the end of the mission. Alongside the fighter jets, he could only see one of the two of C-130s that brought people and equipment from Tel Aviv on the tarmac. Arriving at the hangar, he saw that the other C-130 was in there. His first reaction was to note the unusual contraptions on both wings, saying to himself: "they're hiding it so that the Saudis don't see the Koveshes being tethered to the C-130."

When he entered the hangar and saw Marvin, his first question was: "Where are the drone pilots, by the way?"

"Safely south of Tel Aviv, on Palmachim, in the hall you visited. We didn't think it made sense to bring them here. It's not necessary. Would've created yet another risk. The Saudis are nice, but this ain't home."

As they walked around the cargo plane, Simon could see that the two drones were still on the ground. Marvin told him they had been loaded with all the equipment needed plus a few small arms, ammunition and a couple more tarps that the team might need to hide equipment while on the ground. Marvin pointed to the structures on each wing of the C-130, explaining that the bits that were attached to the wing were strong enough to hold three times the weight of each drone. So, needless to say, as he said, nothing really bad could happen. By the way, he added: "Simon, just in case you're wondering, the reason for the margin of safety is that the wings of the drones interact with the air flow. They can have a higher effective weight than they do on the ground in certain flying conditions. . . ."

He pointed to the top of each assembly where one could see

something that looked a bit like a flattish cradle. He explained that this was where the drones were attached to the cargo plane.

Simon asked how they would be "launched" to which Marvin said, without missing a beat and with visible delight, that about ten seconds before planned release, the C-130 pilots would contact the ground pilots of the drones and ask them to turn their engines on. About a second before release, they would have them rev up the engines to 35% fuel flow; then they would trigger a pneumatic anchor which released both drones at the same time. The C-130 would immediately dive about 500 feet, while the drones were powered up and started climbing. The drones should almost instantly clear the tail of the C-130, but Marvin still added: "We're talking a second or so here."

Both drones would bank in opposite directions and to the outside. Then they would complete their turns, until they were lined up, more or less one in front of the other. Once at 50,000 feet, they would vector into Kashan and start a gentle glide path at reduced power.

Satisfied with his lecture, Marvin had asked: "Any news of the other members of the team?"

Simon replied: "Final part of the countdown . . ."

CHAPTER.21

Back to Qom a few days earlier, Minoo was still trying to get Farid fully on board with the plan. In the end, his love for Minoo won out and, in an almost dejected tone of voice, he said, "You know what, I'll do what you want—something tells me there's a plan. But, if this isn't proving my love to you, I don't know what will."

Adding: "Minoo, you owe me one . . ."

Minoo beamed and simultaneously burst into tears. He was coming through and proving to her that she was making the right choice. So, she gave him a huge kiss and stayed snuggled in his arms for what seemed like an eternity. Then, she returned to the topic at hand and "explained" that he needed to be at the airport on May third, because she needed to have someone who had seen the Germans before and who could transmit two sets of keys.

"Wait, what's with the keys?"

Minoo knew that she had not given him a vital piece of information. She knew she eventually would have to. But she was worried doing it now would risk starting the fight all over. In the end, she did what she had to do and told him, with as genuine a smile as she could muster: "The Germans would be using both my car and Dad's flat."

This triggered Farid who, again, was lost and angry, "What now? A new twist?"

"The Germans need a quiet place to stay . . ."

"Are they involved in the attack?"

"Technically, I do not know . . . But, in a way, I've got to think they have to be"

"Minoo, you told me the terrorists were homegrown . . ."

"I know, that's what I heard. But, there's some outside help. In fact, honey, I know that some of what the Germans do is to facilitate the work of the terrorists . . . Please, do not ask me more. You would not want me dead, would you?"

Farid really looked lost for a minute, and even Minoo who knew him so well was not really sure how this was going to end up. He looked at her, then looked at the ceiling, then looked at her again. The internal conflict he was living was obvious. She drew herself as close to him as she could and waited; what else could she do?

Farid dejectedly raised his eyebrows at her last statement but nodded his understanding. Minoo could not hold back tears again, but quickly regained her composure as she knew time was of the essence. She then turned to the task of packing. She said that she had found a way to ship a suitcase full of things he did not want to leave behind but could not be seen taking with him abroad. She admitted that it may take a few days longer than if he had taken it along, but she could guarantee it would arrive.

Farid argued that he probably did not have much that he would like to take along, but he said he was sure that he would not need more than two suitcases. In fact, he added that he would rather take the rugs and a few of his books than more clothing. They agreed that they should go to his flat and complete the packing. Another surprise awaited Farid when Minoo told him that they should take the suitcase and packages he would not have with him on his flight to her Dad's flat. She added that it was where she would leave her own extra suitcase and her car, too.

She told him the story of the meeting with Dr Amid, her rector, and said with a smile that she was leaving on May third at 8:10 a.m.

She added that she was going through Istanbul because it gave her an almost decent connection. So, the plan would be for him to take her to the airport, greet the Germans and hand them the keys and then make his flight out as well.

As they were searching for options for his own flight, Farid came back with the obvious question: "Why are you not flying Iran Air?"

Somewhere deep in her mind, someone said, "not again . . ." She was fully aware that she was on a "suspended sentence" as she put it to herself. She explained that she wanted to be safe the moment she was out of Iranian airspace, adding, "With Turkish Airlines, I don't have to worry about the flight being recalled if something should blow up here. I think that's a risk with Iran Air. That's also why I think you should leave on the same day, but in the afternoon, after you've greeted the Germans and via another airline; how about Emirates?"

Farid picked up on "blow up" and Minoo kicked herself. If she was trying to quiet him, she was obviously failing. How was he going to react next?

CHAPTER.22

MAY 5
TEHRAN AND QOM

The flight from Istanbul to Tehran landed safely at Imam Khomeini Airport at 14:55 as scheduled. Doctors Dieter Hinterland and Nikolaus Reinhardt, who were traveling in First Class, in keeping with their supposed status, were among the first off the plane. They were accompanied through the local formalities by a local Turkish Airlines agent, as is frequently the case for VIP travelers. The two scientists were whisked through immigration. Their trip less than one month earlier had been duly recorded on the passports that were then being presented to the official. *Two visas into the country, in such a short period of time . . . These must be important people,* the immigration official thought before stamping and handing the passports back to Dieter Hinterland, a.k.a. Daniel Himmel. Their clearance at customs was equally uneventful: the officer waved them through with a simple couple of questions; "What is the purpose of your trip?" and "How long are you here for?" They spoke of important conversations with fellow scientists near Qom and said that they were returning to Germany within a week.

Once in the international arrival hall, Daniel spotted Farid at some distance. He motioned Nathan, a.k.a. Nikolaus Reinhardt, to follow him.

"Doctor Kashani, a pleasure to see you."

"It's indeed a pleasure to see you both . . ."

"We weren't sure we'd get the chance, as the invitation came from Mr. Amir Mashhad. "We thought you might be traveling."

Farid replied that he was in fact about to travel. He said he was leaving in the evening for the Middle East, Dubai to be exact. He said he had two envelopes for them. The first contained the key to an apartment they should feel free to use while in Qom.

"It's a bit more comfortable than a hotel and gives you more privacy. It belongs to my fiancée's father who is also out of the country, on vacation in France."

The second envelope, he added, contained the keys to her car . . ."

Nathan could not resist pretending that he did not know the plot and asked, "Don't tell me she is also traveling."

"Well, she is. She went to attend a conference in Geneva. Actually, it's a presentation at the CERN of their work on the Higgs Boson. I'd have loved to be in her suitcase . . ."

They thanked Farid, who then moved away quickly from the arrival hall as he did not want to be seen by too many officials. This was his second trip to the airport today, and there would be a third later that afternoon.

He had already tried to be as inconspicuous as possible that morning as he dropped Minoo off. But he had wanted to stay around, until he'd seen that she was safely through passport control and flight security screening. His heart was heavy as he saw her leave, as he was still a bit worried that something could go wrong. *She certainly knows something I don't, and I really don't like this feeling of total lack of control,* he had thought, but he had maintained as even an external demeanor as possible, fearing that she was hiding her own fears as well. He did not want to spook her, certainly not as she was about to go through passport and customs control. She had been quite clear in her suggestion not to be too visible to officials who might recognize him later on when he would be boarding his own flight. He was increasingly tempted to think that there was something of a spy in her, but she ostensibly would have none of it. He was pretty sure that no one had stared at him, and that he himself did not see anyone then that he might have seen that morning.

He decided to get the car and drive into Tehran. First, he could not think of a good reason why he would be so early for his flight. *I would look desperate and invite special attention*, he had argued to himself. Second, he worried that someone might notice a car that had not moved for an extended period of time in the parking lot. While this might not be totally unusual at large or even mid-sized western airports, the majority of vehicles in the parking lot at Tehran Airport were in for a short time—dropping off or picking up passengers. Tehran's was not like airports in the developed world where it was common for people to use long term parking. Here, flying was definitely a luxury. Most people used trains or even buses. So, air travelers were often taken to and from the airport by family or friends as was the case fifty years ago in the Western world, when air travel was still a novelty. As he drove away from the airport, anxious and lonely, he settled on a visit to the University Campus where he had received his bachelor's degree. He had decided he would drive down memory lane, as people at times do during stressful times in their lives. He drove past where he had lived, where he had studied and maybe even a few places where he had had fun with fellow male students. He even stopped to grab a bite at a place where he had eaten in his youth.

Daniel and Nathan went straight to the car rental agency. They had reserved a Peugeot 206, the same as Minoo's car, which they had been told was the most popular car in Iran; it would get them used to a car that they would later have to drive. *With this, we can't be noticed*, Daniel had thought. The light blue car they had booked for a week was there, awaiting them.

They waited until they were in the car to send a message to Amir: "We're in town and driving to Qom. We'll first get to the flat where we're staying. Then, we need to run a couple of local errands, nothing urgent. So, can see you at any time. Let us know."

They also sent a message to David and Mike: "In country. On our way from the main airport to the city where we're staying. Should see our contact later this afternoon. When should we meet you? Is everything OK with the airstrip?"

This done, they drove prudently on the highway, careful not to attract any attention to themselves. They recognized a few of the sights, although they had come in on a Lufthansa flight the first time around and thus landed just after midnight. This time, they were able to see the details of the landscape in broad daylight and noted that it was pretty barren except near the towns where local farmers benefited from better access to water and grew the food for local consumption. Halfway to Qom, they were surprised when they saw a police checkpoint. They did not remember seeing it the last time they travelled the route; Nathan asked, "What the hell is that?"

"Don't know, but we should be OK . . . Remember, we have the invitation."

They eventually made it to the front of the line. They played their roles of German scientists to the hilt and produced the invitation to visit the Fordow plant, together with their passports. The "conversation" with the officer was quite abbreviated as his English was virtually non-existent. They were allowed to proceed. Nathan made a note that this could be a major issue on their next trip.

"What if we are stopped again when we drive back from the airport in a few days?"

"You're right; we need to let Simon know. My bias would be to have another letter from Amir, but . . . We'll see."

They recognized the fact that the road initially climbed as they left the airport, to be followed by a long, downward incline as Qom was almost nine hundred feet lower than Tehran Airport. Briefly looking back toward the north, they saw the majestic Elburz Mountains towering in the distance. *And right beyond them, you find the Caspian Sea,* Daniel thought to himself.

They heard from Amir first.

"Leaving the office at 5:00 p.m. this afternoon. Can be anywhere you want me to be in Qom after 6:00 p.m. Let me know where you want to meet."

They agreed that there was no need to show him Minoo's dad's flat. Simon had indeed mentioned that he had kept Minoo and Sarah on totally separate tracks. He said the reason was because Amir and Farid knew each other. He wanted to have separate access to the facility and to make sure that they wouldn't trip each other up. Nathan thought to himself: *Divide and reign . . .*but kept quiet.

Dan and Nate began discussing Amir, again. Nathan still harbored mixed feelings from the earlier trip to Fordow. Dan repeated the simple explanation which Sarah had given to Simon, who had relayed it to them. He also reiterated the point that Simon was prepared to let Amir have their lives in his hands. They needed to trust him completely. After all, he was a *Mossad* agent from what Simon said. He had a flashlight tool and had met Simon on a trip to Greece.

But Nathan noted that Amir did not have the same "deal" as Minoo and her family on the luggage front when he escaped.

"Where does that take you, Nate?"

"*Caveat emptor* as they say in Rome."

As Dan was driving, he asked Nate for directions to Minoo's dad's flat? Nate replied that it was in the north central part of the city and near what looked like a study center; it was called *Madinatolelm* on the map. It looked like a good location for Minoo and her dad. It would've been easy for Minoo to go to see her father from the University of Technology, which was due north and a couple of miles outside of Qom. Mischievously, he added: "The story doesn't say where Minoo's flat is . . ."

Dan smiled at the joke and then suggested that they should tell

Amir to pick them up at the Jamkaran Mosque. Nate was startled and asked: "Why in the world did you pick that place?"

Daniel seemed not to understand the question and replied, "Why not . . . ? It's the one I've heard about."

"Well, you always surprise me, Daniel. I sure would've thought that the Golden Mosque, or Fatima Masumeh Shrine, would be better known; but, whatever."

Dan wondered out loud why this should matter and asked, "Where is it in relation to the flat?"

Nate, who had his GPS app working overtime, simply said, "Well, see. Let's put it this way; it'd be hard for you to pick a point that's further from the apartment and still in Qom."

"Serious?"

"You bet. It's not perfectly diametrically opposed, but pretty damn close. One is in the north central part of town and the other is in its southwestern corner."

A bit chastised, Dan asked whether his teammate wanted to pick another location. Nate thought for a minute and then said that they should stick to it. First, and somewhat jokingly, he said that first impressions were often a signal from "on high." But he quickly added that he liked the idea. The Jamkaran mosque was a tourist attraction, and it had a large esplanade. Also, it was not in the center of town, so they could be sure it should be much easier place for them to park the car than a site that was buried into the center of the city. He added that the cherry on top of the cake was that there should be plenty of people there that were not from Qom.

They kept driving and found themselves on the ring road. They first turned west and then south. Reaching the building where Minoo's father lived, they found it, as advertised, close to a very modern, Islamic, study center, the *Madinatolelm* complex, which was indeed quite visible and much more modern than any of the buildings in its immediate surroundings. Cyrus's building did not appear particularly luxurious, even by local standards, but certainly seemed quite comfortable. It was exactly the kind of place where a retired senior civil servant would be expected to live. The flat was on the second floor and looked very well-tended. They appreciated the fact that the building had an underground parking garage; this was important, given the moving in and out of suitcases they knew they had planned.

The apartment was nicely decorated with colorful curtains hanging around each window, and walls that were painted in shades of beige, with more or less orange or blue in the mix. The furniture was very typical of the region; most of the wood was stained in dark colors, with arabesque decorations carved or simply painted on panels.

A few very finely woven carpets, with intricate designs, served to delineate certain areas on the floor. One was in the sitting area; another was in the main bedroom where the double bed was pushed into a corner of the room perhaps to make the room appear larger. It seemed to be made out of wool and silk; it was stunning. The master bedroom was a bit dark and had a large number of photos of Cyrus, his wife and Minoo on the chest of drawers. A dark, tall armoire towered in the corner, just to the right of the sole window. A third carpet was also in the living room; it was a masterpiece. Though it looked a bit larger than many traditional prayer rugs, that's exactly the use that Cyrus initially had for it.

There was another bedroom with only a single bed and parquet floor, with a relatively inexpensive tribal rug. The room looked like it might have been a teenage girl's room, with pastel colors and simple decoration. This was, in fact, where Minoo had grown up; her parents had never wanted to change its decoration once she had flown from the proverbial nest. The Islamic art pieces that hung from two of the walls in the living room and near the dining room table completed the décor, one which exuded a sort of welcoming simplicity.

Walking into the main bedroom, they located the three suitcases neatly aligned at the foot of the double bed. Dan decided he would use this room and left Nathan to fend for himself in what had been Minoo's room. Next to the suitcases, they noticed two rugs, neatly rolled. They noted that this made five rather than the three rugs they initially expected. They unrolled these two, added Cyrus's three rugs and even included the Bokhara rug in Minoo's room, thinking that, at worst, Minoo and her father could always get rid of it if they truly did not want it. Having the six carpets in one roll would make them easier to load; Nathan noted that they should fit in the space in front of the rear seats of the car.

They decided to use the extra time they had before they went to meet Amir to dye their hair back to its natural color. Now that they had passed Customs and met with Farid, the disguise was no longer essential or in fact needed. Indeed, darker hair would fit much better into the local scenery. They went back and forth on the issue of facial hair as that was pretty prevalent in Iran. They still elected to shave the mustache and goatee. They sent a message to Amir to tell him to expect them dark-haired and clean-shaven.

The message from Amir came in on Daniel's flash tool at almost the same time as the reply from David to their first message from near the Tehran airport. Daniel chose to read David's message first. It was longish and detailed, but the question required some level of precision in the reply: "We've had a bit of a minor scare, but it's resolved. The plans are unchanged. We need to have you come here before 2:00 a.m. tomorrow morning to help unload the drones and pick up your stuff. Take the road to Kashan, about thirty-five miles south of you. Then drive south toward Amir Kabir. The strip is two miles south of Amir Kabir on your left. The site will initially look impressive, but we've confirmed it's deserted most of the time. Drive to the hangar on the right when you get to the fork in the road, after the cluster of small buildings on your right. We'll be around the back, and the Koveshes should be landing at 2:00 a.m. We've asked the pilots to glide them in as much as they can to minimize noise."

Dan replied with a simple question: "Are police roadblocks frequent here?"

He explained that they had been stopped on their way from the airport and wondered whether this in any way changed the plans for their highway travels, adding, "Should we stay off highways?"

David replied that they had not been an issue for them.

Amir replied he would meet them at the front of the mosque at 7:00 p.m. He said that he remembered Dan's and Nate's faces and added that he could imagine them with a different hair color but wondered why they had changed.

CHAPTER.23

MAY 5
QOM

Dan and Nate left the flat for the mosque thirty minutes after receiving these messages. This would provide a cushion in case they got lost—somewhat unlikely thanks to the GPS—as well as allowing them to scope out the neighborhood around the mosque. They reminded themselves to take some of the bottled water they had bought early, with Dan adding; "I'm sure we'll need it. And I don't want to drink the local water if I can help it."

Given David's reply on the highway issue, they decided to drive back to the ring road and then take it around to Jamkaran to meet Amir. It was not the most direct route by far, but, at prayer time, traffic can be crazy. They preferred to be on time, if not early. It was one of the habits that all field operatives learned quickly; they familiarized themselves with the surroundings as much as they could, before meeting anyone anywhere.

The history of the mosque was quite interesting. It was dedicated to Sheik Jamkarani who was believed to have met Muhammad al-Mahdi as well as a prophet when the place was simple farmland. They instructed him to have the owner of the land cease cultivating it and build a mosque to celebrate the fact that this was holy land. More recently, the mosque's reputation had spread particularly among the young. The back of the mosque had a "Well of Requests" where it was believed that the Twelfth Imam had once appeared. It functioned very much like the Trevi Fountain in Rome. Right after his election, a previous Iranian President had donated $15 million to fund plans to turn what had been a modest mosque into a massive complex.

Though journalists—even local Muslims—were no longer allowed on the site (because of comments that had been made in the press about the opulence of the place), Daniel and Nathan felt they could come close enough while still on the esplanade to meet up with Amir.

They parked near several of the tourist buses that seemed to be everywhere and started walking in the general direction of the mosque. The esplanade around the mosque was indeed impressive and quite beautiful. They were once told politely but firmly that foreigners were not allowed into the site, unless they were Muslim pilgrims accredited as such, and they respectfully complied; they could be Muslims, but they were not accredited pilgrims. They asked whether they could take a few pictures and were told it was OK, provided they stayed outside of the mosque area itself. They explored the surroundings as best they could, but truth be known, there was not much to the area beyond the mosque. Jamkaran was indeed a spot that only recently became a part of the "greater Qom." It started as a small village of less than 10,000 people and was now a part of a city with upwards of 1.2 million inhabitants.

Amir noticed them before they saw him. In fairness, how else could it be? He blended in with the locals and his face had been one of several at the plant. On the other hand, if the person staring at them at the plant was Amir, he would have had all the time to take mental photographs of them and recognize them despite the change in hair color.

"Good to see you two here. Guess we can dispense with the doctors or the German accents for you. We all know why we're here."

Daniel swallowed hard: "Well, Amir, you're pretty direct. It's a good thing we recognize you from our brief first encounter. Otherwise, I might have had to kill you."

Amir smiled, and simply replied: "Are you Daniel or Nathan? That, I don't know."

"I'm Daniel and he's Nathan."

Amir suggested that they should get into his car and drive to a quieter place. He offered to take them to his flat in the other end of town. In passing, he noted that it was in a part of the city that was closest to the Fordow complex. He commented further, "Good for my commute."

He continued, saying that, they should be able to talk freely, once at the car. Dan replied that Nathan would go with him while he would follow in their car. His point was that he did not want to have to come back to the mosque to retrieve it. Amir seemed surprised that they would have a car; they simply noted that they needed mobility. Nate asked Amir where he had parked and he said that the car was quite close, "I always park near the tourist buses; it's always better guarded. Although, it's not that there's so much crime here. Sharia law is not kind to thieves. . . ."

Nate could not help himself and said: "So we've heard, indeed."

Dan replied that they were parked in the same area but not for the same reason. As they were walking in the direction of the car, Dan asked Amir to enter his address in his GPS so that he could find the place even if the two cars got separated in the traffic. They found Amir's car first, a Peugeot Pars, the same car as Farid's. *This must be their normal executive sedan*, Nathan thought to himself. Daniel could see his car from there and pointed it out to Amir.

They drove back to the north end of the city, but Amir did not select the ring road. Rather, he took them through the main avenues. After traveling straight, alongside a construction site destined to be the next cross-town expressway, they came to a roundabout and took Moallem Street into the center of town. They veered right on Imam Moussa Sadr Boulevard, along the river and then left onto Imam Khomeini Avenue. Fortunately, neither of these major arteries within

Qom was terribly busy. They arrived at Amir's flat, just off Imam Khomeini, in less than forty-five minutes. The building looked quite similar to all the surrounding buildings and seemed neither modern nor terribly old. It really was totally nondescript, with three stories and small balconies at all the windows. Amir seemed quite pleased with himself: "I'm on the third floor, the top floor. We haven't got an elevator, so, we must use the stairs."

"It's good for our hearts," Nathan chimed in.

Upon entering the flat, Nathan asked to use the restrooms, so Daniel waited for him to return. Nathan had a secret application on the tablet he seemed always to keep with him; it would detect any microphone or other listening device within about three hundred feet, by emitting a high pitch ultrasound and checking any return vibration. He would not be able to pinpoint their exact location, but he would at least be able to warn Daniel that something was amiss if he thought Amir's place was bugged.

Nathan's face was severe and drawn as he emerged from the bathroom. He said, "Amir, this flat is bugged . . ."

CHAPTER.24

Minoo immediately realized that she had not presented the challenge to Farid in the right way. She corrected herself. She explained that she was being overcautious, adding, "This is the first time I have feared for my life . . ."

Farid moved a couple of steps closer and put his arm around her shoulders. She gratefully noticed his reaction but carried on. She needed to clarify what she had meant by the idea of someone finding a link between the three of them. Farid had indeed asked, "Three of us?"

"Yes, Papa, you and me."

She immediately continued although Farid ostensibly had a question on the tip of his tongue. Her point was that the link was ridiculously small. Each of them had a good reason for leaving Iran for a short while: holiday for her father, business for her, and some combination for him. She added they went to three different places: her father to Paris, herself to Geneva, admittedly via Paris; as for him she suggested to Farid that he might go to Dubai, adding: "Nobody should imagine a link between us, other than the fact that we are all out of Iran at the same time. But that can't be the first time . . . I'm overcautious, sorry."

For once, Farid seemed satisfied. So, she suggested that he should book a roundtrip ticket to Dubai and then a one-way from Dubai to Paris. He could use Emirates for both but under two separate reservations. She gave him a credit card number to use for expenses outside of Iran. She added that it was in her name but should be no big deal. She warned him not to use it for the roundtrip to Dubai; he should pay for that in Iran, either at the airport or at a travel agency in town. Continuing her litany of advice, she said that he should not check himself to Paris at Tehran's airport, just to Dubai using the roundtrip ticket. She said it would be great if he could avoid checking any luggage as keeping everything as carry-on would increase his flexibility, adding: "But don't panic if they won't let you carry it all on. It'll be just a bit longer of a process for you in Dubai. But, if you can do carry-on only, then, when you get to Dubai, simply go to the transfer desk, and check in for the next flight."

"Whew. This sounds more and more like a spy story. You wouldn't?" She just smiled.

Farid tried one last objection, arguing, "But, I haven't gotten my flight yet and haven't told Reza anything."

Minoo just replied that they could book the flight right then and there and get the ticket in the city the next day. Then he could tell Reza when he got to the office. He asked, "Isn't that going to look odd?"

"What . . . ?"

"For me to leave at such short notice."

"Tell him you found out I had been invited to a CERN presentation in Geneva and you want to surprise me. That's almost true. He might even check it with my rector, and have it confirmed. By the way, are you close enough to him that you could imply that there may be more than meets the eye between us?"

Farid admitted that Reza knew how he felt about her. He said he was not a close friend, but they did talk, and they had talked about her. Changing tone on the spot, he added: "By the way, your excuse . . . A brilliant idea. It explains everything. Thanks. Are you sure you're not a spy?"

Minoo smiled broadly and coyly replied: "Me, a spy . . . ?

They started working together on his laptop. The first airline they tried was indeed Emirates. They were lucky. They laughed like teenagers. The flights were not only available, but the timing was feasible. Sure, Farid would have to wait almost seven hours after having greeted the Germans before flying out. But there was no real alternative. All other Middle Eastern airlines had him either wait just as long, or longer, for his next flight in Tehran or were simply not serving Tehran. So, having to wait in Tehran was not a big deal. While he said he might still change his mind about what he would do for that extra time before his flight, he mused at the idea of driving a bit around the city, though he did not want to get caught in the traffic of the city. They decided he would leave on EK 978 at 9:20 p.m., which would put him into Dubai just before midnight. He would have to wait until 8:00 a.m. the next day to take the new Airbus 380 flight EK 073 to Paris, arriving around 12:30 p.m. Dubai Airport offered hotel rooms within the terminal, so that he could actually sleep there while waiting for his Paris flight. Minoo told him he could book that hotel room now, with the credit card number she gave him; they would surely accept an internet reservation.

They knew that Farid would need to pick up his roundtrip ticket to Dubai at the downtown ticket office, as was the rule in Iran—no e-ticket. She said she would not accompany him. Though she had not been with her father when he bought his ticket to Paris, she had recently bought a ticket to Istanbul and did not want to attract attention. The ticket from Dubai to Paris was electronic; they charged it to Minoo's foreign credit card, which Farid believed was related to her mother's family. They did the same for a hotel room in Dubai Airport. The two electronic confirmations would be in Farid's inbox and would only be activated when he got to Dubai.

Farid seemed quite content. But, for a second, he looked quizzical.

Minoo felt a whiff of panic at the thought that the whole edifice could still collapse. Yet, she maintained her composure and asked why.

He answered with a smile that she had not told him her flight details. He would love to have them, if only so that he could follow the flights on the Flight Tracker app on his phone. She replied that the university had booked everything. She had asked to be routed through Istanbul as they had earlier discussed, but there was another reason. She could have flown directly to Europe on a European airline, but they left Iran at the wrong time. She asked to fly via Paris so that she could get to Geneva on the superfast train, TGV, from Paris. Since there was no direct flight from Iran to either Geneva or even Zurich, the University didn't find the routing she had asked for odd. So, she said her flight would be leaving Tehran at 8:10 a.m. and arriving in Istanbul at 10:15 a.m. Her next flight would leave Istanbul at 2:25 p.m., arriving in Paris at 5:10 p.m. She would be supposedly staying at the Sheraton Hotel at Charles de Gaulle Airport and taking a TGV at midday the next day from the station at the airport almost right under the hotel.

But she added with a large grin that she could privately tell him that she would NOT sleep at the airport and that she would NOT be on that train. She would be in Paris when he landed in Dubai and would pick him up at the Paris airport the next day. And she added: "I'll be wearing my best smile, which won't be hard, as it'll be the second-best day of my life," as she winked . . .

"Second best?"

"Have you forgotten already . . . ? Remember the day you proposed?"

CHAPTER.25

MAY 5
QOM

Daniel was surprised to hear Nathan's verdict that the flat was bugged, but not nearly as much as Amir; Dan knew that Nathan was checking for microphones in the bathroom, while Amir had no idea.

"What?"

"There's an open mike nearby my friend."

Amir was lost for words. He stuttered that it was impossible. But Nathan calmly told him he was absolutely sure. Amir asked, "Where is it?"

"That, I can't tell you, my friend. I don't know. It could conceptually be in your neighbor's apartment. But the signal seems too clear for that."

Daniel was by now moving into Amir's "physical space" as both he and Nathan were getting ready to get him to talk, one way or another. Nathan discreetly tried the app a second time and noted that the signal appeared stronger. He concluded they had to be getting closer.

All of a sudden, the proverbial light came on in Amir's mind: "YouTube."

Daniel and Nathan looked at each other quizzically. Dan asked Amir what he meant. He took them both to what might have at one point been a second bedroom and had been converted to a den or office; this was where Amir had his computer. He pointed to the computer and showed them that he had simply forgotten to switch off the sound after he had watched a clip, on YouTube.

"The mike and the speakers are on the same switch."

He switched them off and invited Nathan to run another test. Nathan nodded to him and to Daniel that they were OK. They sat down in the living room with its heavy upholstered furniture, protected, they assumed, from all prying eyes or ears.

Daniel told Amir that they would be getting a couple of suitcases which they would need him to take into the complex for them. He asked Amir if there was any space in his office where they could safely be stored, adding: "No risk that someone finds them out or worse discovers what is in them."

Amir replied that he had a couple of closets that he could lock. And he was the only one with the key. He asked: "What's in them?"

Without displaying any emotion, Daniel answered with a short description of their job: "As you know, our job is to engineer a full blow up of the two enrichment halls. We want the whole facility to be crippled, if not totally destroyed."

Amir looked a bit shocked and conceded that Afri—aka Sarah—had told him to expect something big, but he hadn't anticipated anything that big. He added that he now understood why she told him to book an airline ticket out of the country for May eighth.

Daniel explained that they were going to deposit custom-designed bombs under thirty-six centrifuges in each hall. Nate corrected him, adding that there would be thirty-six bombs in one hall and forty in the other. Daniel explained that they needed the bombs to do enough damage but limit the time placing them in the halls to the absolute minimum. This led to the determination of an optimal ratio of bombs to centrifuges. He added that the reason there were more bombs in the second hall was because of the additional fifty-two experimental centrifuges in that hall.

Amir then asked where the bombs were at present. Daniel explained that they were not yet in Iran. He added that they would come into the country not fully assembled, with Amir interrupting: "Wouldn't want them exploding in transit . . ."

Daniel nodded and continued that they indeed needed to finish putting the parts together after they had collected them. Looking directly into Amir's eyes, Nathan added that he, Amir, would not need to be involved then. Daniel could read the fact that Nathan still harbored some suspicion vis-à-vis Amir. He chose to ease the tension by arguing that Amir had to be kept out of the limelight as much as possible, for his own safety and the ultimate success of the mission. Nathan picked up on his teammate's sensitivity and added that they had to protect him.

"Your role is absolutely crucial. We need you to smuggle the bombs into the plant so that, early after midnight, we can set them up and eventually trigger them. We also need you to smuggle us out of the plant. Big job, big job."

Nathan concluded by explaining the final step of the plan: Amir would need to take them back to their car that would be parked a couple of miles outside of the main gate on the way back to the main highway. Once that was done, Amir would need to drive to the airport to catch his flight. Nate asked: "Which flight are you on?"

"Atlas Jet to Istanbul leaving at 5:30 a.m."

Daniel noted the information, adding that it should work just fine. He indicated that their work should be done by 2:00 a.m. or so. That should give Amir plenty of time to get to the airport and check in for his flight. Yet he noted: "But you won't have too much time to waste either."

Given the fact that Amir normally left for work around 8:00 a.m. each day, they agreed that they would meet him downstairs in his parking garage, on May seventh at 7:45 a.m. Daniel added that he would send him a flash if they needed to change and asked him to send them a flash if an issue arose on his end between now and then. As a final instruction, he asked Amir to let them know as soon as possible of any change at the plant that appeared unusual or big, whether it be people or activity.

Before they left, Amir confirmed that the surveillance camera work was well in hand. He had gotten the equipment from Afri. The most difficult part was the connection to their system, together with the relatively short recording time. As he had told Afri, he reminded them that they needed to worry about four cameras, one in each hall and one in each plaza. The tunnels were not monitored. There was nowhere to go other than to the office building, the halls or the plazas. All of those were covered by video surveillance, except the office building. Since they only had slightly more than two hours of capacity on each tape, he needed pretty precise timing so he could have the correct time window for the recording. Daniel replied that they expected to start their work at around 1:00 a.m. and be done at 2:00 a.m. He commented that they had taken less than an hour in rehearsals but admitted that they were not constantly checking whether someone was coming. So, he concluded that Amir should record a two-hour period 12:30 a.m. to 2:30 a.m.

"It should cover the whole gamut with plenty to spare."

On a different note, Nathan added that they would give him a small wireless mike that connected to ear buds they would be wearing; he indicated that Amir would have ear buds, too. He explained that it was a three-way system, so they could all stay in touch. He noted that they should use it as sparingly as possible, as there was always a risk of external detection. Yet, it was the only advance warning system they would have. He asked Amir to remind either of them to give him those buds and the mike should they forget in the heat of the moment.

Once back in their car, Nathan blurted out that he might believe that Amir was trustworthy but added that, if he was a double agent, he'd want to project the same image. So, he argued that they should continue to be very careful and watch their backsides. He added: "I'll be the first to thank him after the fact, but until then, I'm not willing to bet the bank on him. I'll keep my eyes wide open. There's something odd about him—can't quite put my finger on it though."

"Can't tell you the idea hasn't crossed my mind, Nate. But we have to trust Sarah and Simon."

"Agreed, but . . ."

CHAPTER.26

Both teams arrived on time at Kashan airport, though David and Mike were there first. It was their responsibility to ensure that all went smoothly.

At Cyrus's apartment, Daniel and Nathan had loaded the three suitcases in the trunk of the 206. They were quite heavy, one of them in particular. It was Farid's who, as he had previewed, had preferred to take his favorite books, even if it meant leaving clothing behind. The suitcases fit easily in the trunk, which, Nathan observed, should not be a surprise as Minoo had the same model of car and thus knew what you could and could not put in the trunk. As planned, the rugs were rolled up in a big cylinder, leaving Dan with the hope that his colleagues would have a bit of rope to tie them into better rolls. They hid the rugs behind the front seats. They had even found a dark underlay under the largest rug in the apartment and used it to wrap around the outside of the package. This way, everything fit nicely with the dark grey interior. They satisfied themselves that no one would see them unless looking for them. They felt safe driving down to Kashan. As usual, they were careful to respect all speed limits and road signals, without looking obsequious; that might have made them suspect.

They turned left toward the terminal. Daniel noted: "Boy, I understand their first reaction. This looks like an access road to a perfectly functioning airport. I sure hope they've been thorough checking it all out."

They passed by what David and Mike had called the garrison, saw the two buildings in the distance on the left and turned right toward the larger hangar that the team was now calling "the terminal" or "the hangar" interchangeably. They turned off their headlights, using the 2:00 a.m. moon to give them the light they needed to stay on the road. A short flash of light followed by another two, slightly longer ones told them that at least one of their teammates had seen them and was waiting for them. Nathan lowered his window and replied with two quick light flashes. They parked the car immediately behind the hangar, alongside the Land Cruiser and walked around to the side that was hidden from view of the other end of the airport.

They greeted one another, although Dan and Nate were initially surprised not to see David. Mike reassured them, answering the question that Nate had asked: "He's there," pointing to the far end of the hangar, "he's watching for a sign of the Koveshes."

"What's that, next to him?"

"Oh, that's the heli-drone, Nate."

"Heli-drone?"

"Yes, it's true; you guys didn't see it when you were in Tel Aviv."

"Looks sharp. What does it do?"

Mike went on to explain that the heli-drone was there to help them deal with heavy stuff. Its principal role was to ferry what they could not carry between the camp they had set up near the plant and the area within the plant where they had to work, during the final stage of the operation on site in Natanz. Nate could not resist asking: "Two places?"

"Yeah."

Mike explained that the area within the fences around the plant needed to remain as "normal" to the eye as possible, because there was a permanent risk of patrols. Having a staging area outside of the plant allowed them to keep all their equipment with them, even when not in use, but to avoid having to hide it within the plant, which he added would simply not be possible. Nathan nodded with visible admiration. David called out to Mike, Dan and Nate: "Guys, I think the drones are arriving."

They all turned to peer at the night sky to watch the arrival of what would, ultimately, be their transportation out of Iran—hopefully . . .

The drones had found the Kashan air strip without difficulty, and more importantly had not experienced any issue throughout their inbound flight. David initially was pointing to something in the air, over the mountain range on the east side of the valley; he was in fact somewhat guessing the spots he was seeing were the drones, but it was too dark for them to be sure, despite the moon and the multitude of stars that illuminated the firmament. Yet, they had agreed with the pilots that the leading drone would turn on an outside light, like that of a transponder, for five seconds as it was abeam the runway. David had picked the first one out of the night sky and that something appeared to be moving, in the right direction. They certainly could not hear anything that sounded like a jet engine. They all thought the same thing: *Thank God, these things are not as noisy as we feared.*

Eventually, the first Kovesh was making its last turn and lining up with the runway. It was visible, but, even then, the minimal cross section of the drone made it look more like a mosquito a few feet away than a 65-foot wingspan aircraft a mile away. Nate queried their ability to land without lights and David explained that the remote pilots were using the night vision cameras they had seen in the hangar at the base.

"We'd said they had to be discreet. No noise, no light and maximum precautions. You can bet you won't hear any reverse thrust when they brake . . ."

Suddenly the first Kovesh swooshed onto the far end of the runway and proceeded to slow down to a fast crawl. The second Kovesh was now visible, following on virtually the same trajectory and with similar landing procedures. It touched down as David guided the first to the spot he had chosen, behind the hangar, but still on the tarmac. They only started to hear the gentle sound of an idling jet engine as the drone was no more than 300 feet from them. David concluded that he was certain that none of the local farmers on the other side of the highway would have heard anything: "And we're operating in the dark here. They couldn't see anything unless they knew exactly where to look."

David blurted out, "Not again . . ."

All four of them had turned toward the South and saw a landing light approaching. They immediately took cover and waited, praying that the light would not come close to seeing the drones. It was another helicopter which landed neatly near the other end of the runway, in front of the last building. It stayed on the ground a short amount of time. Yet, the team, who had not retrieved anything from the Koveshes yet, was unable to see what was happening without the night-vision goggles which were part of the inbound cargo. They could see the lights of a car driving out on the road and turning toward Kashan at the T-intersection. Soon thereafter, probably not more than five minutes later, the helicopter took off and never came close to seeing what was going on at their end of the runway.

"Where are the AWACS?" was all David could say. He elected to unload the drones first, send them on their way, and then warn Simon. It was clear to him that minimizing the time the Koveshes were on the ground was now a top priority. They unloaded the drones simultaneously, to save time on the ground and allow them to return home as fast as possible. Mike was appointed to take inventory, while David recited from memory what should be in the cargo bays: "In each drone, we should have a fully fueled up excavator, with its cutting head and an additional gas tank, a jet pack, some extra gas for the heli-drone and the excavator, a set of acid containers, eight bombs and one suitcase filled with pre-assembled bombs for Nathan and Daniel.

They should also contain four sets of small arms and ammunition, plus night vision goggles and various miscellaneous items: a couple of shovels, extra tarps and the like."

Daniel confirmed, "Everything present and accounted for here."

"Thanks, mate . . . Nate?"

"Same here."

"Perfect."

Dan and Nate packed one suitcase and the rugs in one drone and the other two suitcases in the other. David pointed to the hooks and straps that the designers had located throughout the cargo bays, with the advice that anything they put in them should be well tethered. Daniel worked on his suitcase and the rugs which were now a single roll not much more than five or six feet in length. And then, he closed and locked the cargo door. Nathan on his side had also completed loading, closing and locking.

The team proceeded to clear the area around the drones and move them into position. Mike took control of one plane while David controlled the other to drive the Koveshes to end of the runway. Mike asked the remote pilots whether they needed to take off into a head wind. The reply came within seconds: "Guide us to the closest end of the runway. We'll take off in the opposite direction we landed. We've got so much power and runway length that the initial heading won't matter."

They told the pilots to hold off for a few minutes, until all the equipment remaining at the airport was safely hidden away. Mildly changing the original plan, they decided, after having looked at the sky in every direction and seeing no incoming light, that they should drive back to the main drag before sending the planes off. Mike relayed the plan to the remote pilots but clarified that they could take off anyway, if they saw anything worrisome on their 360-degree infrared cameras.

The excavators and the jet packs were loaded into the Land Cruiser; the suitcases plus the detonators into the 206. They were ready to go in less than fifteen minutes. David inspected the cache behind the hangar by himself; he was fully satisfied with what he saw. They instructed the remote pilot of the heli-drone to fly it to their staging area near the Natanz plant.

They made sure that the two drones were now at the end of the runway heading northwest and that their pilots were ready. The last flash indicated they would initiate the take-off sequence in five minutes, or earlier if they saw an emergency. This would give the two cars plenty of time to get back on the road to Amir Kabir. Mike and Nathan, who were not driving, confirmed that the two drones took off and immediately veered off to the east, starting a long turn that would take them due west. The take-off was a lot noisier than the landing as the instructions to the pilots were to climb as fast as they could to avoid any risk of radar detection. David asked Mike to send a message to Simon to tell of the helicopter landing, adding: "Tell him we need AWACS cover. This was close, way too close. The Koveshes were on the ground . . ."

CHAPTER.27

When Simon and David visited the Palmachim Base and discovered the Kovesh, Marvin had also demonstrated a machine that would allow the team to drill into the protective layers of dirt which the Iranians had piled on top of the centrifuge halls. After having seen both the drones and how they would be remotely piloted, they had left the drone control center. Marvin had then led them to a much smaller hangar, a few hundred yards away. This was what the lab called a test hangar. It was a small one-story structure and it, and others like it, were built for the sole purpose of testing new pieces of equipment and providing training in their use. Three of the four sides of the building were constructed of corrugated steel attached to a visible, steel frame, while the fourth backed onto a mound of dirt. It was only when they got inside the hangar that they could see that the fourth wall had a huge glass window.

Marvin had played the role of proud father as he pointed to the features of the excavator. It was a camouflage-painted machine whose section was barely larger than one square foot. It looked like an elongated box with two caterpillar tracks, one along each side, running nearly the full six foot length of the machine. Two larger wheels were found at each end and on each side; they were virtually as large as the body of the excavator, measuring ten inches in diameter. Two smaller wheels, in-between and with an axis lower than that of the larger wheels brought the caterpillar tracks down. This was to create space for the engine and the gas tank behind it. At the front of the machine, a cylindrical cavity held the external power drive. This particular excavator was equipped with a large, frontal drill, about eighteen inches in diameter and no thicker than a few inches—a miniature version of a typical tunnel boring machine. Its axis was higher than the center of the cylinder containing the drive. The rotating cutter head was equipped with a number of small disc cutters set at an angle perpendicular to the head; their job was to dig into the soil while the rotation of the head itself helped remove debris by propelling it backwards. Marvin explained that the foot-wide ring they could see behind the head was pneumatically activated. Every foot or so, the excavator would stop, and hydraulic pressure would push the ring outwards to stabilize the walls of the tunnel.

Marvin ended by explaining that the operator would simply shift the machine into reverse when he wanted to remove the debris. The plates at the rear and to which he had just pointed served to push the debris back up the tunnel and outside. He added that it was probably a good idea to shift the machine into reverse every ten to fifteen feet.

Marvin then demonstrated the camera function. He prefaced his exposè with the statement that one can never expect to see what was in front, given the size of the cutter head, hence there were no headlights or front camera; plus, there was nothing to see. However, pointing to a half sphere set on the top and at the back of the excavator, there was a camera and LEDs to provide the light needed.

At the front of the machine, he explained that they had engineered a solution so that, once the cutting head was removed, one could attach other implements for the spraying of the acid they would need to dissolve some of the reinforcement steel bars in the concrete structure above the top of the enrichment hall.

The excavator was positioned on a ramp leading to a mound of dirt; the ramp was about ten feet long and had an upward slope that would bring the drill in contact with the earth about two feet off the ground. Marvin ushered Simon and David into the hangar. He picked up another tablet and launched the appropriate application. With it, he turned the engine on, and his two visitors could see the excavator move forward, crawling slowly up the ramp. As the excavator reached the mount of dirt, Marvin triggered an operation that surprised Simon and David. They saw the front end of the machine rise up a bit and the drilling axis angled downward. He then explained, "The cutter head is attached to a ball joint that can be turned up, down or sideways; it helps you set the boring angle for the excavator. You can't angle the cutting head more than 30 degrees relative to where it stands. But, within that constraint, a small hydraulic pump pushes the axis up or down so that the angle of the drill doesn't interfere with forward progress. That's important when you need to drill up or down . . ."

The excavator was now moving forward, and they could follow its progress through the single pane, glass window. Every thirty seconds or so, Marvin was activating a scraping blade that moved from right to left and back to its idling space on the external surface of the glass. This was meant to clear up the small remaining layer of earth; they didn't want the cutter head to break the glass. The demonstration allowed the two agents to keep seeing what was happening on the other side. They could see the head gradually come back in line with the main body of the excavator, and its front end settle back to its original position. Once they had drilled about three feet, Marvin put the machine into reverse and they all could see the debris being forced out of the tunnel.

Marvin was beaming. Simon and David congratulated him on his "baby" noting that he had been absolutely correct when he had told them: "I think we have a solution for phase one in Natanz."

CHAPTER.28

While Daniel and Nathan headed north back to Qom, David and Mike first went north but then turned south as they reached the ramp to the highway three miles north of Amir Kabir. They went straight to the perimeter of the Natanz complex as they had planned.

They were happy to find the heli-drone already there when they arrived, as they had requested. The personal jet packs that had just arrived would allow them to leave the complex in a hurry, if needed. These had two operating modes. In normal operations, they relied on relatively quiet air jets to move; the power for these came from the central turbine rotating at low speed. There was also a true jet move, relying on compressed exhaust gases, which would literally jet the individual wearing the jet pack up in the air at a speed such that he could avoid bullets were he discovered and shot at—a similar principle to that of an ejector seat on a jet plane. The plan called for both Mike and David to have their personal jet propulsion devices near them at all times to provide them with the ability to escape safely and rapidly, if needed. As a precaution, Simon had all four agents train on the use of the jet pack; they had good fun with that.

The plan had Mike flying into the complex first and positioning himself in a small depression about nine hundred feet south-southwest of the main fence. Satellite pictures had shown that there were quite a few trees which, they thought could provide further shelter from view.

Though he would be close enough to the first target, the northern enrichment hall, he would be hidden from the view of the barracks which lined the west end of the area. Once the material for that first site was assembled and hidden under a camouflaged tarpaulin, he would move about four hundred fifty feet west-southwest to another small depression, close to where their second effort would start.

The initial load contained the first of the two underground excavators. The plan was to drill a foot-and-a-half-wide tunnel down through the estimated seventy-two feet of dirt which had been packed on top of the first enrichment hall. Weighing four hundred fifty pounds, the excavator stretched the carrying capacity of the heli-drone near its five hundred-pound limit. The first trip proved to be totally uneventful; the excavator arrived in good shape, and there was no visible reaction from the barracks. The next trip ferried the equipment needed to hide the activities from external views when the first few feet of drilling had been completed: tarps, shovels and the like. Mike sent the heli-drone back to David and proceeded to hide the equipment on the first site.

As Mike moved to the second site, sounds came from one of the barracks. His heartbeat accelerated and he immediately checked the straps on his jet propulsion system, ready to escape if needed. For the next few minutes, he remained as well-hidden as possible and sent a pre-arranged signal to David. The noise was certainly not coming any closer; in fact, at one point, it started to abate. A false alarm. Both Mike and David breathed a large sigh of relief and returned to their tasks.

The next two trips brought the same equipment to the second site. Still no sound from the guards. A couple of mishaps made this process a bit longer than planned: the second area which Mike selected had no real level ground. This made the unloading of the excavator more challenging. Four hundred fifty pounds, even for a very fit man working with the mini crane attached to the drone, were not easy to handle. *This is fragile cargo,* he thought to himself, *and this is NOT the time to destroy it.* Once the equipment had arrived in good shape, Mike hid it using a similar tarp to the one he had used on the first site. Then, he air-jetted back to base, to discuss the next steps with David.

Initially, they had hoped to be able to start the first phase of the drilling immediately. Despite their extensive training for this first operation and planning for how long it would take, the terrain difficulties as well as the false alarm, brought them too close to daylight for comfort. Thinking out loud, they calculated that they needed at least two hours to drill the first two yards, which was the minimum depth necessary to be able to hide the material in the tunnel. Although they hated the idea, they elected to wait until the next evening and run the risk that the material might be discovered in the daylight. As Mike had put it: "Better they find the material than either of us."

They agreed they would start an hour earlier than originally planned the next day and send a message to Simon to inform him of their decision. They sent the heli-drone on its way to the place David had selected to park it, about ten miles to the southwest, where hills would provide a natural cover. Before sending it on, they had topped off its tank, with gas from the Land Cruiser. Nathan made a joke about what people might think of the consumption of the Land Cruiser if they kept siphoning from its gas tank to fuel the heli-drone. David replied that they were businessmen looking for sites and that the Land Cruiser was not known for its frugality when it came to gas consumption.

The remote pilots of the heli-drone were charged with permanent monitoring of the surroundings, with the 360-degree, night vision camera sitting on top of the main rotor. They were under strict orders to escape if there was any intrusion and to be prepared to trigger the self-destruct mechanism in flight if there was a risk of being shot down. The self-destruct mechanism plus the fact that the equipment bore absolutely no markings of any sort, either on the machine or any of its components would minimize the risk that any finger could ever be pointed to Israel. Admittedly, not too many countries, other than possibly the U.S., were known to be able to engineer and manufacture such a machine, but, at least, it could not be displayed with great fanfare as had been the case with a U.S. Sentinel drone, allegedly captured by Iran a few years earlier. Any attribution would therefore be mere conjecture. Further, Israel had never displayed this equipment nor used it in a way that it might have been photographed; it was as secret as anything could be.

They loaded their personal jets, as they called them, into the Land Cruiser and made sure that they couldn't be seen from the outside when the car was in the garage. They then retreated to the apartment in Kashan, about twenty-five miles away. The early part of the morning was not a problem as they both had no trouble sleeping, given the efforts of the night before. The mid- to late-afternoon was a bit harder. They were wide awake and could not help shaking the worry that the plot would be discovered on the Natanz site and the mission compromised. They had rehearsed their escape in such a case many times, but this was a scenario which they certainly did not want to have to play out. But they couldn't go to the site too early—the risk of being caught rose dramatically when operating in full daylight. They had to bide their time and were left having to play out the roles dictated by their cover. And this was very tedious for people anxious to get into the real action.

CHAPTER.29

Daniel and Nathan had no difficulty on their trip back to Qom. They were pretty much by themselves as most people were asleep at 3:00 a.m. And they thankfully did not have to contend with any police roadblock. They parked the car in the garage and took the two suitcases together with the smaller cases containing detonators and small arms up to the apartment. Immediately, Nathan noted that they did not remember the suitcases being so heavy in rehearsals. Dan simply replied that they had had a busy night so far, and that the sixteen bombs they had rolled into the small depression behind the hangar were not lightweights, "We're both tired; that's all . . ."

They were still speaking in German as they absolutely had to maintain the cover that they were two scientists involved in some way with the Fordow plant. Not a difficult requirement and, in truth, they actually enjoyed the opportunity.

They first decided to grab a bit of sleep. They did not want to start assembling bombs then. They were tired as they had had virtually no sleep so far that night. Additionally, they noted that they would rather do it during natural daylight even if they had to use the electricity then to avoid people seeing them through the windows. Dan added: "There's no point drawing attention to our windows being the only ones lit up at this ungodly hour."

"Agree. The first one that wakes up, calls the other."

"Hold it . . . How about this, Nathan . . . The first one who wakes up after 8:00 a.m. calls the other."

They retired and chose not to take a shower—no need to wake neighbors. They had determined to be model tenants so that people who did not know that Minoo's father had gone on a holiday would not ask themselves why he was doing things he never did. Though the call for the morning prayers from the nearby mosque was pretty loud, they both barely woke up. They simply turned in the bed and went straight back to sleep. Daniel was the first to wake up and it was already past 9:00.

They decided first to have breakfast. Then Dan said "Let's take showers and start working. We've got seventy-six bombs that we need to assemble."

Nathan smiled, knowing full well that the process of assembling the bombs would be a lengthy one. These bombs were in fact the brainchild of Simon. His idea was to create small, flat bombs that could be slipped under a few of the centrifuges. The bombs would have two different components.

The base would be classical C-4 explosive, with a small, radio-activated detonator in the center. The goal for that base would be to create damage in a horizontal dimension to all the neighboring assemblies as well as an upward blast. To maximize the damage from the blast, a second layer of different explosives would be placed on top of the base and around the detonator. It would comprise four, small bombs, one on each corner of the base, which, when exploding, would send small projectiles—small ball bearings—at 30- to 45-degree angles, whatever the lab determined would be most efficient. The impact of the projectiles would be twofold. First, hitting other centrifuges, they would destabilize them relative to their carefully assembled and maintained vertical axes. Second, punching holes in pipes linking them to one another would further damage the overall installation. With any luck, they might even punch holes in the walls of the external cylinders, destroying the internal vacuum the inner cylinders need to operate.

∎∎■∎∎

A while back, in Tel Aviv, Marvin had first told Simon that he thought that the idea of having two different actions was great. He then delved a bit deeper into the engineering aspects, arguing that describing each of the five elements as different "bombs" was not all that necessary. Marvin suggested that the assembly, whatever you called it, should have a single source of explosive, and this would have to be the C-4. The blast would do two things. First, it would damage the assembly under which it's placed as well as those around it, just as Simon wanted. Second, that explosion would trigger the breakup of the containers housing the projectiles and the blast needed to provide enough impetus for them to travel the desired distance. He agreed that the side containers could be angled any way one wished around the horizontal axis so that the balls would go in the desired direction. He finally added that, at most, they would test using a small strip of C-4 inside each of the lateral containers.

∎∎■∎∎

Now, Daniel and Nate feasted on the fresh fruit, yoghurt and breads they had bought. They missed milk in their fresh coffee, but they had been warned not to look for skim milk. It would be whole milk and not always cow's milk. And the coffee would be instant rather than freshly brewed. They had also bought Persian Pistachio brittles, *sowhan,* a local delicacy, which they enjoyed sparingly, as they had been warned it could be addictive.

They were now ready to start their work. Though tedious, it had to be done perfectly. In fact, training had suggested that they should test each detonator before they installed them. Obviously, they could not test whether all the various elements of the bombs were in the perfect spot, but they knew how the whole assembly was supposed to line up. The key was to make sure that the radio receptors on top of each detonator were operating freely and had not been damaged in transit. Then, they needed to plug the detonators in, using a small depression on the shaft so that they could feel the detonator engage. They agreed that the effort would probably take them the better part of the whole day.

They agreed to separate the work into two distinct tasks, one testing the detonators and the other inserting those detonators that had been cleared into the bomb assembly, testing the corner bombs and setting each fully assembled bomb in the suitcase. And they would exchange roles every twelfth bomb or so. Though this was not the way they had trained in Tel Aviv—where they each worked on a complete bomb assembly—they thought *this would reduce the risk that they might make a mistake out of habit.* Daniel had mentioned that the risk existed but was largely mitigated as they needed to switch on the bombs one by one as they placed them under a centrifuge. A small, red light should shine right next to the radio actuator and it should turn green when the actuator was rotated 90 degrees to the right. He added: "I've got to assume that the light won't come on if something is askew in the assembly."

Nathan concurred, up to a point: "Right. But I want to find any error while we're in this flat; not when we're setting the bombs down and trying get the hell out of there."

They set the first suitcase down on the floor, right next to the dining room table. The table was modest and could probably sit at most six people, but there was enough space on it to pile twenty bomb assemblies. Each assembly consisted of a square sheet of C-4 that measured a bit less than an inch in thickness and eight inches on each side; it weighed almost one pound. At the center of each sheet, there was a hole in which the pin of the detonator was supposed to fit. At each corner of the sheet, there was a container that had five sides, one of which was curved inwards. Together, these containers created a depressed cylinder at the center of the sheet, where the detonator would slide in.

Two of the five sides of the containers ran along the perimeter of the sheet of C-4; they were longer than the other two, measuring half the length of each side of the square sheet, or about four inches. The other two sides were shorter and measured about two and a quarter inches. They left a central cylindrical hole, three and a half inches in diameter, which was just enough to plug the detonator, which was about three inches in diameter. Inside these containers, one per side, you could see small darkish balls. They were made out of carbon fibers. The original plan had called for metallic balls, but they decided on carbon fiber, simply because they would be lighter than metallic ones yet just as strong. This would increase the speed at which they would impact their targets. The upper face of the containers was not parallel to the base; rather, it was set at a 30-degree angle, as originally planned, to create the up-and-out dispersion pattern they desired for the carbon-fiber balls. Additionally, it increased the volume of the containers, thus allowing a few more balls in each of them.

The design of the overall assembly called for the simultaneous ignition of the plastic base and the lateral containers. For the latter, the explosive charge was quite small and simply involved breaking the container open so that the blast from the C-4 could project the carbon fiber balls with as much power as possible. Each container slid into a small depression in the C-4 sheet, and that depression contained a wire that was itself connected to the central detonator plug. Thus, the initial ignition of the plastics explosives would create a large blast, which was tested in the lab to have a twenty-five-foot radius, with greater damage occurring within the first fifteen- to twenty-feet. This blast would destroy both the centrifuge under which it was placed and at least eight or nine others, if not more, within each row, and stretch across two and, possibly, hopefully, three rows. The simultaneous explosion of the containers would send the small balls up and away, which would damage piping, centrifuge containers and related installations. The combination would lead both to the destruction of the equipment and to the releasing of radioactive gas which would make any effort to deal with the explosion by internal or external security teams all the more difficult, at least until someone could stop the flow of gas into the centrifuges.

Nathan started testing the small detonators. He needed to do two things. First, verify that the lithium-ion batteries providing the power were fully charged. He had been provided with a simple voltage measuring device to make sure that the batteries were all good. They had a supply of additional batteries, if necessary. The batteries had already been tested before they were sent, but this was a part of their fail-safe approach to the project. Second, he needed to check that the radio receiver was activated and capable of receiving on the required frequencies. They had indeed decided that they needed ignition also to be fail-safe; they had thus provided for three redundant receivers, each working on a different frequency. As Daniel kept saying, "The point is efficiency, not miniaturization."

A small testing kit, which had been hidden in the suitcase containing guns and ammunition, was provided to test each of the receivers and make sure that they were able to receive the frequency that was assigned to them. Though certainly not rocket science, it required a great deal of attention to detail. While the initial testing in the lab had them assemble the bombs in five to six minutes or less, it would in fact take longer. The testing of the various components was a dimension that had not been originally considered and was thus added later. They now estimated that, at a minimum, it would take closer to seven to eight minutes per assembly at least.

Daniel was verifying that the four containers were solidly attached to the base and, much more importantly, that the connection between them and the detonator was working. He had a simple, screwdriver type tool that sent a low voltage electrical current into the plug where the detonator would slide. This was supposed to illuminate a small LED within each of the four containers, if the connection was still valid. Though it would take him less time to perform his test than Nathan would need to do his work, he would be busy once he had done it, as his job was also to place the completed assemblies in the suitcase; they were supposed to fit two across and three lengthwise in the suitcase. Thus, each suitcase could hold thirty-six to forty-two assemblies.

The plan called for them to set a bomb every fifteen centrifuges. This way, each bomb would be required to do damage within a seven to eight centrifuge radius. It would, therefore, take twelve bombs to cover the whole length of the hall. The first hall would only require thirty-six bombs, which allowed them to target three out of the eight rows, which would be plenty. Though the implicit radius built into this plan was not even half the full power they tested in the lab, they wanted as much of an overlap across the individual bombs as possible. This would cover a possibly malfunctioning bomb, or component, and create more havoc in the fine mechanical and concrete work that served as the infrastructure on which the centrifuges were set. The second hall would require an additional four bombs that would be placed in the two smaller, experimental cascades. The need for the bombs to work flawlessly reinforced their determination to have their individual bombs tested as thoroughly as possible under the circumstances.

At one point, they had considered doing the testing at the plant, just before placing them, as there was always the possibility that the trip to the plant and the handling of the suitcases might dislodge one or the other small component. In the end, it was decided that they could not do the job with enough focused attention while they were in "enemy territory." Plus, it would have added too much time on site with the potential to be discovered.

As they were working, they joked that the one thing which they knew for sure is that mishandling could not trigger an explosion; they had to rotate the actuator at the top of the detonator before it would work, and the bomb explode.

They took a short break to grab lunch at one of the street merchants outside the flat and returned quickly to finish the job.

CHAPTER.30

MAY 6
FORDOW

Once both the assembly and testing were completed, Nathan and Daniel decided to drive in the direction of Fordow. They had two goals in mind. The first, and most urgent, was to do a bit of terrain reconnaissance. Their first trip to Qom had been too short and shepherded for them to do much of what they would eventually have to do. They were concerned that some police activity might cause some trouble but were still relaxed as there was nothing in the car that could give away the fact that they were not German scientists.

They knew they would be driven to and from the plant by Amir, but they also knew that they would drive Minoo's car to a spot nearby. As they had briefly explained to Amir, they would split up shortly after he had extracted them from the plant. He had to drive himself quickly to the Tehran airport to flee, while they still had other work to do. For the obvious reason of not disclosing anything that was not mission critical, they didn't tell him that they had to join their colleagues at the air strip near Kashan to fire the six missiles.

Their first order of business now would be to find the best side road to hide Minoo's car but make sure that it didn't look abandoned. It had to be there when they returned and needed it.

A secondary goal was to get a sense of the topography around the plant. The key to any successful operation, as they had been taught, was that they should know exactly what to do if things went wrong. The plan obviously was critically dependent upon Amir. What if he failed to perform for any reason? There could be so many such reasons that one could spend a long time running through them, the instructors had explained; but, in practice, they ranged from something as silly as Amir having a heart attack while they worked inside the halls to something much more serious. If Amir fell ill, one could assume that guards and other people at the plant would focus on him and would not be looking for intruders. This would give both of them a chance to escape. They needed to know in which direction to go and how to find their way back to a place they might know and where they would be safe. But what if he was caught doing something which immediately created suspicions? Would they be able to use the same escape route? Would they need a different one? If yes, which one? There were a number of permutations on that theme.

Finding the perfect location for Minoo's car was not hard, though they could not initially decide between two spots. Both were side roads that led south from the road on which they would be driving from the highway to the main gate of the plant. They were on either side of a small hill that rose a couple of hundred feet above the road level. The guys opted for the one that was a little farther from the valley in which the plant was located. They chose it because there was a small kink in the road not more than three hundred feet from the main road; the car would not be visible from the main road, unless you were driving on the side road or looking for it. A bit farther on, the path took an almost 90-degree curve around the base of the hill which revealed most of the complex down below in the distance. *This would make a great observation post to get their own takes on what activity at the plant looked like*, they thought.

They decided to return to that spot later to spend time observing movements within the plant before being picked up by Amir for the final stage of the mission. They briefly considered this second location a better spot to park the car, but decided against it, thinking that they did not want to have to run for a half mile to get to the car and then drive back that same half mile to the road, particularly if they thought they had guards looking for them. It was now time to drive back to Qom.

They were still brainstorming escape possibilities, though they fully appreciated that any escape from the plant was going to be tough under virtually any scenario. The rocky nature of the terrain and the large area that seemed to be protected by several fences along the perimeter made the plan for such an escape, at best, dicey. But, as Daniel observed, "We've seen this kind of stuff before." The idea of cutting through the external fence was seen as a last resort; through their goggles, they could discern wires from afar. At this point indeed, they would not take the risk of being too close to the fence and in the open, and thus had to carry out their first inspection tour, as they called it, from a safe distance. There was no immediate explanation for the wires other than to conclude that the fences were alarmed in some way. Whether this was an alarm to indicate that the perimeter had been breached or designed to give someone lethal, electrical shocks was not terribly material. The fences had to be avoided. Since they could not cut through them or climb over them, they could not think of how they could consider any escape from the guarded perimeter. Nathan had added: "I agree and there's no hope digging under the fences either. Let's make a note to ask Amir what the fence protection system is when we give him the suitcases tomorrow morning."

Daniel mentioned that he had just had a thought of an initial line of defense. He was thinking of asking David and Mike for the use of their heli-drone, if they no longer needed it. He conceded that they would be really busy in Natanz and have other priorities. Still, there might be some flexibility for the timing when they could help extract their colleagues: "They could get their work done and help us afterwards."

Using the heli-drone could be a big help. It could extract them from the complex, carrying both of them at the same time. Dan's original idea rapidly ran into a snag: without an oxygen system for Dan and Nate, the drone could not carry them high enough for them to avoid potential unfriendly fire. Nathan was smiling. He had just thought of an alternative: *Why don't we use the drone to bring the jet packs to us?*

This would allow for a faster escape and, as a bonus, split the targets for potential Iranian fire. Dan and Nate would simply aim to fly to a point higher up in the hills, which would naturally take them back, toward Minoo's car. He added: "By the way, that's one more reason to select the side road we picked. The more distance we have from the main entrance, the more of a chance we have to get to the car before they start looking for us further down in the valley around Qom."

They kept talking as they were driving back to Qom. Daniel, as often was the case, was driving, so Nathan sent the messages to David and Mike, as well as to Simon. They didn't have to wait more than a few minutes. Simon was the first to respond: "Glad you guys saw the problem this early. Will talk to Marvin and revert. Your plan shouldn't be a problem. Let's see what David and Mike have to say."

David and Mike followed a few minutes later: "Sounds like a perfectly decent plan, but still don't like the odds. We'll wait for more from Simon."

CHAPTER.31

As the sun set over the region, David and Mike drove back to their base near the highway and parked the Land Cruiser in the same spot as they had the prior day. Everything was exactly as they had left it earlier that morning. They had set a few traps to ensure that they would know if the base had been discovered. Their inspection proved that either no one had been there or that whomever had been there was both particularly careful and particularly diligent. With this, they retrieved their jet packs from the trunk of the Land Cruiser, donned them and flew to the two sites beyond the fences where the excavators would soon be busily working.

Their pocket GPS allowed them to locate the exact point where they were to start the drilling. The excavators were both rugged and complex. They were rugged because the team knew that they would need to operate in challenging conditions. The complexity came from the fact that they would be called upon to do a number of different things during the mission. In this first phase, they were to start digging while Mike and David, each at his own location, were immediately spreading the earth they dug up around the area in as unobtrusive a way as possible, using the shovels that the drones had brought. Mike and David controlled the excavators from the outside near the mouths of the tunnels they were digging; they kept their jet packs on their backs in case they needed to leave in a hurry.

Once the first six feet of tunnel were completed, the process changed. The excavators were to continue to operate, but they were now totally inside the tunnel. David and Mike had affixed the extra gas tanks to the rear of the excavators and flipped the switch to make sure they were connected to the fuel system. These extra tanks would provide sufficient gas for the excavators to work continuously through the rest of the digging process. David and Mike knew that they would need to spread the dirt that the excavators would push out of the holes when reversing as neatly as possible.

David and Mike each triggered the reversing process to ensure that whatever dirt had been dug up would be dispersed; there was no need for it to accumulate further while the rest of the digging process unfolded. They spread it out as nicely as they could near the mouth of the tunnel and sent the excavators back into the tunnel. They each pulled another camouflage tarp, about three feet in diameter and secured it tightly over the opening to the tunnels they were digging. They were very careful to ensure that no light would escape from the tunnel. The excavators had their lights on such that their operators could see what was happening: Was the dirt still flowing by the central camera? Were the walls of what had just been dug still holding in place? Was there even any change in the color of the earth indicating the possibility of some unexpected complication that the Iranians might have added? If not properly hidden, any light leaking out could be sufficient for guards and other security personnel to notice and come take a close look. The sound of the engine was muffled by the debris accumulating between the excavator and the surface; this prevented guards from being alarmed by an unusual noise. The team in Tel Aviv, where the equipment had been tested, had confirmed that the sound of the boring could not be heard beyond a distance of thirty feet from the opening, unless there was absolutely no ambient background noise. They had also estimated that it would take the machine about an hour to dig three feet, which meant that they had quite a bit of time ahead of them.

David flashed his infra-red light upward three times. This was the signal he and Mike had agreed they would exchange when the first of the two of them was ready to leave. Mike flashed back four times, which told David that he was almost ready, but not quite. Six times would have told David that he was having difficulties relative to the agreed-upon schedule. A few minutes later, Mike flashed his light three times. David replied with a single flash. With this, they both started their jet packs and flew back in the direction of the Land Cruiser. Finding it where they left it and ostensibly by itself, they landed nearby. They confirmed they were indeed alone and then loaded the jet packs back into the cargo bay and started the drive back to Kashan.

One of their first observations was that it was amazing to see that the color of the dirt, six feet below ground, was not really different than on the surface. They assumed that it had to be because the Iranians only covered the halls with dirt in the last five or six years. It was still fresh. Mike added that it probably was also why they were not encountering any large rocks—a very good thing as such obstacles could compromise the mission. David summarized their common thought: *Imagine having to divert and start another hole.*

They agreed that kudos were due to the team who reached that conclusion just on the basis of the satellite pictures taken when the complex was constructed.

As they were planning their next steps, David noted that he was ready to leave the site at around 1:30 a.m. At that time, the excavator was already nine feet down. Given the angle of his tunnel, he knew he needed to drill about eighty-two feet to get to the top of the reinforced concrete. That meant that he had another seventy odd feet to go, which would take about twenty-two hours, if there were no problem. The first phase of his work should therefore be finished around midnight tonight, May seventh. He turned to Mike and asked him what his estimated time of completion was. He replied that he was about fifteen minutes behind, but that he only needed to dig seventy-nine feet as his tunnel was more vertical. In short, they concluded that they were pretty much on the same schedule. They agreed that they should return to the camp at around 11:00 p.m. David added that they should check on the progress of their excavators throughout the day to make sure that there were no issues. They did not want to wait until the evening to discover that one or both of the excavators was stuck. Also, they had decided that they did not need to evacuate the debris during that period as it seemed quite loose.

Once more, they reviewed what they would need to do when they returned, again to make sure that everything was down pat. When they returned to the camp, they would both don their jet packs and go to their respective tunnels with gas containers. There, they would remove the cover and reverse the excavators to have them push the debris from their work. Once the excavators were at the surface, they would use the maneuver to top up their gas tanks with the gas from the containers they had just flown in with. They would spread out the debris around the site, noting that they would not need to leave much debris to cover the sound of the engines since they would then be operating deep enough.

At this point, they would split up their duties. David would jet pack out to the camp while Mike stayed at his site. They estimated that they should be at that point around 1:00 a.m. on the next day, May eighth. They agreed to ask the remote pilots of the heli-drone to have it at the camp by 12:45 a.m.

The immediate next mission-related step was for them to leave the apartment at around 10:00 p.m. At that point, they would drive to the airstrip. There, they would retrieve the acid canisters that were hidden next to the big bombs behind the hangar, after which they would drive back to the camp near the Natanz plant. The canisters would stay in the Land Cruiser, until they returned from the first trip to the tunnels, as there was no point ferrying them to the tunnels should they find they had problems there. That was the point at which David would jet pack back and load the canisters onto the heli-drone. They agreed that they would need two trips, since each canister weighed about two hundred pounds and they would have to fly in at least another forty pounds of gasoline to top up the excavators. The team in Tel Aviv had concluded that the gas topping up was probably an unnecessary precaution, but neither they nor Simon wanted to take the risk of either excavator getting stuck for lack of gas going down or backing up.

David would thus send the heli-drone to Mike first who would unload it and send it back to him. David would then load the second set of canisters and the extra gas for his excavator and send the heli-drone to his site. He would jet pack there alongside the heli-drone. He was going to keep the drone with him, although the remote pilots would cover them if anything were to happen. He argued that he could not flee and fly and destroy the heli-drone all at the same time. The remote pilots would have to take care of the drone, if an emergency occurred.

Continuing on the recitation of their plan, they would then wait by the mouth of the tunnels, until the digging was finished. Mike added: "That should be pretty close to when we get there if the schedule holds."

"Agreed."

They would get the excavators out of the tunnels when they had reached desired depth but wait to spread what was left of any debris around the site, as it was not a time-sensitive activity and just needed to be finished before they returned to camp. They would then remove the front end of each excavator and slide the acid canisters into the base of the spraying system that was behind the cutting head. They would pull the two spraying tubes out of the body of the excavator and secure them so the sprayers at the front of the tubes were clearly beyond the canisters; they did not want any acid sprayed on the canisters. That would be the point when they topped up the gas tanks of the excavators and sent them back into the tunnels for their spraying mission. Once completed, they would seal the top of the tunnels with the tarp. They would then tie the gas containers and the cutting heads to the heli-drone and fly them back to the car. As David pointed out, that meant that the heli-drone would have to fly from him to Mike before flying to the car, as David's site was the last site to receive the supplies for the acid spraying phase. It would only fly once back to the Land Cruiser with the load of the two cutting heads, the canisters and shovels. The total weight would be well within the drone's carrying capacity. David would be the first back at the car and would load his jet pack. Mike would then, with David's help, unload everything from the heli-drone into the car, then the two of them would drive back to Kashan.

As Mike was the one driving the Land Cruiser back to Kashan this morning, he asked David to check on the two excavators on their respective tablets. Looking at his tablet, David confirmed that his excavator had drilled an extra meter since they'd left.

"I'm on track. Let me check yours . . . You're on track, too."

He added that he could see that the excavators were both well within normal gas consumption range.

By then, they had arrived at the flat. They decided to go to bed and get some sleep as they knew they had a full day ahead of them. Then, Mike blurted out: "Just thought of one contingency we didn't cover . . . When we get to the airstrip . . . What if the canisters aren't there?"

David, who was about to fall asleep, perked up. He asked Mike what he was thinking, and Mike simply replied that someone could have found them. David's face grew serious as he realized that if someone had found the cannisters they would have found the bombs, too. So, someone would be looking for them. Mike quipped, "Unless they're thinking of ambushing us . . ."

"Wait a minute . . . That's bloody true. Let's make one change to the plan. We'll tell the heli-drone to fly below radar and near the air strip before we get there, to check out the weapons cache."

David explained. Assuming the Iranians were smarter than they had given them credit for, all they needed to do was to wait patiently for whoever was collecting the cannisters and bombs. "Two birds with one stone. They get our stuff and they get us."

They agreed that they would tell Simon about their change in plan. They figured he would immediately be mad at himself for missing that possibility and learn from the lesson. Mike, with his natural optimism, argued that the Iranians would have to have tightened security around the two enrichment sites for the scenario to make sense and occur. And, since they apparently had not, the bombs and canisters were probably still safe. David agreed, but added, "Better safe than sorry."

Before finally turning in, David sent a signal to the remote heli-drone pilot, using the same flash of light technique he had used for prior distant communication, informing them of the change of plan. The reply was virtually immediate and simply said: "Fine."

He looked at the portrait of his wife and two children that was password protected in his tablet. *This thing's going too well*, was the last thought he had before falling asleep. Despite all the adrenalin that was flowing through his veins, he slept soundly.

CHAPTER.32

Albert, one of the Palmachim-based pilots of the heli-drone, thought to himself that *it was a good thing that Mike and Dave had siphoned gas from their car into the tank the prior day.* He was going to have to stay aloft longer than originally expected.

He flew the drone out of its hiding place toward the airstrip near and to the southeast of Kashan. To avoid detection, he chose to fly low and in the mountain ranges first in the direction of Ghamsar, about fifteen miles to the northwest. Once abeam Ghamsar, he continued following the terrain and was soon forced to fly very low in the flatlands, staying to the south and the east of Amir Kabir Industrial Town where he'd been told there were more risks of being noticed. He also avoided the farms that David had noticed south and east of the strip. He did not worry about radars: the heli-drone was small and covered with radar evading material. His biggest worry was the proverbial person in the field who might report seeing some unidentified flying object looking like a small helicopter to authorities. There were no remote-controlled toy helicopters around Kashan. So, they might be looking for the real thing and the plan could unravel. At the same time, he kept thinking that the night had already started falling. So, he also counted on the reasonable assumption that people would be praying *Isha* (the evening prayer Muslims must recite between twilight and midnight). That should minimize the number of people wandering outside. Plus, though the airstrip appeared not to be active, there was always the risk that it would be in use at that time—the odd military plane or helicopter landing.

David and Mike were able to capture the images from the heli-drone's two onboard cameras on their tablets. They obviously became much more focused on them as the drone was over the tarmac at the end of the runway and near the hangar; it flew a bit further toward the garrison as well and then hovered for a few seconds over the tarmac at the other end of the runway. They looked for any sign that something looked out of place. They saw nothing and concluded that either anyone waiting for them was particularly well-hidden, probably in the hangar, or that they had nerves of steel. The most reasonable conclusion had to be that there would be no surprise. David took over the heli-drone and turned it toward its hiding place. The remote pilot understood the signal and retraced its steps toward the mountain range, still working to avoid any detection. He did not go as far as the hiding place as the heli-drone needed to fly to the camp near Natanz where it would be needed for ferrying canisters to the excavators and cutting heads back to the Land Cruiser.

Mike and David parked the car farther than usual and still approached the hangar with a great deal of care and guns drawn. David went first in the direction of the front door of the hangar with Mike covering him. He noted that the door was still partially opened. Yet, more importantly, he confirmed that there was nobody in sight who could warn anyone inside the hangar of their arrival. *Better and better news,* he thought to himself. He then slowly and carefully pushed the door to the hangar wide open and saw that it was as empty as it had been the last time they were there: "All clear, Mike . . ."

While Mike returned to the Land Cruiser to park it in its normal spot, David walked around the hangar first on the tarmac in front and on the dirt path that led to the place where they had hidden the part of the load that the Koveshes had brought and which they had not yet taken with them. Mike quickly joined him. They were happy when they removed the camouflage tarp and saw that the canisters as well as the rest of the equipment were still there. They loaded the four acid canisters into the cargo bay of the Land Cruiser and reset the camouflage tarp over what was left to stay hidden and made way for the camp near Chaleh Qareh. They knew they would be a bit early vis-à-vis their original schedule but felt that it would be safer for them to wait there for full darkness than anywhere else.

When they arrived, they were quickly satisfied that, as usual, their "camp" had not been disturbed; they parked the car and waited for darkness to fall so that they could resume their operation. The heli-drone had already arrived and was waiting for them at a short distance, dictated by the fact that they did not want its rotor unnecessarily close to the trees that partially hid the truck from view. They checked the progress of the excavators on their tablets from the car and were delighted to see that they were right on schedule, and right on target with their gas consumption estimates. They would be at their target depth in the next half hour at most, so there would probably be some extra gas at the end of the mission.

"The extra gas in the tank will definitely help the explosion into the tunnel when the time comes." Mike noted.

They got out of the car, retrieved the jet packs from the trunk and donned them. They flew to their respective sites. Once again, luck seemed to be with them as they went totally unnoticed. They stopped the digging of their respective excavators and backed them out of the tunnel; they had to do this slowly as there was a fair amount of accumulated debris behind each of them. This debris had to be pushed back to the surface; this required a minimum of precaution to avoid any damage to the engines of the excavators from over-exertion. They allowed the debris to accumulate around the mouth of each tunnel as they had planned.

Turning to the reconfiguration of the excavators, they removed the cutting head fixed at the front of the machines, as well as the fan-like structure at the back, as it was now useless. They attached one to the other to minimize the number of loose parts; the circular fan was tiny and weighed next to nothing compared to the more substantial cutting head. The cutting head, in fact, accounted for at least a third of the four hundred fifty-pound weight of the whole excavator assembly. They noted that the two holes into which the canisters were supposed to fit were in perfect shape: no scratch, but a little bit of dirt that was easy to clean out. They verified that the spraying arms that would deploy were also in full working order. The cannisters would fit into the small holes, once cleaned up, and snapped into place; the back end of the canisters had a small female cavity into which a male protrusion would be mated. This snapping action would start the flow of acid into the spraying system. There were protective caps set on the nozzles at the tip of the spraying arms; their purpose was to ensure that nothing could damage them when the arms were folded along the sides of the excavators. Mike and Dave removed them, such that these nozzles could spray the two combined chemicals from the front of the excavator. All seemed to be in order. They signaled each other when they were done, with Mike beating David this time. They quickly spread the debris around the site, being careful again to have the new dirt dispersed in as even a manner as possible. They both reserved a small amount of dirt for future use.

David used the jet pack to fly back to camp while Mike stayed in position at the mouth of his tunnel. A set of three infra-red flashes in the air told Mike that things were on track when David returned to camp. David loaded the first two acid canisters and one of the extra gas containers onto the heli-drone. He flashed his infra-red light three times again to alert Mike that he was ready to send him the heli-drone. Seeing Mike's three-flash reply confirming that all was still clear, he dispatched the heli-drone. Mike unloaded the canisters and flashed three times. Three more flashes indicated David's acknowledgement, so Mike sent the heli-drone back to camp. Seeing the heli-drone over the last fence of the plant, David took over the controls and brought it to camp, where he loaded the last two canisters and the final extra gas container. He then took off at the same time as the drone in the direction of his tunnel.

For some reason he could not explain later other that sheer intuition, he changed the usual flight path and dove into the depression located just on the inside of the major fence at the north side of the protected perimeter. Something startled him. He could see activity in the barracks in the distance and hoped that it was just a minor issue. He hovered a couple of feet above ground, until he was sure that no intruder was in sight. He then continued to fly very low to the ground as he made his way, slowly so as to produce as little engine noise as possible, toward the entrance to his tunnel. Fortunately, the activity, though continuing, seemed to be heading in the opposite direction: *What in the world are they doing up and about at this time of the night? This is a Muslim country and those are Revolutionary guards; they can't have been drinking. Must be some sort of maneuver,* he thought to himself.

Once at the entrance to his tunnel, he quickly removed his digging screw and mounted the two canisters onto the excavator, topped up its gas tank and sent it on its way with its 400 pounds of chemicals which were designed to weaken the reinforced concrete structure.

Although no acid can do the trick perfectly, hydrochloric acid has the property of being able to dissolve both concrete and steel. Mixed with nitric acid, it makes a solution called *aqua regia*, which is even more powerful than hydrochloric acid alone. When exposed to steel or concrete, the chemical reaction will produce nitrogen oxides which are very toxic, but the team was not worried. They would be in Kashan while the acid did its trick; there was no risk that they would breathe any of these gases. Each canister contained about eighty liters each of the mixture which was scheduled to be released steadily over the ensuing twelve hours. The team in Tel Aviv expected that this would weaken considerably the massive reinforced concrete walls which protected both halls. It would make the next and final phase of the project much likelier to succeed and to inflict massive damage.

The excavators and their canisters were then sent back into the tunnels; they would start the spraying action at the bottom and slowly work their way back up when finished. As usual, they covered the hole with the tarp so no activity could be noticed from outside. But, to avoid the risk they would be overcome by the nitrogen oxide fumes as they came back and removed the tarps, they did not tuck the tarps as closely into the loose dirt around the mouth of the tunnel as they had earlier when the excavators were digging. They wanted to allow the fumes to escape as much as possible while they were safely away. In practice, that was not a problem as they did not need to see what was happening in the tunnels during the spraying phase; so, they switched off the lights and the cameras on the excavators, eliminating the need for the tarp to be as tight as it had been during the drilling phase. There was no light that could betray the activity.

Mike, whose work site was closer to the barracks, noticed again that there was noise from that direction, and he guessed that those were troop movements. His instincts told him they were getting closer. He spoke a quick note on his tablet and sent a flashlight message to David—two flashes—that told him to look at his computer tablet immediately. David read the message: "Put on the jet pack immediately. I see movement in the barracks. Let's be ready to escape before they get here. The moment you hear me start mine, start yours and fly due east, and as low to the ground as possible. No lights."

David replied with the same tool in the same way: "Roger; shame to get interrupted so close to the end. Send an end of caution signal— three flashes—as soon as you can: I've still got to fly the heli-drone back to you. Thought I saw and heard soldiers move as I was flying in . . . But they appeared to be going in the opposite direction."

"Roger; think they're moving closer now."

Mike came back on: "Moving still closer but coming for me . . . Not for you."

Keeping his attention on Mike and a possible signal from him, David fixed his cutting head onto the heli-drone, laboring a bit more than normally would be the case as he was doing it with the jet pack strapped firmly to his torso and his body tense with caution. He waited for Mike's signal for what seemed like an eternity. Mike was still not ready to give the all-clear. The noise was not getting closer but was not moving away either.

David noted: "Definitely from the barracks. Saw a light, but nothing now."

"Hope they're not ambushing us."

"We've got the jet packs. Let me move a few steps to get a better view . . ."

A few seconds later, his message came back: "I see them. They're in front of their barracks. No search light."

A minute or two later, Mike flashed three times, when the noise from the troops seemed to be receding. David thought to himself, *Must be a part of some patrol rotation routine, but, if it is, don't understand why we haven't seen them anywhere near the fences between here and the camp.*

David picked up the signal and flew the heli-drone to Mike who attached the cutting head and fan. He did not wait for Mike to be finished with his work but flew back to the Land Cruiser; he waited for Mike to join him, with the heli-drone in tow. They unloaded the materials and put them in the cargo bay together with the jet packs and the empty gas containers while the heli-drone flew back to its hiding place up in the hills.

They noted that it was a shame that they had to get the cutters out of the perimeter of the plant when they knew that they would have to get them back into the plant area and eventually send them down the holes. But taking them along now was needed; they could not risk them being discovered. They had to send them down the holes, since they had no way of taking them with them back to Israel and would certainly not leave them out in the open to be eventually discovered: "No trace" was still the *modus operandi*.

Within a second of noticing that the excavators had reached the lower end of their tunnels, Mike and David triggered the start of the spraying from their tablets and returned home while that work was going on. On their drive to Kashan, Mike observed that he might have an explanation for the occasional noise they'd heard from the barracks.

"What if it simply was some sort of patrol rotation."

"Exactly what I'd thought, my friend."

Discussing why they had not ever seen any patrol anywhere near the area between the camp and the tunnels, they agreed that this might simply be due to the fact that they had the no man's land between the two fences somehow protected, maybe by a mine field. So, the Iranians thought that the sector was safe, which, the agents noted, their team and its actions so far had proven a faulty assumption. David concluded: "They might just be running their patrols, if that's what it was, between the barracks and the main gate."

As they were getting close to the flat, David as the good leader that he was, reminded Mike that all the work they had done so far was only the prep work. He added: "The real thing comes when fire and brimstone rains on the place."

"Yeah, I know and I'm looking forward to it."

CHAPTER.33

MAY 7
QOM

As planned, Nathan and Daniel arrived at Amir's apartment building at exactly 7:45 a.m. Amir was already downstairs, near the garage door. When he saw the car approaching, he came out on the sidewalk and motioned them into the parking garage. After the usual greetings and small talk, which Nathan was trying to keep to a minimum, they asked Amir how the work with the cameras and the video surveillance system had gone. He replied that it had worked like a charm, and that he was able to get everything done, and done well the first time. The four play-back machines were programmed for 12:35 a.m. the next morning, or on May eighth. He explained that he wanted to give himself five minutes leeway, if he needed to banter a bit longer than usual with the guards at the main gate, or any other unplanned delay.

Both Nathan and Daniel showed appreciation, though, as usual, Nathan was visibly more reserved. Daniel asked Amir how the external fences were protected at Fordow. He replied matter-of-factly that there was an electrical system, adding that it was not meant to electrocute and kill an intruder, but just to stun him and, more importantly, to alert the guards to check that general area.

Turning to the business at hand, they showed to him the two suitcases that were still in the trunk of their car. Daniel warned him that they were heavy but not insurmountably so. He added that one was a bit heavier than the other, but the difference was minimal. Also, since they were on rollers, he told Amir that he shouldn't have to make more than one trip. Amir concurred arguing that two trips might look a bit suspect. He told Dan and Nate that he had already made up an answer should anyone question the contents; he would say that they contained extra surveillance equipment that he would be testing. Daniel and Nathan congratulated him.

Amir asked whether they were locked. The guys looked a bit surprised, wondering why one would worry about that. He replied that he wanted to have trouble opening them if he was asked to show the contents. It took a while for Dan to appreciate the smarts behind the question and the desire to have the suitcases locked. Amir explained that he would not be able to open the cases readily, if they were locked. Rather, he would have to be fumbling through his pockets for the keys. He added: "Knowing the people around here, they'd tell me not to worry and I'd move on."

Finally understanding Amir, Daniel congratulated him for the idea and told him that they were actually not locked but could be. They each had a lock and the keys were attached to the handle. So, he could easily lock them and remove the keys.

Daniel and Nathan each unloaded a suitcase from the trunk of their rental and placed them, standing up, next to Amir's car. Amir opened his trunk and lifted the first suitcase. He let out a small cry: "Sharks. You weren't kidding when you said they were heavy."

Nate replied that they weighed between seventy and eighty pounds each. Though it surely was more than a standard suitcase, it was not inconsistent with Amir's proposed explanation that they contained surveillance equipment.

As they needed to create space for the second suitcase, they moved Amir's own suitcase, the one he would take on his flight out of Iran, further back into the trunk. Daniel observed that he was not taking much along. Amir said that this was Afri's instruction. He had to be credible as someone going on a vacation. So, he could only have the one suitcase with whatever one would expect him to wear on vacation, plus a carry-on that had a few personal items. He confessed that he had hidden things like pictures of his late wife and a few others that he would really like to keep; he added that these were among the kind of things that one would expect him to take with him from the plant. The idea was that he could react if anything happened at the plant and someone there called him. With a smile, he concluded that he did not need much: "I'm starting a new life . . ."

Seeing the surprised look of Daniel, he explained that he hoped that Afri would agree to become his wife.

"She's so wonderful. She's saved me from this place, from these murderers who killed my poor Nina, my dear, first wife."

Daniel replied that they had not known any of those details and were sincerely sorry about his first wife. Nate added that they had never met Afri either. They wished him the best of luck. Switching gears, Dan reminded Amir that they would meet him at the corner of the second road on the left, after he turned onto this main drag at 12:30 a.m. tomorrow morning. He added: "Is it still OK to count on thirty minutes to go from here to starting the work in the hall?"

"Absolutely, I'll meet you then."

Amir asked them what their plans were for the rest of the day. Nathan answered in as flat a manner as he could that they had a number of loose ends to tie up. Amir left for the plant.

They drove back to the apartment and started packing. The day was going to be pretty full. They knew that their main task was to find a way to appear to be leaving Iran without truly leaving. This was going to be very interesting and almost as challenging as their work at the plant, but not quite . . .

Once they finished packing, they first did a complete sweep of the apartment to make absolutely sure that they'd left nothing behind. There could not be anything that could remotely be traced to unknown persons that might have used the flat. They noted to each other that they had been incredibly lucky not to have run into anyone in the building. That removed the need for them to explain their presence. So, no one could possibly tell the police anything that might give them the idea that they should comb the flat, though "you never know" as Nathan had said. Still, they felt that they should not take any risk. They went as far as erasing any fingerprints that they may have left behind; they wiped virtually everything probably cleaner than it had been in a while. They directed most of their attention to the dining room table and its immediate vicinity. C-4 powder or residue might have rubbed off the explosive sheets as they had been placed on the floor or on top of the table, awaiting their turn for testing and final assembly. Forensic experts would love to get their hands on anything like that.

Since both of them had had some experience on the "other side," investigating crime scenes, they knew where to look, and had particularly well-trained senses. Through the years, their teachers had explained to them that what makes a great detective was not what he or she saw directly. A keen sense of active observation was a given. The critical difference between normal observers and great detectives was brains that were trained to notice unusual patterns. They called it diffuse attention, or involuntary observation. Thus, they might be looking straight ahead while their brain would be noticing something in their peripheral field of vision that, somehow, did not look right. It was very much like the engineer who saw that a particular formula could not be correct or the business manager who knew that a forecast or a set of numbers could not be right even if the junior person who prepared it swore it was accurate. Thus, they made at least two, full passes each. The first, they were looking for anything visible. The second time around, they were casually looking around, without directing their attention to anything in particular, hoping to notice the unusual; it could be a light reflection that should not be, a dot that was the wrong color or a couple of things that did not line up the way they should. Suddenly, Dan exclaimed: "Well, am I glad I found this baby."

It was a lithium-ion battery. It was one eighth of an inch thick and no more than a third of an inch in diameter. It would have been so easy to miss, but it would surely be enough to get people's juices flowing. He said that he had thought they had put the three that they found to be defective directly into the suitcase. But he concluded that this one must have rolled out somehow. He added that it was a good thing that it had rolled off the suitcase but didn't go any further.

When they were fully satisfied that they could not and would not find anything further, they decided to leave the flat. First, Nathan went out by himself, carrying the same piece of luggage he had when he arrived. Only a very astute observer, who had been there and looking at him at the beginning, would notice that the color of his hair was different than when he came in and that the goatee was gone. Also, his second piece of luggage, his carry-on, looked a bit heavier. Where else would he have put the ammunition for the gun that the first Kovesh flight had delivered, together with the night vision goggles?

He went down to the garage. Satisfied that he had not been followed, he stepped out onto the sidewalk to make sure he had a direct satellite line of sight and sent a quick "all clear" message to Daniel. He, too, left and locked the flat, and went straight down to the garage. They had agreed that he would drive Minoo's car while Nathan would drive the rental. They loaded their luggage in Minoo's car and drove together to the rental car agency on Emam Khomeini, the nearest avenue.

They took the time to stop at the gas station and fill up the rental car. They drove to the agency and parked the car in the space provided at the front of the shop. The agent was a bit surprised that they would return the car not only early, but also in Qom rather than at the airport. As all good customer service people do, he asked whether there was something wrong with the car. Daniel replied in German-accented English that all was well, but that they were lucky to be able to finish their work much faster than they thought. They flattered the agent with a compliment about Iranians and how they were very smart and worked quickly. Nathan added a further layer saying that scientists in Iran were very advanced, knew their work well and could do things at twice the speed of Europeans.

The clerk's English was not great. So, in truth, he probably understood less than a third of what they were saying, but they looked sincere and smiled a lot. So, he smiled back and nodded with some local pride as he had understood the piece about Iranians being smart. He asked the normal questions: "Is the car full of gas?"

Nathan could not reply because a nasty thought linking beans and being full of gas came to his mind. He almost lost it. But Daniel answered that they had just filled the car up at the nearby station.

"Gasoline's pretty cheap here," he added.

"Locals don't think so," the clerk replied.

The clerk asked them to wait while he printed the bill. Commenting on the bill, he pointed apologetically to the fact that there was a penalty because the car was returned in town and not at the airport, in Tehran. Daniel said he understood and they both exited the agency.

There followed a short "explanation" between them, with Daniel asking Nathan what was wrong with him.

"I don't know, Daniel. But the "full of gas" got to me. Sorry."

"Well, I guess it shows you're human. What self-respecting professional field operative would do something as dumb as that?"

Daniel winked at Nathan who understood it was all a joke. Nathan was still somewhat mad at himself for having almost lost his self-control. He mentally blamed it on stress and filed it in a remote corner of his brain "for further review," as he often said. They walked around the block until they reached the spot where they had parked Minoo's car. They had thought *it should be somewhat out of the way; there was no need for the clerk to see them return a car and immediately drive the same model out.* "Too many questions; too many unnecessary questions" they had agreed.

Dan's and Nate's next jobs were to pretend they were leaving the country, though they obviously were not. They had to make it appear they would be going through immigration and security control and then be boarding their flight. However, they also had to find a way to stay in Iran. They would have preferred to return the car in Tehran, at the airport, as that would have been the normal thing to do. But they did not want to risk being seen entering the airport parking lot with two cars: "Why would two foreign guys flying together drive two different cars?" they had asked. Hence, the decision to return their rental car in Qom and to drive to the airport in Minoo's car. That was now done.

The next steps would by far be the most difficult.

CHAPTER.34

MAY 7
TEHRAN AIRPORT

The first order of business for Dan and Nate was for the two of them to exchange their air tickets so that they could be leaving today rather than in four days, as originally planned. That, they felt, would not be terribly hard. Yet, the short time between now and the boarding of their flight might still make it problematic. People change their flights, even at the last minute, all the time; but they usually give themselves a bit more time. Clearly, changing flights was less likely an occurrence in a place like Tehran than at any major airport in Europe, Asia or North America where it happens every day. Still, it had to be done. Once they had their new boarding passes, passport control and airport security should not be terribly difficult. The most challenging would be to appear to board the plane without really boarding it, and then to find a way to exit the terminal without being noticed.

They parked the car in the parking lot and took the two bigger suitcases. These contained the clothing and toiletry items which people would expect the two German scientists to carry back with them. They left their carry-on luggage in the trunk of the car; they kept their guns as everything was made of ceramic: the guns, the silencers, the magazines and a round of bullets for each; none of these would be visible on any security camera, particularly since they had deemed that security arrangements were somewhere between poor and abysmal.

They went straight to the Turkish Airlines ticket office and asked whether they could have seats on the next flight, leaving at 3:55 p.m. The flight would take them to Istanbul, with a connecting flight to Frankfurt, at least that was what their tickets indicated. These were actually the same flights and routing as the original itinerary. When asked why they were changing their plans, they gave the clerk the same story they'd told the car rental agent. They were pleased when they heard there were two seats left and even more pleased to know that they would have to agree to fly economy. Under normal circumstances, this might have been unpleasant news, as their original tickets were for first class. However, considering their intention to "disappear" before take-off, the limited number of passengers in first class and the added attention paid to them by the cabin crew, would have made their absence more noticeable.

They accepted the two seats which the clerk offered and waited for her to print their boarding passes. They asked the ticket agent to check them only to Istanbul. Nathan explained that it was an old superstition of his never to book the connecting flight, until he had landed at the intermediate airport. The agent looked at him quizzically, but, in the end, did as she was told, mentioning that she could then only check their luggage to Istanbul as well. They would have to retrieve them in Istanbul and recheck them. Dan and Nate said they understood and were OK with that. They received the appropriate luggage receipt tags for their suitcases. They would eventually scan these tags with their cell phones and send them to a *Mossad* agent in Istanbul so that someone there knew to claim and pick the suitcases up.

Their decision not to be checked through to Frankfurt and for the luggage to be picked up in Istanbul obviously had nothing to do with superstition nor the desire not to lose whatever was in the suitcases. Rather, they assumed that their absence from the Tehran to Istanbul flight would not be noticed. They further assumed that their luggage being picked up in Istanbul together with the office in Istanbul cancelling their Istanbul to Frankfurt leg even before their first flight had landed in Istanbul would remove any risk that anyone would find something odd. The only odd bit could be the late cancellation or change of flight in Tehran, but that was minor. This was much better than running the risk of the suitcases being left on the carousel at the airport, either in Istanbul or Frankfurt, or for someone to notice that they had not made their flight to Frankfurt. Someone would be bound to check immigration records and see neither of them having entered Turkey. The suspicion would have to arise that they never were on the initial flight and thus that they had stayed in Tehran.

Once checked-in, they proceeded directly to passport control. They were a bit early for the flight, but not so much as to arouse suspicion. Passport control went smoothly; the officers only looked at the passports and the boarding passes. As anticipated, the change in departure date was not an issue; the officers could not know about it. Also, the guns went through security unnoticed, which did not surprise them. These guns had been tested through security at Ben Gurion where the equipment reflects the latest technology. If you could get through security there, you could get through security anywhere.

This was the fourth time Daniel and Nathan had travelled through Tehran. They had twice flown in and departed once. As trained agents, they knew to keep their eyes wide open, particularly as they knew they would eventually have to deal with the problem which was now theirs. So, they kept observing the way security procedures were implemented, what seemed to be tight and what appeared looser; where there were police guards and where there were none. They had, in particular, made a note that security seemed very tight getting into the actual terminal, until you were in the concourse and gate areas. Once there, it looked noticeably lax.

Their plan was to try and get an early boarding onto the plane and then to find a way to disembark before the plane left the gate. The idea was simple. They wanted their boarding passes to be entered into the system, failing which the airline would be calling them on loudspeakers and wasting time removing their luggage from the hold. This would undoubtedly draw the attention of the security agents. More ominously, the fact that their luggage had been taken off the plane would give a clear indication later on that they had not left Iran. In short, they had to get off the plane, but not their luggage. This would underscore the assumption that they were indeed on the flight and had left Iran.

Managing to come off the plane should not be hard; they had seen people do that in several airports around the world. The challenge would be to stay off the plane, until it left the gate. The risk that remained was that a flight attendant might notice they were not on board and start looking for them—being in the economy cabin made that easier. They had two seats that were not next to each other; that would help, too. With the airplane, as usual, only about 50% full in the economy class, cabin crew personnel would be much less likely to notice that two passengers were missing if they were not seated together. People frequently changed seats before take-off. *Mossad* had Minoo and Sarah confirm—and both Daniel and Nate had noted it on their earlier flights—that Turkish airlines did not seem to perform a passenger count before closing the aircraft door. They relied on boarding passes being swiped as passengers came in, as well as a manual count at that time to confirm the number passengers boarded matched the flight manifest. The assumption was that everyone was onboard if those numbers matched. Many other airlines, El Al among others, routinely did a routine headcount of passengers as the aircraft door was about to be closed. Such a routine would have made Nate's and Dan's plan unfeasible. So, they were pleased that all airlines were not equally meticulous.

Daniel approached the agents at the desk about forty-five minutes before flight time and asked if they could board early. He explained that his friend needed a bit more time than others to get settled. He said he needed to take medication because he was afraid of flying and being on board early allowed the pill to take effect while the environment around him was still calm. The fact that the story was consistent with the "superstition" that Nathan had claimed at check-in was a nice touch though unlikely to matter. At the same time, the story did not seem to fuss the boarding agent, who immediately indicated that this would be OK and accompanied them on board; she even provided the glass of water that Nathan would need to swallow his medicine which, in fact, was only a sugar pill. They settled in their seats. The moment actual boarding started, they made their way back to the door and asked to go briefly outside to look for a cell phone they thought they had left either in the concourse or in the gate area. Daniel continued playing the role of the person watching over his friend, Nathan, mumbling that it was stupid to have lost his phone and smiling a lot.

The phone had to have fallen while they were waiting in the gate area or when they bought a coffee a bit further back in the concourse. Surprisingly, but also fortunately, the flight attendant did not object. She let them both deplane but reminded them to have their boarding passes with them when they returned. They checked that she made no manipulation that would remove them from the passenger count. They emerged from the jet bridge without being noticed by the gate agent who was busy checking the other passengers onto the flight. They first pretended to check around the gate area and then moved away in the direction of the concourse as quickly as they could without drawing attention. They found restrooms one gate area down toward the terminal. They walked in and waited there. They took turns going into and out of the stalls. They busied themselves washing their hands, listening for any announcement that was made in the concourse.

Daniel was amazed that the ploy seemed to be working so well, but he gave the credit to Minoo and Sarah. The two women, as instructed, had tested boarding early, deplaning airplanes and re-boarding on other Turkish Airlines flights or on their own and had found it quite uncomplicated. They had never done it with two people simultaneously nor had they ever not re-boarded a flight, which was where the additional information about the airline not doing a final passenger count was so important. Yet, he was still amazed that making a final passenger count was not standard procedure for all airlines.

They waited in the restrooms until the flight was called, and they had concluded that the gate finally closed. They then proceeded to walk down the concourse back toward the main body of the terminal. Daniel noted that Phase 1 was complete, to which Nate replied that Phase 2 could be more difficult.

Another observation they had made in prior passages through the airport, also confirmed by Sarah and Minoo, was that most of the doors from the concourse to the tarmac were neither secured nor even locked. The two agents were used to the alarmed doors with keypads that are prevalent in the West but only found plain doors with what appeared to be locks that were not even used. Employees appeared to walk to a door and open it without so much as turning a key. They had, therefore, decided that they would escape through one of these doors. They would find their way downstairs and eventually look for the domestic part of the terminal. They assumed that the lower level of the terminal contained the luggage handling complex, something which Minoo had confirmed based on broad architectural drawings, though neither she nor Sarah had been able to check this personally, given the obvious questions and suspicions that this might have prompted.

They had concluded that hiding in a luggage handling area would not be too hard, given the confusion that often reigns in there, though obviously it would be less congested in a small airport like Tehran than in much busier places like Atlanta, Amsterdam, Dubai or Singapore. What would be hard, they were certain, would be to exit from the international complex and enter the domestic side. This was where security appeared to be, by far, the tightest.

So, they sat near one of these doors, waiting for an opportunity.

Nathan jumped when they saw a worker come back into the terminal. He politely held the door for him and smiled at him. The employee returned the smile and went about his business walking to one of the nearby gate areas as if nothing had happened. Nathan slipped behind him and through the door, out of the concourse, without triggering any obvious reaction. He was immediately surprised to see that the door did not lead to an external staircase, as he had expected. He cursed himself for not having looked at the outside of the terminal as they had taxied to it the prior times. He would have seen then that there was no external stairway. This would have given him a warning. Here, he found himself at the top of an internal staircase, which led down to what looked like a small, landing area with another door on the right-hand side. He made a sign to Daniel through the small window on the door to wait a while. He reached out to his gun in the holster against his left calf, verified that the silencer was screwed on properly and went down the stairs. The next door had a rectangular, vertical window nearly eight inches wide and two feet tall; he looked through it to assess the situation on the other side. He saw a big hall, with a lot of luggage carts and what looked like a few conveyer belts. He breathed a sigh of relief, "Just what the doctor ordered."

He ran back up and gave the OK sign to Daniel. Daniel approached the door with caution. Once he was sure that no one was watching, he made a sign to Nathan who opened the door. Dan slipped through it, too. Nathan joked that Dan really did not need him to open the door. He could simply have pressed the handle down and he could have opened the door by himself. Daniel noticed the obvious at that point: the staircase was internal. He immediately mumbled that *"whoever had designed it could have saved themselves the trouble and built an external staircase like everywhere else. It would be a lot easier to secure and police."* Nate countered that Dan was absolutely right from the point of view of security, but that, Thank God, it was not their job to make Tehran Airport more secure.

Fortunately, it was exactly as they had hoped: a luggage handling hall, as big and cluttered as one would anticipate. Seeing no one nearby, they checked their guns and silencers, before again making sure the coast was clear and opening the door. They walked quickly to the first luggage cart they could find; it was less than twenty feet away. Nate whispered: "So far, so good"

Looking around, they could not see any obvious sign of where the domestic side of the terminal was. However, based on the layout of the upper part of the terminal, Daniel assumed that they needed to go left. He added: "From here, can't see anything that looks different. But, upstairs, I counted six gates, three on either side before ours. So, we've got at least that far to go, before we get to the split, between domestic and international areas."

Nathan looked in the direction indicated by Dan and said that a good guess would be that the split, between international and domestic, might well be at the far wall they could see. Dan gave a sign that he agreed. They still could not see how to go from one area to the other, but decided they had to move and get as close to the wall as they could. They chose to move as inconspicuously as possible and one at a time while he was being covered by the other, until they reached the wall, they had both seen when they entered the hall. From where they were, they could see a door about 100 feet to their right but had no idea where the door led. It also had a small window on it, but they had not observed it long enough to know how often it was used.

They were debating whether it was or was not a door to the other side of the terminal when they heard a small noise. They crouched down behind luggage carts nearby. The door opened slowly, and someone entered . . .

CHAPTER.35

MAY 7
KASHAN AND NATANZ

By late-afternoon, Mike and David were repeating the steps they'd taken the prior day, but with a different goal. They made a last, detailed search of their Kashan apartment to ensure they had not left anything behind that could betray either their identities or national origins. When they had initially rented the apartment, under their assumed identities, they'd indicated that their stay, which was planned to last no longer than a week to ten days, was a research mission. The fact that they had worked at their real mission during the night and slept in the early morning hours still gave them plenty of time in the late morning and afternoon to conduct mock research and remain believable, if anybody had been watching.

However, now that they were leaving, they had to make sure that nothing was left that could possibly be traced back to Israel. In fact, their search produced absolutely nothing as they had been extremely careful the whole time not to have anything that could be incriminating. Most consumable toiletries and related personal items, for instance, had been bought locally as one would expect to be the case for local businessmen. Anything that was not, had been bought in Dubai, to fit with their story. Similarly, the *Mossad* had been careful to procure clothing that they could have bought in the United Arab Emirates and would be in the middle of the available price range there, as would fit the social status of their official cover. They planned on leaving consumables in the apartment as well as any dirty clothes. Thus, any subsequent search of the apartment by the lessor would only reveal that the lessees had left in a hurry.

They had sent the heli-drone ahead of them from its "resting location," as they called it, to the airstrip to check that all was still clear. As the images from the drone seemed to indicate it was, they drove in and parked as usual at the back of the hangar. They still conducted the same search of the area, approaching the front of the hangar with guns drawn as they had the previous time, but felt considerably less anxious now. They reached the cache at the back of the hangar and retrieved the sixteen bombs which had been stored there. Before loading them into the Land Cruiser, they were careful to check the security of the black plastic rings which prevented anything but a massive impact from causing the detonators to trigger the bombs These were tightly fastened around the vertical pin which would trigger the bomb if it were depressed. Typically, a shock would be enough to trigger the mechanism, for instance as the bombs drop from the air onto their targets. The team, therefore, had to find an engineering solution to ensure that the bombs did not explode until they were supposed to. The plastic rings had been engineered specially for this mission and were thus designed to withstand an impact of five hundred pounds hitting at more than ten miles per hour. The plan was to roll the bombs down on top of one another into the tunnels, and, hopefully, into the cavities in the ceilings of the two enrichment halls that had been created by the action of the aqua regia on the reinforced concrete. This could create quite an impact and they needed to hold off detonating the bombs, until the first missile hit and detonated them all simultaneously.

After the bombs were loaded into the car, the heli-drone was sent to the camp at Chaleh Qareh, via the mountain ranges to minimize the risk of detection. Once at the camp themselves, David and Mike were preparing, first, to ferry the bombs from the camp to each of the two sites and, then, to roll them down into the tunnels. They elected to use what David now called "the low route" for the heli-drone; staying close to the ground, in the depression just south of the main fence, minimized the risk of detection. That risk was especially important as they calculated they would need four heli-drone trips, each carrying four bombs which would be placed into a net fastened to the hook under the drone.

Once there, they rolled the bombs gently into position at the mouth of each of the tunnels. They had planned for a length of rope to be used to lower the bombs rather than dropping them into the tunnels; they worried that the speed these might gain over the ninety-five odd feet to their final location, combined with their own weight might create a force strong enough to test the resistance of the plastic rings. A small, circular handle near the pin was used to thread the rope. They pushed the rope through it and let the bomb move slowly into position until a depth of around eighty-five feet, the original depth of the tunnel. They released one end of the rope and thus the bomb allowing it to free fall the last few feet into position. Though it slowed the execution of that phase, it eliminated the risk of involuntary explosion. At the same time, some downward momentum for the bombs was necessary. Mike and David needed the bombs to build some speed as they got to the lower reaches of the tunnels. The walls of the tunnel in the area that had been melted or eaten away by the acid were likely not smooth; in fact, the agents fully expected the odd reinforcement bar might still be protruding into or remaining across the tunnel opening. They needed the bombs to have enough momentum to be able to bend or displace whatever steel reinforcement or semi-loose concrete blocks might be there or be tumbling.

By the time the last bomb rolled in, and David was still able to let it drop beyond the eighty-five-foot depth point, he was visibly elated. He thought to himself that *even if the excavators did not stop at their maximum digging depth, the depth at which it seemed the last bomb settled had to mean the acid had melted almost exactly the amount of steel or concrete that the lab guys expected.* He concluded that it probably left only a limited amount of concrete over the actual ceiling of the hall and that a small layer of concrete should not be an issue for the bombs to burst through when they were detonated.

Once the bombs were down each tunnel, David and Mike, each at his own site, threw the remaining unneeded material into the tunnels. First, they removed the acid canisters from the excavators and flung them into the open holes. Then, they folded back the spraying system against the sides of the excavators and re-attached the cutting heads and their tiny fans and sent the excavators down the tunnels. They felt it was a shame to waste such great equipment, but, if the choice was between having themselves or the excavators onboard the Koveshes, it was the world's easiest decision. They also dumped the shovels, netting, ropes and extra minor equipment they had been using.

David then carefully replaced the tarp on top of the entrance to his tunnel and secured it with the same small rocks he had been using for the last three days. He then swept the small amount of dirt he had reserved onto the tarp to further hide it. Finally, he slid a small piece of metal just under the dirt and on top of the tarp.

"This isn't the time for anyone to find the tunnels"

As he finished his thought, he caught a glimpse of three infra-red light-flashes from the area where Mike had been carrying out exactly the same maneuvers.

"Mike's ready too." he immediately concluded.

He flashed his reply to his partner as pre-agreed and the two of them flew with their jet packs back to the Land Cruiser. Maybe by force of habit or simply not wishing to do anything silly near the end of a mission, they flew very low to the ground into the depression between the mounds hiding the two halls and the fence, over the first fence and almost at ground level through the no man's land, being careful not to touch it now that they thought that *it might hide a mine field*. Once over the last fence, they made a slight right turn and flew into the small stand of trees which had become their base camp for nearly a week. There, they loaded the jet packs into the car and drove back to Kashan. They sent a message to the heli-drone operator that they should keep it at the camp for another half hour or so and then fly it to the airstrip. They were thinking that there was no point having the heli-drone fly to the strip and being detected before it was absolutely necessary. The final phase of the mission was going to be the most complicated—and one where no error was allowed.

CHAPTER.36

MAY 7
TEHRAN AIRPORT

Nathan and Daniel walked carefully in the direction of the man, using the cover provided by luggage carts strewn about the place. They noticed that he seemed unarmed and that he was wearing a uniform that suggested he worked for the airport and not for the police or the army. They saw him move to the other end of the hall. They kept watching him carefully but started to move slowly toward the door. Daniel moved parallel to the wall to get closer to the door, but also to position himself between the door and the man, who increasingly looked like a luggage handler. What was he doing? He moved around the hall but did not seem to do anything. Initially, it appeared as if he was moving a couple of luggage carts, but, in the end, he left them untouched. He looked at a pile of luggage sitting near the back wall, but, again, left them untouched. Neither Dan nor Nate could make any sense of his activity.

As Nate was getting to the door, it opened again, and another Iranian came through. He saw Nate, who managed to intercept him immediately and sting him, with a needle hidden in the crest ring he was wearing on his right pinky. The drug put the poor luggage handler to sleep and would erase from his memory any trace of the encounter.

Unfortunately, as Nathan grabbed him, he let go a small cry which his colleague picked up. He could not see what was happening, nor could he see either Daniel or Nate, but he started walking toward their end of the hall. As he came within jumping distance from Daniel, Dan caught him and administered the same drug, with the same effects. At the same time, Daniel and Nathan now had to worry about the fact that they were leaving some trace of their passage behind. The men would not remember them or what had happened, but something had to have happened for both of them to "fall asleep" at the same time and on the job.

Nathan dug into his pocket and produced a business card of the Espinas Hotel in Tehran. Simon had asked Sarah to get a couple of these business cards for the team in case they would need them. With the card conveniently dropped near the second sleeping luggage handler, any action which the Iranians might undertake to look for a potential aggressor would likely, initially at least, be aimed toward Tehran to the north rather than Qom to the south. Plus, neither of the two luggage handlers would know how many people were involved in the attack. For all they both knew, it could be the work of a solitary wolf. That might even add to the terrorist storyline . . .

Nathan took the risk of looking through the window on the door to see whether there was any sign of more activity on the other side. He concluded that it was indeed the domestic luggage handling hall that was on the other side of the wall and the door.

Nathan told Daniel then that the space on the other side of the wall looked identical to the one where they were, but less well-maintained, but maybe more active. They peered through the window again and could see some activity some distance away, but there was no one near the other side of the door at least. They quietly and discreetly snuck through the door into the domestic luggage hall. Not only was the space less well-maintained, but the luggage was much more ragged. They looked down and peaked at a luggage tag; they saw that the flight on which it came had originated in Isfahan.

"We're in the low-rent district."

For the first time in an hour or so, they felt that they had done the hardest part. Yet, they knew they were still not home free. They might be on the domestic side of the terminal, but still in the luggage handling area, not in a truly public area. They still needed to get to baggage claim, on the other side of yet another wall. They looked around and saw a couple of large openings in the opposite wall, with what looked like a number of dark rubber strips hanging down from the frames around them. They immediately concluded that these had to be the openings through which oversized luggage was hand-carried to passengers. They wondered why there were two rather than a single opening and simply concluded that this had probably been the original baggage delivery system and that carousels had been installed later. In fact, there were a couple of more traditional carousels a bit further to their right. Dan and Nate briefly debated what would be safest way to get to the arrival hall, the carousels or the old windows with rubber strips; they quickly concluded that latter had to be the best solution. Not only would they have to walk in the opposite direction of where they eventually wanted to go if they chose the carousels but arriving passengers would also likely be congregating around them, not to mention the risk of coming face to face with a luggage handler.

So, they each approached one of the two rubber strip window openings and put their prayer caps on, thinking that this would allow them to be as innocuous as possible. Daniel stuck his head discreetly through the strips to make sure that no one was on the other side. It was deserted, except for a few travelers who, as expected, were waiting for their luggage near the carousels, some distance away. They returned their guns to their holsters and carefully slipped through the rubber strips. They breathed a sigh of relief without saying a word to each other. They exited the arrival area following the signs that pointed toward the parking lot and carefully walked to their parked car, making sure they were not being followed. Once in the car, they both let out an audible sigh of relief.

"And we didn't even have to fire a gun."

"Good thing. They'd be looking for the killer if we'd left a body behind."

They paid the parking fee and began the drive back to Qom, feeling cautiously optimistic. So far, the plan was unfolding exactly as designed. No snafu, only their concern about Amir, but that was something they thought they could manage. At least, Simon didn't seem worried about him. They would have to control their feelings but remain very cautious. There was no remaining trace of them in the Qom area, and they had managed to leave the country officially. They still had a few hours before they were to meet Amir, so they decided to take the drive leisurely. They could feel their blood pressure rise a bit each time they passed a police car on one side or the other of the highway, and Nathan could not help but keep his gun on his lap rather than tucked in the holster. Dan noted: "Man, you're really nervous . . ."

Nathan argued that nervous might not be the right word. He just wanted to be ready if anything happened. Dan remarked that he would only become nervous if he saw several police cars. That might signal that the Iranians had figured the whole thing out. But he added that, if that happened, it would not make much difference whether the gun was in his lap or in the holster. They would be "cooked." Nate remarked that he would rather be able to kill a few of these guys before they killed him, because one thing was for sure: "You know what it means to be arrested by these guys . . ."

Daniel agreed, but trying to calm the nerves of his friend, he made the point that the car was pretty unassuming. The license plate was pretty ordinary, too. The university sticker on the windshield wouldn't be visible to a passing police car, but, even if anybody noticed, that would probably make them more innocuous rather than not; it could not be taken for a rental car. Nate replied that he knew all that, but that Simon's words were etched in his brain: "A good agent is a live one."

They kept bantering back and forth on the same theme, most probably because talking of the obvious risks and the fears that normally went with a mission allowed them to feel gradually more secure. It is indeed one of the great fallacies spread by spy novels or movies that agents should be viewed as daredevils and almost fearless. In reality, fear is a very important emotion that agents are taught not to deny or suppress. Instead they're trained to control and manage it. They're taught to avoid allowing it to paralyze them. In fact, they're told to channel it positively, for instance, by staying on their toes and allowing their instincts to operate in milliseconds when the adrenaline is flowing.

They ran again into a police barrage, pretty much in the same spot as the last time they travelled that road. Nathan fumed and swore. Daniel told him to cool it, in the hope that they would be able to proceed with no problem. They were still ready for any eventuality, as the roadblock was only manned by two police officers. Dan and Nate knew they were on a mission and always needed to be on their guard. They needed to be able to act and use their weapon if needed and yet look "normal" if the stop did not lead to a confrontation.

CHAPTER.37

As they approached the officer at the roadblock, he caught sight of the university sticker on the windshield. He waved Dan and Nate through without requiring them to stop. This confirmed to them both that they looked quite a bit more local than foreign, particularly with their prayer caps on and that they shouldn't worry for as long as they acted naturally.

The sun had set on the valley by the time they arrived at the point, north of Qom, where they were to veer off and drive in the direction of the Fordow plant. They had grabbed the bits of *sowhan* that were left in their carry-on luggage together with a couple of sandwiches they had bought, as they were walking to their boarding gate in Tehran. They started munching on the sandwiches and reserved the sweets for later. Though certain field agents did not like to be early on the scene of future activities, Dan and Nate were the opposite. They thought *it was sheer superstition that made people not want to fill themselves with the environment.*

Daniel kept saying that he wanted to be on location as if he had always been there. Every sight had to have a second-nature dimension to him. Nate agreed and noted that they did not want to discover something that they should have known and did not, simply because they had not taken the extra one, two or three steps. He added that he would love to be doing more reconnaissance work around the plant and within the fenced-in perimeter but knew they could not do that. Yet he had suggested that there was plenty of stuff just outside the perimeter that they should know better. Dan had readily agreed. Nate argued that working in such low light circumstances should also help their eyes get better adjusted. Dan did not disagree but made the point, however, that they would wear their night vision goggles, once they were in position. However small it might be, the one or two milliseconds advantage it might give an agent could mean the difference between shooting first or being hit.

They had parked the car beyond where they had planned to park it and near the spot where they had a virtually unimpeded view of the complex and decided to eat the last of their *sowhan* brittles while walking up the hill. They wanted to explore, each of the three dirt paths going beyond the clearing where the car was now parked and that they had noted on their last pass. Two of them, those that were the farthest left from their point of view, actually converged soon thereafter. The third, though seemingly starting uphill, eventually quickly went sideways and around the hill and ultimately led to the next side road where they had initially considered parking the car. So, it offered absolutely no escape.

They took the leftmost path and walked all the way to the top of the hill. From there, they could see at least three different ways to go back down. But the real benefit was that, standing nearly five hundred feet higher than the entrance to the complex and about as high as the crest of the hill into which the enrichment halls were dug, they had a particularly good vantage point from which to conduct their observations. Further, given the distance and the fact that they had been careful to avoid having any reflecting surfaces on their clothing, they felt they were not running any serious risk of being visible from the guardhouse.

They sat around and observed the activity around the plant from their vantage point. In truth, there was precious little activity they could see, other than what looked like the occasional truck moving up one or the other of the ramps that were carved into the side of the mountain and, which, they knew, led to the halls inside. Turning their attention closer in, to the guardhouse, they noticed limited, but regular guard movements. Obviously, they could not make out facial features from this far. So, at best, they could see that guards seemed to be following a set pattern that looked like some sort of troop rotation.

"Let's time their rotations, Nate."

They did not have to wait terribly long before they could start the stopwatch for the first. Not more than five minutes later, another truck drove to the main gate from inside the barrack compound and seemed to deliver troops there. It quickly turned around and drove back to what they assumed was its base. They started asking each other what they might be doing. Having discarded the notion that they were rotating guards so frequently, they worked on a different hypothesis which Nate offered: "What if they have troops walking the perimeter? They would need to be collected and deposited at periodic intervals."

"And that would be what those truck movements are."

Nate thought *that was reasonable.* Yet, they debated how feasible that idea was. After all, the perimeter of the whole area was six or seven miles long as per the satellite and GPS maps they had seen in Tel Aviv. As they were going through their thoughts, the next truck arrived. It had been fourteen minutes and thirty-two seconds, since the last one had arrived. They agreed to assume that troops are dropped at roughly fifteen-minute intervals. Going back to their initial assumption, they discussed the idea that they might have troops do a walk around the whole perimeter and collect them when they're through. Then they would be taking them back to the barracks just beyond the gate to rest. They agreed that it would be feasible, even if they had to walk six or seven miles. Dan had noted that Marine Corps training had their recruits do more than that. So, settling for a while, or at least until proven wrong, with that scenario, they immediately saw two implications that would concern them. They were glad to have learned of them before doing their work inside the plan.

The first would mean the Iranians must have fewer people assigned to guarding the inside of the plant other than those manning the gates at the entrance to the tunnel ramps. They had arrived at that conclusion simply by counting the number of troops taken up by the rotations. It appeared the Iranian protection strategy was focused on defending the perimeter and key strategic points, such as the entrances to the tunnels.

The second implication had to be that any escape for them would be much harder. It might be hard for people to get in, but the same forces that prevent intruders from getting in could also prevent anyone from getting out. At the same time, they were somewhat reassured by the fact that there seemed to be no more than four men in each patrol; Dan and Nate should be able to hit them with their handguns before they could be hit; this is because Dan and Nate thought *they would have the benefit of surprise, as they would know where the guards were, not the reverse.* Further, if the groups were spaced about fifteen minutes apart, it would mean that the closest patrol would be about a mile away, in either direction. Dan surmised that this would make the guards much less effective if they elected to flee upwards in the heli-drone scenario, as he could not believe the guards' guns would have the required range.

They concluded that they had seen virtually all they could. They certainly would have liked to do more, like walking down to the perimeter fence to see it closer up or going around the full perimeter of the installations. But they immediately agreed that getting closer to the fence would be stupid. They knew from Amir that it was armed and that would not really help them. But they still decided to take a walk around as much of the full perimeter as possible, if only because they were dying to see what was beyond the back of the mountain.

They started downhill having figured it would take them about a mile to reach the general area of the fence. For some reason, they both donned their night vision goggles. They found the walk initially relatively easy as the dirt road was quite practicable. The terrain was very flat once they were down from the top of the hill where they had been monitoring the plant. They reached the fence and turned right on another path that was gently climbing for another half mile until they reached what they had called the valley between the enrichment mount, as they called it, and the next small peak. They turned left and kept hiking when Nathan who was walking in front suddenly stopped: "What's up Nate . . . ?"

"Shhh. Danger ahead . . . Oh, my God . . ."

"What is it?"

"Small guardhouse . . . four hundred feet away . . ."

Nathan motioned for them to retrace their steps carefully.

They could not know that the path they were on eventually led to the Soltanyeh Mine, which provided some of the uranium ore to Iran's nuclear projects. The whole area around the Fordow complex was indeed a massive mining and processing area of which the enrichment plant was but the local culmination. In fact, had they continued on the path, they would have encountered small guardhouses, not more than thirty to fifty feet long and fifteen feet wide which served as advance warning posts, despite the fact that one never got to within less than three hundred feet from the actual first fence around the enrichment plant. They asked themselves why geothermal imaging did not show those guardhouses and concluded that they had to be too small; they still decided that they should report the mishap to the lab in Tel Aviv.

Fortunately, having arrived late in the evening, with night vision equipment, had given them the margin of safety that they had needed. They returned to the car and drove it closer to the main road right behind the kink they had initially observed. They began to complete their last important task before entering the plant: remove any and all identification numbers or plates from Minoo's car. They would only keep the license plates, until they arrived at the airstrip; they would not want to be stopped by the police for driving a car missing its license plates. But they had to eliminate plates that had any vehicle numbers or other identification markings. They had, in fact, gone on their small topographical exploration first, before getting to the plates, as they needed the engine area to cool down. They were going to use some of the left-over C-4 to booby trap the car and would have it eventually explode into bits that were as small as possible. They could not, however, be sure that each and every bit would be small enough that an identification plate could not survive. In part, they thought that *it would be very difficult to blow up the chassis or the engine of the car. At best, it would break up a bit and burn, which would be made easier by the fact that the fuel tank was at least half full.*

Thus, they removed the usual plates found on the engine block, the door frames and just under the front left part of the windshield. They placed these small plates into their carry-ons. Without these identification plates and, eventually, without the car's license plates, it would be virtually impossible for anyone to link the car to Minoo. There were simply too many of this type of cars around the country to determine who might have owned a carbonized carcass broken down into a large number of parts, strewn around at least a fifty meter-radius. They prepared the plastics explosives they were going to use and connected them to one another with the main fuse cord. They reserved the spot where they would put the detonator but kept the assembly in Daniel's carry-on and the detonator in Nathan's. They had no desire to blow themselves up by trying to plan ahead.

They chose this time to send two messages. The first, to Simon, was simple: "In position, waiting for the pick-up to penetrate the location. All other steps completed. BTW, we are officially out of the country."

The second to David was a bit more expansive: "Awaiting pick-up to get into facility. Almost all worked according to plan and everything in order and ready. BTW, no possible escape south and east of plant. Real activity should commence at 1:00 a.m. and be complete no later than 2:00 a.m. Should put us at strip around 3:15-3:30 p.m. and probably earlier. Still OK?"

David replied almost immediately.

"Not on location yet but getting there. Packed and left the apartment definitively. On our way to the strip to retrieve last pieces of equipment. Going to camp for last time and last local manipulation. Should be done by the time you finish. The Heli will follow us to strip for gas for return flight. Should put us at strip at same time as you, probably be ahead by fifteen minutes. Don't worry. Best of luck."

Simon's reply was equally simple to the original message: "Great . . . Anxious for details. Wish I was with you."

CHAPTER.38

As they left the camp near Natanz for the last time, David and Mike let Central Command know that they would be at the airbase at or near the precise time provided in the most recent plan, if not a few minutes early. Central Command had ordered the Hercules into flight, circling over the Khafji area so that they would be ready to release the drones as soon as needed.

Prior to sending the Hercules up, Central Command had launched two simpler, propeller powered IAI Eitan drones. The Eitan—which means "steadfast" in Hebrew—is a mid-altitude, long endurance aircraft, which can operate at altitudes above commercial air traffic, though about 5,000 feet lower than the Koveshes.

It is a high-wing monoplane with a pusher propeller at the aft tip of the fuselage, but ahead of the rear stabilizer. It carries a wide array of electronic equipment and its main mission revolves around intelligence, surveillance and target acquisition, military speak for laser guidance, though it hadn't yet been used for that purpose in real-life situations. It can stay aloft for an extended period of time and has a range which extends as far as four thousand six hundred miles, which substantially exceeded the requirements for the current mission.

The Eitan's primary role in Operation Kovesh was to help direct the six missiles which were going to be fired at Natanz to their precise target acquisition. These drones, however, had to be released substantially ahead of the Koveshes as the maximum speed of the Eitan was barely over 200 knots. It would therefore take them about two hours to get into position, while the Koveshes would need less than an hour. The Eitans were sent as planned and initially told to circle high over the location until the time of the strike was fixed.

Though the six missiles were in fact of Iranian origin, they had been carefully modified from the simple use which Hezbollah expected to make of them. The goal was to render them fit for the mission at hand. The first modification related to the explosive charges which had been tailored to the needs of the mission: high blast, limited need for projectiles, for the first four, lesser blast and high shrapnel damage potential for the last two. The second change, which had proven more difficult to execute because of space considerations, was to provide them with laser guidance capability. Thankfully, the missiles would not need to fly more than ten to fifteen miles, at most, if one counted the total length of the trajectory, not the ground to ground distance from launch to target, which was less than ten miles. That was less than half to a third of their normal range. This reduced the need for fuel and made space for a laser guidance system.

The plan called for the drones to set up position veering back toward the southeast, as they flew over Namak Lake, almost abeam Qom, or about seventy-five miles northwest of the Natanz site. At that point, they would fly in a southeasterly direction toward Natanz and start figure eight holding patterns when they were forty miles out. Once the team at the Kashan airstrip was ready to start firing the missiles, the Eitan would resume their southeasterly course, substantially decrease air speed and descend to a lower altitude to guide the missiles to the entrances of two tunnels. The small pieces of metal that David and Mike had left at the center and on top of the tarp at the entrance of each tunnel were intended to be a second safety element to help the Eitan accomplish its mission. The small layer of earth on top of the metal pieces was meant to minimize the risk that wind or some small animal might move them. These pieces of metals were designed to facilitate the acquisition of the appropriate target through the use of magnetic verification of the original coordinates provided by the global positioning system.

Once the missiles were fired from Kashan, they would initially fly almost vertically so that they could intercept the laser beams from the Eitans and be guided down onto both the right attack angle and the right impact point to each of the two tunnels. The correct angle of attack was important in that the explosion of the missile charge needed to be as close as possible to the bottom of the tunnel rather than against one of its sides. The correct target was equally important for the same reason: the closer the missiles hit to the center of the hole (which was only a foot and a half in diameter), the higher the likelihood that they could travel to their intended destination and their explosion would have the intended effect.

In fairness, the accuracy of the first strike on each tunnel was considerably less important than it was for the next two. The first strike was indeed only intended to detonate the eight bombs which had been rolled into position inside each tunnel. Any serious blast was going to do the trick with or without direct impact on the last bomb at the top of the pile they had dropped. The second would need to penetrate further into the cavity created by the first strike. Together, these two strikes were somewhat like a poor man's version of bunker bursting bombs. Though Israel had these heavy bunker busting bombs in its arsenal, these were much too heavy to be launched in any way other than from a conventional bomber. This would have required overflights which would likely have been detected and could be traced to Israel (or to any partner it might have chosen for that part of the mission). Also, they might have been attacked by Iranian fighters before they hit their target. Whatever the scenario, it would have left no room for Israeli or coalition plausible deniability of its involvement.

Once the go ahead was given, Central Command ordered the

release of the two Koveshes. The pilots, who had already done the trip twice, once to and once from Kashan, knew the flight plan literally backwards and forwards. Though they were always ready to react to any unexpected interest in them by the occasional radar or fighter pilot, they followed the same operating mode as the previous times. They'd be using the same flight path, the same flying speed and thus the same gliding approach into Kashan.

David and Mike expected to arrive at the airstrip at least twenty minutes before the drones were to land. One element of the plan they did not originally like was that the heli-drone would wait at the strip. Indeed, once the issue of potentially having to rescue Dan and Nate if there was a mishap at Fordow was no longer relevant, the heli-drone was no longer needed. So, they would have liked to send it on its way. Also, sending it earlier would have been one fewer thing to do when the time constraint was the highest. Yet water had flowed under that bridge. The heli-drone needed the four extra gas tanks, and these were coming on the Koveshes. So, the heli-drone had to wait for them.

As they were driving from Natanz and nearing the airstrip, a sixth sense seemed to be warning Mike, who was driving, and he had slowed down. Then, he blurted out, "What the fuck?"

Mike's reaction jolted David. He had noted that they had slowed; but as Mike had kept driving, he had not attached too much importance to it.

"What's up?"

Mike answered by motioning ahead at the road they were supposed to turn into to get to the airstrip. David immediately saw what Mike had seen. A vehicle, which they could only make out from its headlights, was driving from the airport toward the main drag on which they were themselves. Somewhat incredulous, David said: "Another delivery?"

"What do you mean?"

"Another copter drop . . . We've seen two already."

Mike said that he did not feel he had any option but to stay the course, drive on and see what happened—whatever the option he was going to choose, turning toward the airport was not on the list. He speculated that the car and whoever was in it would turn left if they were going to follow him and right if they were going anywhere else, most likely Kashan.

Unfortunately, the car did not go toward Kashan this time, but turned left, effectively following Mike. Mike slowed down but could not obviously stop. The car caught up with them and passed them; it was a light military truck. A few hundred yards later, Mike turned off all the Land Cruiser's lights, did a U-turn, and started driving slowly back toward the airport. As they started back, both David and Mike heard a loud noise. Instinctively, they lowered their windows to get a better look. A light was rising from what should be the runway of the airport. David immediately said, "It's a copter, another one . . . Goes with the car that just passed us . . ."

Mike stopped the car on the right-hand side of the road. David reached out to the remote pilots of the heli-drone and told them to approach the airport very carefully as there might be danger. In particular, they should first make a wide circle around the whole of the perimeter, lights off naturally, to allow the team to see whether they could discern any sign of unwanted presence. At a minimum, it could tell them whether there were other pieces of equipment. They indicated that they had just seen a helicopter take off and a few minutes earlier a car driving out of the airport. Simon who, coincidentally was monitoring the communications channel, sent them a message with two thoughts which he meant as advice to his troops. The first was the obvious: "remain very careful." The second was meant to calm them down a bit: "We've seen this three times now. It is probably bringing some political or military big wig back to the area. This one is more worrisome as it did not go to Kashan. Could it be going to Natanz?"

He added that they should confirm asap what was happening—the Koveshes and the Eitans were well into their flights.

CHAPTER.39

Amir arrived right on schedule and picked up Dan and Nate as requested, about two miles before the main entrance to the Fordow complex. He could not see their car, so he asked where it was. Daniel replied that they had left it just around the small kink in the road; they didn't want someone casually driving to or from the base seeing the car and becoming suspicious and asking the guards to come investigate.

As they were driving, Nate asked Amir about the movements of guards to the gatehouse almost every fifteen minutes. Amir looked absolutely nonplussed, replying that it was standard procedure. He explained that a patrol was made up of four or five guards, but most often just four. It completed a full, walking tour of a good part of the perimeter of the complex—about five to five and a half miles after which the guards were dropped back at the main gate, close to their barracks. He added: "But don't ask me why they're not walking that short distance from the main gate to their barracks."

Amir continued his explanation, saying that they started walking in the direction of the main facility. He noted that it was bit of a climb, but that the soldiers did not feel it as their legs were fresh then. They walked along the road, which was well-paved and ran roughly northwest to southeast. He added, as an aside, that he had heard that you could land transport planes on that road because it was absolutely straight for about a mile and a half.

"Some people say that you could even land jets, but I can't think of why you'd do that."

Nathan made a mental note about transport planes. This meant they could bring reinforcements in quickly. Amir continued his description of the circuit of the patrol, saying that once they got to the second gate, the one at the entrance of the enrichment complex, they started going almost due east on a ring road, all well-paved with streetlights every one hundred feet. Interestingly, that road ran alongside and outside a fence that protected the entire enrichment complex, but inside the overall perimeter fence. He continued, saying that by the time the soldiers had gone around the mount, behind the office building and back to the second gate, they would have travelled about three and a half to four miles. He added that they finished their walk by going back down the hill to the main gate, then they were driven to their barracks. Nathan asked: "Why not drive them to the second gate and only have them patrol the ring road?"

"Don't ask me. That's military stuff—not my bailiwick. I can see that they're walking further than need be. My guess is that the top military brass wants to have regular, visible patrols along the main drag, so that's the role these guys serve."

Daniel asked whether they had motorized patrols. Amir replied that they usually did not, probably, in his view, because they felt that they needed the slow speed of a walking platoon to pay attention to details in this deserted environment. But he added that there was a guard facility right behind the crest of the mountain where the halls were: "Those guys have the Iranian equivalent of Jeeps. So, any request for quick help would be for them and it'd only take them a couple of minutes to get to the entrance of either tunnel."

Daniel asked the final obvious question: "Any other way into the complex?"

"Not unless you're a goat and one that can dig underground or jump pretty high at that, Dan."

Daniel was surprised at Amir's sense of humor under the current pressure. Amir reiterated that there was a fence inside the ring road and added that it was pretty difficult already to walk the paths in the mountain, unless you knew them terribly well and were a seasoned hiker. But even assuming you could, Amir argued that you would still have to deal with the outer perimeter fence which was armed as carefully as the first and ran more than ten miles around the complex." Amir added: "Also, there are small guard huts at various places in that area . . ."

Nathan interrupted Amir in the middle of his last point, saying that he and Daniel had actually seen one of them when they had walked in the area a bit earlier today. Amir looked shocked and asked what they were doing there. Nathan looked quite cool and simply said that they had some time to kill and decided to take a walk to see the hill "close up and personal." Amir could not believe it but let it go and went back to the security question adding that there were quite a few mine fields in between the various fences suggesting that, even if you knew where the mines were, there was no flat spot where you could land anything. He suggested that at best you could hover a helicopter, but it would be an easy target for the guards. He concluded that, even if you had managed to avoid all the other obstacles, he could not see how you could get in. He added: "It's a very well-guarded facility. That's why I told Afri that only a great inside job could do the trick."

Amir told the team that both suitcases were in his office and said that, indeed, they were quite heavy. As they had arrived near the gate to the complex, they began to execute Amir's plan: He was going to smuggle them into the compound and drive them to the office building. Nathan would travel in the trunk of the car while Daniel would curl up between the front and back seats. Amir had a black parka to conceal him such that only a prying eye, knowing what to look for, would suspect anything. Nathan and Daniel slid into position, Daniel making a joke about the comfort likely to be enjoyed by Nathan, while Nathan was joking that Daniel was more important since he traveled inside the car. Neither spot was really that comfortable, but they knew that this was the only way. Both had their guns at the ready, just in case, though neither really was looking forward to any sort of gunfight. They both knew that handguns with ten-round magazines were no match for machine guns.

The drive to the main gate took a bit longer than usual as Amir was being careful not to shake up his passengers too much. Fortunately, the road they travelled only had two very gentle curves. He stopped at the first gate, the one that had been left open earlier, but he neither spoke to whoever was operating it nor was he asked any questions. Eventually, Nathan and Daniel felt the car go around what they assumed was the roundabout, veer left and come to a stop. Daniel could feel the fresh air from the outside as Amir lowered his window.

The subsequent conversation in Farsi would forever remain a total mystery to Daniel who could hear it and to Nathan who could only catch a few words from time to time. There were a few laughs and the tone seemed friendly. Eventually, though it seemed an eternity to the two clandestine passengers, the car started rolling again, and the window was shut. They both breathed a sigh of relief but remained silent. A few minutes later, the car stopped again. Dan and Nate correctly assumed that this had to be the last gate, the one that controlled close-in access to the facilities; Amir opened his window and did not need to say more than a few words before the car started moving again. Dan and Nate could feel the sharp right turn and were both quite relieved when the car came to a complete stop, in front of the office building, they assumed.

Amir told Daniel to pivot up onto the back seat and exit the car in a normal way, as if he had been a regular passenger that he had driven. They looked carefully, surveyed the surroundings and only opened the lid of the trunk when they were absolutely sure no one was around and looking. Nathan had heard the instructions to Daniel through the back seat and had prepared himself to burst out of the trunk and be standing next to the other two in as natural a pose as feasible under the circumstances.

Before walking into the building, Daniel and Nathan first needed to set the external radio relays for the detonators within each bomb. They preferred to do it when they had some time rather than when they were rushing to get out of the complex. Amir asked them what they were doing. Nathan dryly replied that it was a part of the overall trigger mechanism. He did not want to provide more detail than necessary as he still harbored some doubt about Amir. Dan felt less compulsion against sharing some information. With Nathan looking a bit askance at him, he said that each bomb, including the one in Amir's office, had a detonator that listened for radio signals. It received signals on three different radio frequencies. When the final "go" was given—but he was cautious not to say when that would be and who would initiate it, though Amir probably thought that Dan or Nate would be the ones doing it—a radio instruction would be sent on all three frequencies. It would be picked up by one or both of the relays they were going to place on the trees next to his car. These relays would in turn send the signals to the bombs inside. And then the whole thing would hopefully go up in smoke.

They walked into the office building together, with Amir leading them to his office which was downstairs.

"Gentlemen, welcome to my humble office . . ."

He added that before going into his office they should don protective clothing, stored in an adjacent room. They all knew that this was not an absolute requirement from the point of view of nuclear safety, but Dan and Nate had elected still to put on masks and the full nuclear clean clothing kit. They explained to Amir that this would also enhance their anonymity, especially if he was unable to warn them in advance of anyone who might disturb their activities. He offered ID badges, saying that he had a couple of guys on his team that looked close enough to them and added that they would have to learn their names, to be safe. Nathan immediately started to laugh, saying that it wouldn't help him to know the name of the guy he was supposed to be: "I don't speak Farsi, so wouldn't know if anyone is calling."

Amir looked chastised but then smiled saying that he had not thought of that. He told them not to worry about the names, but still to wear the badges because they would look suspicious without proper ID. Daniel asked whether they could use night vision goggles under these garbs they had to wear, and Amir conceded it would be a bit tight, but they should fit, adding: "The whole head unit is designed to be worn over oxygen masks. Imagine your goggles can't be any larger than that."

Daniel and Nathan felt a little constrained in their movements in the clean suits, which they wore over their normal clothing; but they understood the need and had trained in similar garb back in Israel. Amir was a bit surprised and taken aback when he saw them slide their guns in a spot that was readily accessible in their new garb. To his question of why they would take guns, Nathan simply noted that neither David nor he were friendly visitors. Amir was still pushing back until Nathan brought the matter to a close: "At this point, Amir, it's no longer our jobs to think. We're here to do the job and we'll take any and all precautions we have to take."

Once dressed, Amir led them back to his office to collect the suitcases. He added that he would not dress up, or at least not immediately, as he had to monitor what was happening on the real cameras while the security system was broadcasting what had happened yesterday at this time in the halls and the plazas. He noted that they were exactly six minutes ahead of their scheduled time, and that he therefore needed to adjust the replays so that they showed the correct time.

"It's exactly 12:59 a.m. Ready, set, go . . ."

Daniel handed Amir the three-way radio system that they had

discussed, with the instruction to wear it and make sure he listened to what he and Nate were saying, especially to warn them if something did not look right. He said he had not forgotten and proceeded to lock up the office and lead them to the first plaza. He indicated that he would return to his office and wait for their signal, adding that he would need about a minute to get to the entrance of the tunnel. Then he would show them where to remove the protective suits and go straight back to his car. Before leaving his office, they all agreed to booby trap it now rather than later. Daniel summarized it: "Really don't want any one of us lingering around this place once the bombs have been set."

The job of wiring Amir's office took no time at all. They had concluded that dropping off the suitcases and what was left in them after they'd been in the two halls would do the trick. There was some C-4 and at least one detonator left in each of them; so they would explode at the same time as all the other bombs. For the sake of completeness, they added a small charge of C-4 near the replay equipment; they placed a standard detonator wired to the same radio frequency as the rest and that was it. Once this was done, they took the tunnel that led from the office building to the enrichment complex, with Nathan and Daniel each pulling their suitcase. The idea, if intercepted by anyone, was to say that this was a top-secret security exercise. Failing this, Daniel and Nathan were to dispose of the intruders, using their silencers to avoid any additional commotion.

Once they reached the entrance to the first plaza, Amir was asked to stay and monitor the plaza until Dan returned. Daniel and Nathan had decided that they would stick with the idea of each man covering a hall solo; but they had also concluded that the risk of Nathan arriving at the second plaza alone was too great. So, Daniel left his suitcase with Amir, and accompanied Nathan to the second plaza, covering for him, with his gun at the ready. As expected, the second plaza was empty, and Nathan walked straight into the second hall and began his work. Dan ran back to where Amir was waiting, grabbed his suitcase and entered the first hall; he started his work while Amir returned to his office.

Though they had said nothing to each other, both Nathan and Daniel had mentally put on their game faces. This was it, and the greatest danger to them was Amir. Either he was for real and the danger was that he'd miss seeing a guard or a patrol; or, if he wasn't and was going to betray them, now would likely be the point where he would act. Although they never were able to explain why they were so unsure of his intentions, despite doing absolutely everything they asked and having been vetted into the agency, there was something about him that made them uncomfortable. The moment of truth was at hand.

As he entered the first hall, Daniel simply announced "on location." As expected, no one answered. He walked to the far end of the room with the suitcase and started working. His job involved placing the bombs under three rows of centrifuges. He had rehearsed this many times, but the movements he had to make were not all that natural; the clean nuclear garb made the whole exercise that much more cumbersome. Plus, there was the pressure of the job and the lingering uncertainty with respect to Amir. He stepped between rows two and three and was happy to see that he could pull the suitcase along, though the space was a bit cramped. He placed the first bomb under the sixth centrifuge on his right. Before placing the bomb, he switched it on and saw the red light appear. He rotated the detonator actuator 90 degrees, as planned, and watched the red light turn green, as expected. He moved forward to the twenty-first centrifuge assembly but placed the bomb under the one to his left, switching the bomb on and rotating the detonator actuator as well. He then moved to the thirty-sixth and placed the bomb under the centrifuge to his right. He kept repeating the process until he arrived at the one hundred and forty-first centrifuge on his left, where he placed his tenth bomb.

The last two, respectively under the one hundred fifty-sixth and the one hundred seventy-first centrifuges completed the first set of rows. He looked at his watch and noticed that it had taken him eighteen minutes and twenty-six seconds.

Should be a bit faster, he thought to himself. "First row completed" was his laconic message.

Nathan replied: "Six assemblies into the second . . ."

Daniel replied: "Need to move a couple of minutes faster per row if we can . . ."

Daniel retraced his steps, such that he was now working between rows four and five. He placed the same number of bombs and found himself at the end where he had started. He happily noted that there were indeed five centrifuges left in the row after he had placed the twelfth bomb: "You're the man," he said to himself, happy that he was still on count. As planned, this would give him one last trip, which would terminate directly in front of the exit from the hall. This fit with the goal of minimizing the time spent in the open and the halls counted as open space in his mind. He looked at his watch and was delighted that he had taken only sixteen minutes and twenty-one seconds to complete the return trip.

"Second trip completed."

"Halfway through the third, but still have the two extra cascades . . ."

An unexpected sound came on the radio. It was definitely Amir's voice. But he wasn't alone. He and at least one other person were speaking in Farsi and the tone was rising. Then, the radio broadcasted another sound, a sort of garbling, as if someone had pulled Amir's microphone. Nathan's heart stopped for a second and he pulled his gun. His doubts about Amir skyrocketed. "You bastard," he said under his breath. He was sure he was going to have to shoot the patrol and that miniature hell would break loose. He added: "Dan, be ready; this is it . . ."

"Could be. I'm ready . . . Do not shoot unless you have to . . ."

CHAPTER.40

Simon was awakened from a light sleep by a message. It was from the Americans. The AWACS has detected some aircraft activity in the Isfahan region. They could not yet tell whether they were just exercises or a response to something else, but they wanted him to know. Simon immediately called his U.S. counterpart, John Suffolk, and asked him for his thoughts, adding: "In the middle of the night . . . Stinks."

Suffolk was a solid CIA operative who had risen through the ranks, including having been on a number of covert operations. In fact, he had started his military life as a U.S. Navy SEAL. He was known for being calm under pressure and to be able to make decisions rapidly if needed. Suffolk told Simon he would call him back within fifteen minutes, once he had talked directly with the AWACS team and Central Command, a euphemism for the Situation Room at the White House. As promised, he called back quickly and said that they suggested that one should not take stupid risks. The plan called for a couple of missiles to be fired into Isfahan and Arak, respectively to the southwest and northwest of Kashan. These missiles were rebuilt versions of the same missiles that Israel had captured from Hezbollah. The U.S. had extended the range to make sure that they could hit their targets from Iraq.

Suffolk suggested that one option was to fire the Arak missiles early to divert the Iranian attention away from the Qom/Kashan region. The marine exercises being conducted between Israeli navy vessels and a portion of the U.S. Sixth Fleet had already attracted a lot of attention from the Iranians who had complained of warmongering by the U.S. and Israel at the U.N. Suffolk explained that it would not be advisable to bring forward the hits on Isfahan for two reasons. First, Isfahan was closer to Qom than Arak was. Second and most importantly, Isfahan was a known Iranian Air Force base, with a full complement of F-14 Tomcat fighters. Whatever the coalition did, they should try to divert these planes away from Isfahan, and at the same time away from the Natanz airstrip.

Simon agreed that the recommendation made sense and asked how quickly the process could be started and whether this could jeopardize the eventual strike on Isfahan. Indeed, he felt, as did Suffolk, that some destruction of the uranium refining capacity in Isfahan was more important to the mission than a hit on the Arak nuclear reactor. Suffolk replied that the team were ready near the Iraq/Iran border and that it would take about thirty minutes for the missile to reach its target.

As an alternative, Simon suggested that they could trigger some of the mines that had been laid around three of the islands in the Strait of Hormuz. He said he would personally choose Larak, as it was the Southern-most island, almost directly opposite Jebel al Harim, the mountain peaks that create the promontory jutting out from the United Arab Emirates and forming the south side of the Strait. Action there would attract attention that far further from both the action in Iran and where the Koveshes would need to fly on their return trip from Natanz. Suffolk said he also liked the option, as the mines could be remotely triggered by one of their submarines. He added that one of the submarines in squadron 21, a part of the Fifth Fleet, was in and around the Strait and could trigger any and all mines in a manner of minutes. They went back and forth, for a few minutes, and eventually agreed that the simplest and least disruptive approach was to trigger the mines. Depending upon how things proceeded, they might also trigger the mines around Abu Musa, an island to the southwest of Larak, almost directly opposite Dubai. It was not only a bigger island, but it had a large airport; Iran could land planes there if they wanted to bring reinforcements in. Simon knew that Siri Island also had an airport, but its location, further north, made it a distant third choice at this time. He and Suffolk actually planned on keeping those around Siri as a deceptive maneuver while the Koveshes were on their last return flight from Kashan.

The Navy garrison on Larak was sound asleep when the muffled sound of mines exploding broke the quiet of the night. In fact, at the outset, there was a great deal of confusion as to what the noise was. The harbor and the town were located on the north side of the island, facing Hormuz Island and Bandar Abbas a bit further west and on the Iranian mainland. The mines had been placed on the sea floor around the entry of the harbor. They were thus not much more than a mile to a mile and a half from shore. People could not only hear the sound of the explosions, but also experience their tidal impact. As expected by Simon and Suffolk, the explosions triggered a major mobilization, that went all the way to bringing surveillance planes from Bandar Abbas. But, naturally, by that time, the submarine that triggered the mines was safely out of reach. It turned out that it was the same submarine that had originally launched the Orcas that had placed the mines.

Simon waited a few minutes before reaching out again to AWACS to ask for an update. He was delighted to hear that all activities that they could detect were directed to the south of the country. He had not bothered informing the team in Iran of the contingency and thought that *he should not bother them with those details now as this should in no way interfere with their work.* However, he promised himself that he would tell them the story later.

CHAPTER.41

MAY 8
FORDOW

Nathan and Daniel were models of complete concentration. Each in their own hall. Nate was bemoaning that it had all worked out too well so far. Yet, his energy was not on regrets, but on the present.

Two Iranian guards entered the first hall. Dan was crouched between rows of centrifuges, with just enough space to see the guards look around. His gun with the silencer on was drawn and Dan was ready to shoot if the guards made any move toward him. He was almost as far from the door as he could be. They walked around ostensibly looking to see if something was amiss. They did not see Dan, nor did they find anything wrong. One of the two guards motioned to the other they should get out. The moment they shut the door, he warned Nate: "Two guards, coming. Hid between the centrifuges; didn't have to shoot . . ."

Nate's attention was fully focused on the door which he had heard was being opened. The first guard walked a few feet inside. Nathan rested his hand on a pipe going into the centrifuge closest to him, ready to fire. He hesitated for a second. The second guard entered. They both were surveying the place carefully, as if they were looking for something, though did not know what it was. They saw Nate at the same time; his nuclear garb must have been reflected on the aluminum body of the centrifuge closest to him. They spoke in Farsi and moved toward him. Two bullets, two dead guards. Nate called

Dan on the radio: "Had to shoot . . . They were coming for me . . ."

"Any more bombs?"

"'bout five, but I've got to go. I am sure other guards will be here in minutes."

"I've got twelve . . . I'll place them in the middle of the last row. Hopefully the damage will be big enough . . ."

"Meet you in front of your hall. I'm sending a message to Mike and David to send the heli-drone and the jet packs. We're gonna need them."

"For sure. Great, see you in a minute or less . . . I am sending a message to Simon . . ."

They removed their nuclear protection clothing and dropped them on the ground. They ran out of the complex by the exit that was furthest away from the office, as they assumed that trouble would be coming from there. Their goal was to reach the back of the mountain, all the while avoiding the point which Amir had indicated housed the automobile patrol. The back of the mountain would allow them to be as high up as they could be and hidden from the front of the site. It had to be a matter of time before the whole site got into "red alert."

They figured that the heli-drone should be arriving in at most five minutes. They sent a note to the pilots to tell them to fly as high as possible and then drop as quickly as they could. Also, they told them they should avoid the left rear part of the complex where the motorized patrol was. As they were less than one hundred meters from the top of the mountain, Dan told Nate: "I'm sure glad we rehearsed this earlier . . ."

"You better believe it . . ."

Both Dan and Nate had their senses in full alert. They were training their ears for the muffled sound of the heli-drone and, simultaneously, looking for any activity from Iranian guards. The only saving grace of the moment was that the moon was hidden by clouds; it was quite a dark night. Additionally, they were both wearing dark clothing. The

Iranians would not see them unless they shone a projector's light right on them. Dan first picked up the distant sound of the heli-drone: "Think it's arriving . . ."

"Don't see anything . . . Not surprising. It's pitch-black out there. Not a star to light up the sky . . ."

"God is with us, my friend."

The drone approached from the right rear, all lights switched off. The remote pilots were guiding themselves using the infrared camera, which could pick up the heat of the agents' bodies against the cold outside. They brought the drone down as quietly as possible and stopped right next to Dan and Nate. The pilots kept it hovering just above ground while Dan and Nate grabbed their respective jet packs. Nate added: "Good thing we trained with those anyway though we weren't supposed to use them . . ."

The remote pilot could see them donning their packs and waving goodbye. They both flew into the valley and then up the hill in the direction of Minoo's car.

The heli-drone pilots provided a diversion to shield them as much as they could. They flew the heli-drone away and straight up. Rather than using the route they had taken to approach the mountain, they went straight above the spot where they expected the guards to be. They wanted to draw their attention away from the guys for as long as they could. They knew that the jet packs had a jet move, relying on compressed exhaust gases. This would project them up in the air at a speed such that they had a good chance of avoiding bullets if they were discovered.

Once it was high enough to avoid semi-automatic fire, the heli-drone switched its lights on. The contrast between the dark surroundings and the light should make it even more difficult for the guards to see the jet packs and their passengers. Their eyes would accommodate to the light and would be even less able to see anything in the surrounding darkness. The guards switched on a couple of anti-aircraft, light projectors. They converged on the drone and were ready to shoot. But the remote pilots, anticipating that move, had plunged downward fast enough to get away from their beams. They switched off their own lights. The guards had lost them. They flew a few hundred yards away and, more importantly, regained altitude. They switched their lights back on. This again attracted the attention of the anti-aircraft projectors. They repeated the maneuver a few times, until they decided that they had provided enough time to the agents. Then, they simply flew away, back to the Kashan airport where Mike and David were expecting the heli-drone.

Daniel and Nathan flew straight for Minoo's car, which they found with minimal difficulty. They were quite thankful that they had spent the time earlier on their reconnaissance mission. They both had their guns out as they walked calmly but cautiously to the car, with the jet packs in one hand and their guns in the other. They walked closer to the car and made sure that it had not been touched. They had left a couple of twigs near the front left door and right in front of the exhaust pipe at the rear of the car. They verified that they were untouched. Nathan started the engine of the 206 while Daniel sat in the passenger seat.

"What the hell was that?"

"Don't know. Do you think Amir double-crossed us or was he genuinely surprised?"

"Don't know. His voice sounded frightened. But he could be frightened for himself or for the mission. Not sure we'll ever know. One thing is for sure, he did not shoot. So, we have to assume he was captured or left with the guards. I doubt we'll see him again, but again, who knows? Anyway, I'm still worried we're driving into a trap . . ."

Nathan and Daniel both suddenly exclaimed: "Oh, No. Amir, No."

They saw the headlights coming their way at about the same time. They were still a distance away. They could not make out what it was. A comforting thought, at least for a short while, was they did not see any further lights behind them. Yet, all of a sudden, that respite went away; there was at least another set of headlights about five hundred yards behind whatever was in front. They really thought *they might have to ask Central Command to trigger the bombs early. It was hard enough if they were going to get caught. At least the mission would not be a complete failure . . .*

"Wonder whether they also know of Mike and Dave?"

"You know what, Nate, let's first focus on saving our skins and then we'll worry about the rest of the team . . ."

"Understood . . . But, yet . . ."

Daniel got his gun ready and waited, while he also had Nate's on his lap. The military truck kept driving and passed them with no incident.

"Hey, that's good . . ."

"Wait for the other one, Nate . . ."

They saw the second truck come toward them and had less than a second to swerve to the right as the truck was definitely taking his half of the road in the middle. Nate exclaimed: "Bastard . . ."

Instead of joining his friend swearing at the truck driver, Dave started to laugh almost uncontrollably. They could see Highway 7 in the distance. From there, they would be relatively safe, unless the Iranians were planning to get all of them at the Kashan airport. Nate asked: "Why would they want to get us as a group of four when they could first get the two of us?"

"What if Amir was simply surprised or had not told them the whole story. They might in fact be tailing us to see where we are going . . ."

"Good thought . . . But I don't see anyone in my rearview mirror . . ."

"Anyway, I don't like the current smell . . ."

"Not me . . ."

"Nate, I did not mean that . . . It was in a figurative sense . . . Second time on this mission that you're focused on the wrong thing . . ."

Nate simply smiled. There was no need to respond. Obviously, as

Dan was expressing his concern for the safety of the mission, he had no way of knowing that Mike and David were parked by the side of the road near the airport, shocked as they had been to see the truck coming out of the airport access road and to hear the helicopter take off.

Daniel then reached for the flashlight tool. His first message was to David: "Done. On our way. Should be there in an hour or less. We're OK, but it was close. Thanks for the heli-drone . . . It should be arriving any second. Amir probably AWOL . . ."

He also sent a message to Simon: "Easter Egg drop complete; on our way to rendezvous . . . Narrow escape from the centrifuge hall. Don't know anything about Amir's whereabouts."

Simon replied almost as fast as the speed of light. He had been waiting for that news and had not kept his eyes off his flash tool, since he knew the last step of the process had started. He decided still not to mention the action they had had to take on Larak Island. He congratulated them both, adding: "Is Amir alive? Sarah was asking about him a minute or so ago."

Daniel replied that he really did not know: "At this point, there are two possibilities. Either someone betrayed him, and he was arrested. That can't be good for him. On the other hand, he betrayed us and the dialog in Farsi did not reflect fear but excitement. In that case, he may well be alive; I can't believe he won't be in deep doodoo when the whole thing explodes. From Sarah's standpoint, afraid it looks like a total write-off . . ."

CHAPTER.42

As he received Mike's reply, Daniel's heart missed a beat.

"Oh, Shit. Smells increasingly bad . . ."

Nathan turned and immediately asked him what the trouble was.

"Just received this from Mike: trouble at the airstrip. Amir may have sold us all out . . ."

Mike had not told the whole story, as there was no point adding too much clutter. The main point was that there had been another helicopter movement, and that the person being ferried in had not been driven to Kashan, but south. That could be "just a big nothing," but it could also be ominous. He still told Daniel to watch out for any military activity as they approached the general area around the airstrip. He also said that he was asking the remote heli-drone pilots for help. In fact, he had just given the remote pilots a heads-up. Though they would have conducted a general site inspection as they had done in prior instances, Mike told them to use extreme caution this time. He added that there could be snipers, or worse, on or near the runway, or even around the terminal. So, the Heli-drone pilots elected to conduct an initial wide circle, higher altitude overflight, using the infra-red cameras at maximum zoom power to see whether there was anything big, such as aircraft or trucks in the vicinity. The wide circles were intended both to avoid flying too close to the runway and to check if anything was amiss a bit further away from the airport, occasionally zooming out and then back in. Simon had agreed that, though it would not be the most logical strategy, the Iranians might want to stage an attack on their own airstrip after the intruders had arrived.

The heli-drone's first pass yielded nothing. Nothing looked different than usual around the airport, and there didn't appear to be anything large on or near the runway. That left only two possibilities. Either this was a false alarm, or the Iranians were hidden in the terminal. Either way, the good news was that they were not using heavy equipment. The AWACS, which had been warned of the possible problem, confirmed that they did not see anything aloft in the near vicinity, but still cautioned that the Iranians could have turned off any transponder or be using a scrambler to hide themselves.

The Eitans and Koveshes had slowed down modestly to avoid arriving on site too early. Though that might marginally increase the risk of detection, Central Command had agreed that the risk was greater for them to get closer to Kashan if trouble was brewing there.

The heli-drone conducted a second overflight, closer to the airport, but still at a higher altitude than its normal approach. Again, there did not seem to be much, other than a car or light truck that was parked near one of the hangars, near the opposite end of the runway. David let out another "Oh shit."

Simon, who was in on the conversation with the heli-drone told the team to hold off, but not to panic. He told them that Palmachim was looking through tapes of earlier approaches by the heli-drone: "Must know if the car has been there all along and we simply didn't focus on it?"

Within a couple of minutes, the word came back that Simon's intuition was not totally correct. The car had not been there in all prior pictures, though a car could be seen in a few of them. He told the team to resume normal procedures, though with as much caution as possible. He was going to try and see if the car was the same as in prior pictures, but that would take some time as they needed to zoom in to the point where the graininess of the picture made a precise identification dicey. He still told the Eitans and Koveshes that they were all clear on the earlier instructions. Daniel and Nathan understood that they were clear to keep driving, though they continued to be on the lookout for anything that could be a trap.

CHAPTER.43

Mike and Dave found their way to their location at the airport with no further trouble. From where they were, they could see a car parked in the distance. Using their night vision goggles, they zoomed onto the car. They were delighted to report to Simon that the car did not seem to emit any significant heat: it had been parked there for quite a while. Certainly, in fact, for longer than when trouble started brewing in Fordow. Ostensibly, this was no guarantee that it would not start its engine and suddenly drive toward the hangar where the team was. Yet, Simon was convinced that, had the Iranians known of the plot much earlier, they could not possibly have allowed Nate and Dave to place their bombs in the two halls.

David offered a frightening thought: "What if Amir removed or disconnected the detonator from the bombs while they were under his control?"

Simon realized that it was possible . . .His thinking was interrupted by Dan and Nate who "called" from their car. Their view was that the Fordow mission had been partially compromised: "We should advance the time of the explosion . . ."

"Dan, I understand, but we do not want anyone to begin to protect Natanz more as they find out that Fordow was destroyed. We're walking a tightwire here . . ."

"Understood, Simon, but consider the alternative. Amir knew of the function of the external relays. If he is alive, he can easily grab and destroy them . . ."

Nathan added: "Simon, did Amir know about Natanz?"

"Absolutely not . . . That was the plan all along. Have the two missions separate from the point of view of our local agents. Neither Minoo nor Farid knew about it either . . ."

"So, there is minimal risk that they would come looking for us here?"

"I wouldn't say minimal. Natanz is the only other known enrichment location. They might guess that it needs reinforced protection . . ."

Dan concluded: "See, Simon, if you follow that logic, they could well reinforce Natanz anyway and try to stop the explosion in Fordow . . . To my mind, that says that we should trigger the explosion asap."

"Let me think for a minute. I'll let you know . . ."

Within a minute, Simon was back: "Send me a signal when you get to the airport. We'll trigger Fordow then . . ."

As planned, the Koveshes flew at about 3,000 feet alongside the mountain ranges on the east side of the valley, flashed their transponder lights for a few seconds to warn the team of their approach, then made a sharp left turn about ten miles south of Kashan and dropped gradually and noiselessly as they approached the runway. Both landings were as impeccable as the first time. David steered the drones toward the back of the hangar. He was relieved, and so was Mike, when the car at the other end of the runway did not seem to make any move: "It's just parked there . . ."

The cargo bays of the drones ferried the missile launchers, six missiles and the four detachable light fuel tanks for the heli-drone. The rest of the space was taken up by two large flexible plastic tanks, one in each aircraft, which contained the extra aviation fuel the drones would need on their return flights. The four agents embraced briefly. The mission was almost complete—but not quite. And the last exercise with respect to Natanz was extremely dangerous and in totally unchartered territory. There was no room for error.

David and Mike returned to their task as time was still of the essence. They topped up the heli-drone's main fuel reservoir with gas they had siphoned out of the Land Cruiser, which would not be used again. They had decided against blowing it up, as leaving it intact might add fuel to the belief that whoever had used it were home grown terrorists, rather than foreign agents. They then attached the four extra gas tanks to the heli-drone, making sure that they were all properly connected to the main fuel system. Just as had been the case for the inbound flight, the heli-drone had to have extra fuel to fly the four hundred miles to Khafji. The four extra tanks would, in fact, provide enough range for the drone to be able to cover the distance it had taken to fly in, and then some. This would provide more opportunities to take advantage of the natural protection afforded by the topography. Also, it would be able to hover briefly a few miles before reaching the Persian Gulf so that the AWACs team—aided by an IAI Heron reconnaissance drone, which had been serving as the mission's air traffic advance warning system near the ground—could confirm that the coast was clear. At this point, the heli-drone would resume its flight, initially to the point that the Heron had selected for it to cross the Iranian coastline. Then, it would veer slightly eastward and fly directly to Khafji.

Once the heli-drone, which was awaiting the fellows near the terminal building, was fueled up and ready, it took off and was set on a 220-degree vector and immediately picked up by the remote operators. They flew it back to the Khafji base as planned, with an extended portion of the flight passing over the Zagros Mountains, which provided cover as the area is sparsely inhabited; their job was to ensure it arrived "home" safely. Once at the base, the heli-drone would eventually be loaded onto the Hercules and flown back to Israel.

Nate and Dan arrived at the airport and greeted their companions with visible elation. The mission was surely not complete, but the four of them were there, together, and the two Koveshes were on the tarmac ready to fly them out of Iran. They signaled Simon who immediately had Central Command trigger the Fordow explosion.

After their conversation with Simon, Daniel and Nathan unloaded the missiles and two launchers and set them aside on the ground. They then, carefully, folded the external jets of the two jet packs. They placed each of them in one of the cargo bays. The rest of the cargo space was taken up by the soft-sided additional fuel tanks. Daniel and Nathan were responsible for making sure that these extra fuel tanks were appropriately connected to the drone's main fuel system. This involved flipping a safety switch inside the belly of the drone. They also had to check that the gas pressure gauge showed the appropriate reading, confirming that all systems were "go." The engineers preferred that the additional fuel tanks not be connected to the main system until the Koveshes were ready to depart on the return flight. They wanted to make sure that any shift in the cargo during the outbound trip could not, in effect, reverberate into the overall fuel system. With the extra tanks disconnected, whatever happened in the cargo bay stayed in the cargo bay. With the extra fuel, the Koveshes could now ferry the four men in total safety, even if they had to travel nearly twice the distance they originally planned. With a system that allowed the remote pilots to see the balance in each of the fuel tanks, the remote pilots could pump fuel from one tank to another to maintain the appropriate weight balance for the drone. Dan interrupted his colleagues: "The signal's gone out. Fordow must have blown up."

Nathan noted that he expected to see something from where he was then, particularly since they were standing at a higher altitude and should have had an unobstructed, though distant, view. It was odd in his mind that there was no external sign. Daniel noted that it was a long way away when he was interrupted by Nathan: "Wait, there's a bright light, there, in the horizon. And it's expanding. Fordow is blowing up."

David uttered a brief congratulation to the team but returned to the current tasks.

Once finished with the extra fuel tanks for the Kovesh drones, Daniel and Nathan helped the final phase of the mission by carrying the missiles from the drones to the firing location, a few hundred yards from the tip of the runway. The team needed to reserve space around the missile launcher as well as keeping it at a safe distance from the Koveshes. They wanted to ensure that any incident with the missile launcher could not possibly jeopardize the drones and their ability to fly the team out safely.

As he carried the first missile to the launch site, Daniel noted that, as planned, it bore Iranian markings. Mike added that it was ironic that they were going to use launchers and missiles captured from Hezbollah without them ever noticing it, launchers and missiles which Hezbollah had gotten from Iran. And that these missiles were going to hit Iranian targets. Daniel could not resist the joke: "Talk of a boomerang effect."

In terms of identifying who was responsible for the attack, the team knew full well that the Iranians would surely know that it could not be Hezbollah that had fired the missiles. But it would take them quite a while to figure out who did. Plus, the Toyota was rented by two Iranians living abroad and they were making sure that the Iranian inspectors would find it and trace it back to those Iranian exiles. David concluded: "That pushes them in the direction of a local conspiracy, but they'll wonder what the hell the Hezbollah link might be."

David added that the plan provided that a message would originate allegedly from the Iranian resistance in Paris claiming responsibility. Nathan, always the cynic, added that the Iranian Resistance in Paris would be surprised, too, when they saw the message. Mike picked up on Nathan's point: "They would obviously know it did not come from them, but they would also have no idea where it came from."

David agreed, but added that Mission Control, aka Simon, believed that the Resistance would hesitate in denying their involvement. Daniel added: "They'd be caught in a bind. On the one hand, it would make them look powerful and gutsy to have engineered this coup. But, on the other, it would expose them to serious retributions."

"And we know the Iranians don't hesitate murdering people they don't like, even if they're abroad."

While David and Mike were assembling the launchers and securing the first, Daniel and Nathan finished bringing the missiles to the launching site and sorted them into two groups. The first four were conventional ordinance, with maximum detonating power; the tip was red. The latter two were engineered to spread their ordinance around as wide a radius as possible; their tip was green.

Daniel remarked that the first four really only made way for the last two: "The red ones open the way; the green ones are the terminators."

David simply nodded, as he was busy with the job of securing the last of the four legs of the launcher. Mike added that, just as they expected to be the case in Fordow, the havoc caused should release plenty of radioactive uranium gas into the halls at Natanz.

"That'll make them harder to service for a while."

They briefly discussed the risk that some radioactive gas could escape via the tunnels through which the missiles would enter the hall which could create a small risk to the neighboring population. David argued that there might be some escape of radioactive material or even signs of a modest explosion backfiring through them, but also added that Farid had discussed a safeguard mechanism in the case of a radiation leak. He added: "Let's hope it triggers itself instantaneously."

Though the team did not like the risk of radiation exposure for the local civilian population, they observed that Israeli scientists were absolutely certain there was no risk of any true nuclear explosion.

Unless the Iranians had lied and there was more highly enriched uranium in there than what they admitted to . . .

CHAPTER.44

MAY 8
KASHAN AIRPORT

Mike noted with some pleasure that he had not seen any increased activity in their immediate vicinity, despite the Fordow explosion. David tempered his optimism: "Remember that they haven't seen our missiles yet. What I worry about is that they would react very quickly to the first impact . . ."

They all agreed and worked even more diligently to minimize the time to recharge the launcher. Daniel, Nathan and Mike created a human chain to pass the missiles as quickly as possible to David, whose job was to load them into the launcher and fire each of them at its target. To be safe, he had set the two launchers side by side.

With the two Eitan drones in position, the team was to fire the missiles alternately at each site. Though they were firing at two targets, these were close enough to each other that the initial missile launch did not need to be adjusted. The necessary correction to the trajectory would be the job of the laser guidance system. The first missile was intended for the northern most site; the second one to the other site. They were going to alternate on that pattern, until the six missiles had been fired. They counted on being able to fire the six missiles in four minutes or less, which gave them about two extra minutes should anything go wrong.

The Eitan drones were the main constraint. As had been explained to the team, they were not stationary. They were flying toward the site at minimum speed, just above stall speed. Too much time to load or fire a missile might cause one or the other drone to get too close. It would then have to turn around and get back into position. The maneuver, though feasible, was undesirable. It increased the risk of detection or reaction on the part of the Iranian Air Force, not to mention the fact that it exposed the team and their Koveshes to more time on the ground than absolutely necessary.

Though the overflight of four hundred miles worth of Iranian territory by both sets of drones created serious detection risks, the one element of the plan which was still unknown was how quickly the Revolutionary Guards would react to the first missile hitting the first target. The distance between the barracks and the mouths of either tunnel was quite short; the sound of the impact would deafen the guards, and the blast would shake the walls of the barracks. The team had decided that the element of surprise would probably shield the first two or three missiles from any immediate reaction. After that, the key issue was whether the guards had a way of intercepting the missiles. Mission Control had concluded that they probably did not have reliable missile defense batteries. However, they had to have solid anti-aircraft guns. Mission Control felt that the real risk was to the two Eitan drones which could be hit, if the guards managed to locate them; however, they thought that *the risk to the missiles was small and that they should still reach their targets unimpeded.* More importantly, Mission Control was fairly confident that any ground-to-air action against the drones would have to be initiated from another location. Intelligence told them that there were anti-aircraft batteries in Qom and Kashan. The Eitans would still be quite a distance away to the northwest of the Natanz plant, and, in fact, would be north and west of the airstrip from which the team was shooting. Mission Control assumed that guards in Natanz would not immediately call reinforcements from places as far away as Qom; they would likely focus on saving themselves. They hoped, too, that the drones would be flying high enough and have sufficient radar evading coatings to allow them enough time to guide all six missiles and then veer southwards over Kashan and return to Khafji.

The one element that was absolutely clear to all was that the evacuation of the four guys was the top priority. The team had been strictly instructed to move into position aboard the Koveshes as soon as the last missile had been fired. They had already placed whatever equipment they wanted to keep into the cargo bays. As they worked the various tasks during the launch of the missiles, Daniel and Nathan had donned their flight helmets. They also had rehearsed the connection between the helmets and the drone's oxygen system. They had ensured that the cargo bays of both aircrafts were appropriately shut. David and Mike could not prepare for their flight at that point as they were too busy dealing with the loading and firing tasks.

The first missile was fired. They all breathed a sigh of relief; the second launcher would not be needed, unless the launcher failed later, a much lower risk than failure due to shocks or other problem during transport. The team briefly saw the missile depart in the general direction of the plant, but with a sharp upward trajectory allowing it to intercept the laser beam that would then gently guide it to its target. Within less than thirty seconds, they saw it peak out. Soon, they could observe the tell-tale exhaust trace bearing down toward the plant. The second missile had already been sent off before the first one impacted. When that first impact occurred, they heard a huge bang resonate, although they first saw what seemed like a ball of fire before they could hear the sound. David had fired the third missile when Daniel interrupted the group: David instructed Daniel and Nathan to get the drones into take-off position, facing the end of the runway, and to send the agreed signal to the remote pilots. The orders continued with calm and authority: "Mike, position the last missile. Nathan and Daniel run for the Koveshes—take the first one. Mike and I will take off in the second. Shouldn't be more than a minute or so behind you."

David warned them to complete their take-off check list as Central Command would not order take-off unless they got their signal. He reminded them all that once the remote pilots started the take-off procedures, it should be pretty rough at the outset as they would be using full power.

"Safe flight. See you in Khafji."

"Thanks. See you guys there. Be safe."

Daniel and Nathan ran for the Kovesh and had no difficulty climbing aboard. They already had their helmets on but had to adjust their chin straps. They took careful pains to make sure that all was in order as they had been instructed. The checklist was very short, but they had to run through it.

"Oxygen connected?"

"Check."

"Canopy lowered and locked on both sides?"

"Check. Check."

"All clear signal sent to Central Command?"

"Check."

Within no more than a couple of seconds, they heard the sound of the engine rev up and felt the drone moving. They could see through the small window in front of their faces that they were at or near the start of the runway. A massive thrust pushed the drone forward and they felt a very rapid climb. Though they took off on a northwesterly header, they quickly veered sharply to the right doing an almost full circle to start on a westerly vector.

There were three main reasons for this strategy. First, the hills were closest and highest in that direction; while the hills to the northeast of the airstrip did not rise much over 4,200 feet, those to the south were in the 6,500 to 8,000 feet range; also, they were probably only half as far as those to the north side. Second, they were avoiding populated areas in the immediate vicinity, as their flight path would be south of Kashan, though directly above Amir Kabir. And third, they were flying away from the Natanz plant which was south and east of the runway. The immediate sharp right turn would also keep them far enough south and west of Fordow to avoid problems with any anti-aircraft defenses based there. Finally, the trajectory was likely to be far enough to the west that it would not intersect with that of any fighter sent to Natanz or Fordow from Tehran or Isfahan. And, the added bonus, that was the shortest route as well.

About fifty miles after take-off, they would have cleared the highest local peak at almost 8,400 feet; these were the high plateaus in the Zagros Mountains over which they would fly for more than half of the distance they needed to cover in Iranian airspace. Once abeam Shiraz, the drones would leave the high country and the pilots would then set a broadly southward course, in the direction of Bushehr, on the Persian Gulf, flying over the coastal plain along the Gulf. Upon reaching Bushehr, they would bank right and aim for a point about thirty miles south of Khafji to start their final approach. They knew that U.S. Navy and Coast Guard ships were patrolling the area over which they would fly while sticking to international waters to avoid ruffling Saudi feathers.

Mike and David followed them a minute later on the same flight path.

The men found the initial climb quite sharp as the operators were taking advantage of the massive power to weight ratio of the drones; the G-forces were particularly heavy when they were in their long, right turn to an almost perfect westward heading. The idea of a very rapid climb was that once they were above 25,000 feet, they were virtually home free unless the Iranians had detected them and launched fighter jets. The Koveshes indeed flew at a top speed that was, at most, half that of a fighter jet. Worse, they were unarmed. They needed a healthy head start to begin to feel secure. The two Eitan drones, which could shoot at the jets as they took off from bases in Tehran or Isfahan, were the only external protection the Koveshes could claim. But, in truth, they were not close enough to be effective unless the Koveshes were detected soon after takeoff and the Eitans needed to shoot at batteries that were near their current locations. Additionally, with their maximum speed differences, time worked against the Eitan drones: they would be falling further and further behind the faster Koveshes. But the real strength of the Koveshes was in their stealth character and the skill of the pilots who had trained extensively for the mission. They should not be detectable and, even if they were picked up by especially sharp radar, they were highly maneuverable and had about twice as much fuel as needed to make it to the Khafji base.

David, who was on the left pod of his Kovesh, strained to see Natanz after the drone set its westward heading. He could only see a huge cloud of smoke. This told him that at least a few of the missiles had hit their targets, but he would not get confirmation of the success of the mission until later, after they had landed safely.

CHAPTER.45

Forty-five minutes into the flight, the men all started to feel the onset of the descent. Contrary to commercial aircraft, where pilots work to make the descent as smooth and comfortable as possible, military operators only worry about safety. With Khafji being just on the other side of the Persian Gulf from Iran, the small size of the Kuwaiti airspace and the desire on the part of both Saudi Arabia and Kuwait to keep their involvement as secret as possible, Central Command had originally decided that the descent would have to start in international waters and to take place either in Saudi or Kuwaiti airspace depending upon wind direction. Today, their preferred approach was from the south; the need, in this case, to minimize the use of Saudi airspaces also meant that they had to work within a relatively narrow corridor. The pilots thus descended in tight spirals which imposed higher than normal G-forces on their passengers. This virtually eliminated the risk that they might be detected or inadvertently shot down; and the G-forces the members of the team each felt were, in any case, far less than what they would be experiencing when they were in the fighter jets leaving Khafji, though they would, then, have protective G-suits.

As they landed, Simon was right on hand to welcome them: "Well done, team. The news is great. Well, almost."

The last two words were said with a somber tone which the team seemed not to notice in their current high state of excitement. All five of them, with Simon definitely being a full member of the team now, were to travel as passengers on five F-15D Falcons which would initially fly due west and then north over Saudi Arabia, until they reached the Eastern branch of the upper Red Sea. There, they would enter Israeli territory flying over Eilat and continue due north until they were ready to start their descent to Palmachim Air Base. This would allow them to avoid both Jordanian and Egyptian airspaces and thus only use Saudi space, until they were nearly home. The flight would involve almost 1,000 miles, with only the last two hundred over Israeli territory. Simon gave them an initial briefing as they were walking to the hangar where the planes were waiting and where they would need to change into their G-suits.

He first confirmed that both Fordow and Natanz appeared to have sustained major damage, pretty much destroyed. But, obviously, no one could fully know what may or may not have happened inside the halls. For this, they would need satellite pictures, which Simon indicated he had not yet seen. He quoted with obvious cynicism and a sense of understatement the message he had received from analysts who HAD seen the pictures that said: "The external topography of both places has changed," adding, "as per the official terminology."

The size of the craters over the two sites in Natanz apparently told the analysts that destruction was quite extensive. However, he conceded that it was harder to be definitive with respect to Fordow, although some chunk of the mountain seemed to be missing. He concluded with satisfaction that whatever was buried inside the mountain had to be gone, at least partially, and was certainly, at present, impossible to operate. Repeating himself he congratulated the team; they, in turn, congratulated him on the planning.

Simon indicated that he had talked with Ariel Landau, who was over the moon with the results. He imagined the same would be true for the Prime Minister, the U.S. President and the other members of the loose unofficial coalition once they were informed. He reported that the other four Hezbollah-sourced missiles were indeed fired by the Americans at Arak and Isfahan just after the Koveshes had cleared the area and passed abeam of Isfahan. Isfahan was where the Iranians took the enriched gas produced at Fordow and Natanz and transformed it into uranium pellets. These pellets were in turn used to fuel reactors or converted again into gas to be enriched to weapon grade levels. Their entire nuclear sequence would be inoperative for quite some time: in fact, it was pretty much out of commission.

Simon moved on to the other target for the American Special Operations forces which involved the Arak nuclear reactor: it had sustained material damage as well, though that damage was focused on peripheral activities and intentionally avoided the reactor itself. Indeed, of the four missiles that were available to the Americans, three were directed toward Isfahan and only one to Arak. The logic behind the decision not to aim for serious destruction at Arak was that the coalition wanted to avoid any leakage of radioactive gas that could impact the local population. At Arak, they had targeted the external infrastructure rather than the reactor itself.

Needless to say, the team had plenty of questions to ask, though they all knew full well that a formal debriefing would have to wait until they were back in Tel Aviv. David still asked: "Simon, anything from Iran as to who they think was responsible?"

Simon replied that they had not heard much but added that this should not surprise anyone. Explaining his thought, he noted that the hits had taken place barely ninety minutes earlier and in the middle of the night. However, he offered his own view that he was sure that the hierarchy was up and meeting, somehow, somewhere; but there was no official word yet. As the team knew, the plan was designed with a number of diverse moving parts. This was in part to ensure that the Iranians would be completely confused as to who had hit them. This looked to be playing out as anticipated. However, given his professional respect for the Iranians, he added: "They'll come up with something. But don't be surprised if they initially blame it on us or the Americans."

Continuing his story, he indicated that the Iranians were indeed accusing the Americans with respect to Isfahan and Arak, but he thought it was more a knee-jerk reaction than anything else. Simon indicated that a message claiming Iranian opposition responsibility for the attacks on Fordow and Natanz was delivered to the press in Paris at almost the same time as the missiles hit. The approach was totally consistent with prior actions by the Resistance, who always wanted to be first to claim responsibility. In this case, given the fact that Israel wanted everyone to believe that the resistance was involved, there was an additional logic for them to anticipate the last few missiles in order to get ahead of everyone else: as the alleged saboteurs, they would have known when the act of sabotage was planned. Simon added that he had been told that a couple of news services had already made a quick mention of the claim. He expected the story to develop later, as it was only six in the morning in Paris and most everyone must still be asleep, "digesting last night's dinner and wine," as he cynically put it.

He took that opportunity to brief the team on the decision that had to have been made with respect to the mines near Larak and Abu Mousa. He first told them the reason they had detonated the mines at Larak, and the team's reaction was one of complete surprise, followed by relief. He went on and added that they had decided to detonate the second set of mines as well, just to keep the Iranians occupied. He explained that the main reason for selecting Abu Mousa for the second set of explosions was that it was still substantially south of where the action actually was. Simon and Suffolk had banked on the assumption that the Iranians would send fighter aircraft there. The idea was that any fighter jet that went that way would not be available to scramble after the Koveshes or would take that much longer to get to them.

Simon paused and the team this time noted that his facial expression had become considerably more somber. He said that the news was not great all around. On the minor side, their attempt at replicating a few of the features of the Stuxnet worm failed completely. The Iranians must have anticipated that Israel might one day try again and had built serious safeguards within their systems. He claimed that all was not lost, though, since their failure showed them a few of their new safeguards, and their attempt could not in any way be demonstrated to have come from Israel.

The really bad news, Simon said, was Amir. They should know that the service had been quite concerned about making sure that all assets in Iran would be able to escape. All were where they were supposed to be, except Amir. Minoo, Farid and Sarah flew out two days earlier and Minoo's father actually left before the team made it to Qom. He said that Minoo, her father and Farid had all asked for new identities in their new location because Iran has been known to have very long arms. For this reason, he could not give them any more detail, other than the fact that they were safe in their new lives. He also confirmed that Sarah had left as planned and was physically OK and safe. The mood of the team took a turn south when they heard that last sentence. They all understood that she might not be OK emotionally.

Simon added that the news with respect to Amir was a complete blank. Nobody had heard a peep from him, which was not good news, but proved nothing. His voice had become more somber, almost choking. He paused for a few seconds to regain his composure.

Daniel tried to deflect the subject a bit and asked how Sarah was coping. Simon said that he did not exactly know her state of mind, but it was clear that she was upset. He was not certain what that meant for her in the future. Personally, he did not think she should return to Tehran unless they knew with absolute certainty what had happened to Amir, adding with a sad smile: "Which we may never get to know."

He continued: "Whatever happened to Amir, there's no place for her in this area. If he is alive, he was a traitor and Sarah's profile is now known to all. If he's dead, unless it was sheer coincidence that someone surprised Amir and he did not have a chance to talk, why would she want to go back?"

"Didn't he have a cyanide pill?"

"Well, David, he should have. But did he have the time to swallow it? Nobody knows."

Simon however wanted to finish on an optimistic note, at least with respect to Sarah. Simon said that they all needed to take a big step back. He made the point that he still did not know if Sarah really loved Amir and would have made her life with him, adding: "She could just have been leading him on for the good of the mission."

It was not clear by the reactions of all team members whether they believed that angle. But they did not have much time to reflect on it as they were now ready to climb onto their respective jets. Simon brought the initial debriefing to its conclusion: "I still need to have many more conversations with you guys. In particular, I want to know everything that happened before you left Iran, and, especially, how you wiped away any trace of your having been there. Obviously, I'm not talking of the misleading breadcrumbs you left behind to confuse the Iranians, or at least point them in the wrong direction."

He conceded that the major loose ends that they could not avoid were the disappearances of Minoo and Farid, and secondarily Cyrus, Minoo's dad. The Iranians would not look for them for at least a week, since they were supposed to be away on holiday. He added that the only two people the Iranians could and, in fact, should suspect were Mike and David. They should be portrayed as local terrorists and blowing up Natanz with Iranians missiles . . . Simon concluded that his only real concern at present was potential missile activity from Hezbollah, Hamas or even Iran. He argued that the one contingency they could not control was a retaliatory strike. But, he said, "The Iron Dome is on full alert. We're not leaving anything to chance; one bad, dirty missile and the results could be disastrous. That's simply not acceptable."

Before they climbed aboard their respective fighter jets, they still had to deal with the last bit of preflight routine: the pilots had to give them the key instructions, as they were going to ride in a supersonic fighter plane; they also had to run through their checklists. The training which they underwent prior to going on location had surely included several trial runs; more than they would have liked in fact, but it was believed essential that they be totally comfortable on the flight. It was going to be long and could be arduous if evasive maneuvers proved necessary, although none were expected given a flight plan that avoided any use of Jordanian airspace and with the Saudi cooperation. Their training had even included landing on an aircraft carrier, just so that the passengers would know what they would face if they had to land at sea. They had also taken off from the carrier, but that would not be needed now.

Yet, the normal routine was still for the preflight briefing to take place, and they all listened carefully. Mission Control had organized for each of the five to fly with the same pilots they'd trained with, to maximize the teamwork and comfort, but the team was still on an adrenaline high when they climbed aboard the jets. Once fastened into position, the canopies were shut, and the jets were ready to leave. They lined up at the end of the runway in waves of two, with the last jet carrying Simon forming the last wave, with a single aircraft. Quickly, they flew away in formation, in a massive, jet engine roar which shook the ground below.

After the five jets had taken off, Marvin supervised the Israeli officers who were still on the base as they went on with their final preparations to leave. They loaded the Koveshes on the wings of the Hercules after they had fueled them, so that they could be released within range to fly home on their own power; this would not be until almost two thirds into the flight back. The Hercules pilots preferred not to land the big plane with the drones still attached. While attending to the Koveshes, they had to wait almost an hour for the Eitan drones to land, because of their lower cruising speeds. Once on the ground, they were refueled in preparation for their own long flights back to Tel-Aviv. The jet assistance personnel finally gathered all their equipment and loaded everything into the cargo plane. The heli-drone was placed onboard the Hercules C-130 with its main rotor disconnected and the blades arranged in a longitudinal direction. In a short time, after the C-130 had flown away, no trace remained that the Israeli Air Force had used the Saudi airport as a base.

As the team was landing in Israel, Jesse Benaroya picked up an incoming phone call: "Our meeting in Naples was quite fruitful . . . Thank you."

EPILOGUE

As a friend and thus the self-appointed, unofficial biographer of one of the main actors in this incredible adventure, Simon, I feel I must tell the story. If I do not tell it, I'm sure it will never be told and that would be a shame. The action which the story covers and more importantly its outcomes literally changed the geopolitical picture in the Middle East, and possibly even the world. It eliminated the Iran nuclear risk and demonstrated that certain new alliances might be forged that hitherto would have seemed impossible.

After all, enough time has passed since these events happened; no damage can be done by it being told, provided the narrator avoids disclosing details that might still be secret or at least somewhat vaguely understood. My former duties give me the perspective needed to ensure that I can exercise that care. It is a story of incredibly complex planning, with a number of uncertainties on a continuing basis. It is a story of daring equipment innovation which stretched the capabilities of the most secretive and effective secret service agency in the world. It is a story of virtually flawless execution, despite the occasional set back due to circumstances beyond the team's control. It is a human story with the main actor caring deeply for his troops and working to make sure that they all returned home safely, once the mission was completed. The story has been reconstructed from interviews I had with all but three of the protagonists, to whom my former position gave me access. They were able to relate actions as well as the numerous planning discussions they held, thus complementing the insights I had on my own. I could not have written this book without many individuals sharing recollections with me. I want to thank them all very sincerely.

I would like to thank the members of the *Mossad* who participated directly in the mission, in Tel Aviv, Jerusalem or Iran. Their accounts of the many planning meetings I could not attend or of their actions prior to reaching Iran or while there provided the basis of this story.

Many members of the Israeli Cabinet kindly provided me with detailed accounts of meetings I did not attend or of discussions they held in small groups or with their subordinates, as did contacts in the higher ranks of the U.S. Administration. Similarly, I asked all the various participants in the mission I could reach, for details of their thoughts or of words exchanged in meetings I did not attend. These proved crucial to the understanding of the process that led to the mission being requested and authorized, and to my ability to relate its development and execution.

Finally, I want to thank two of the three Iranian members of a family who relocated to a new country. As one of the small handful of people who had access to their new identities, I reached out to them and am particularly grateful that they agreed to participate in my effort. Their stories provided much needed local color and corroboration of other recollections, though I may, here or there, have added a few thoughts of my own, to "spice up" the story.

What was shocking is when we discovered that the real traitor in the operation was Farid. After his suicide, Minoo found a letter where he confessed that he had betrayed the group. The pangs of guilt had led him to inform Reza, his boss, belatedly that something was about to happen in Fordow. Thankfully, he never revealed the Israeli connection. Reza dispatched a couple of guards as soon as he heard. They surprised Amir, killed him when he resisted and went straight into the complex . . .

I trust that this story will not only allow you to learn of a truly daring and exceptionally well-executed mission and to understand why our country, however small, will at times do anything and everything to be allowed to continue to exist in an environment which is often hostile at best.

Also, it will demonstrate how, as the story goes, David can at times help Goliath . . . It will also remind us all that love is not always stronger than anything . . .

Signed: A. L.

www.ingramcontent.com/pod-product-compliance
Lightning Source LLC
Chambersburg PA
CBHW052008020726
47501CB00004B/1055